THE HIDDEN HEART OF EMILY HUDSON

Melissa Jones

WINDSOR
PARAGON

First published 2010
by Sphere
This Large Print edition published 2010
by BBC Audiobooks Ltd
by arrangement with
Little, Brown Book Group

Hardcover ISBN: 978 1 408 46144 0
Softcover   ISBN: 978 1 408 46145 7

British Library Cataloguing in Publication Data available

Printed and bound in Great Britain by
CPI Antony Rowe, Chippenham and Eastbourne

For Neil, Ed and Tom

This novel was inspired by the book
*A Private Life of Henry James:
Two Women & His Art* by
Lyndall Gordon, Vintage, 1999.

'It is so hard for one soul to know another, under all the necessary and unnecessary disguises that keep them apart.'

Minny Temple, 1869

PROLOGUE

*London
Late summer, 1863*

Before daybreak on a rainy August morning a young gentleman, stooped, respectably dressed, was seen to alight from a cab at the Westminster bank of the Thames. He was accompanied by a servant; together, in silence, they carried a substantial bundle of materials of different kinds to a waiting boatman, who loaded them on to his vessel.

In the increasingly heavy rain, mingling with the river mist, an observer could be forgiven for thinking these were rags, perhaps curtains discarded or faded bedclothes. But by the light of the lamp the boatman carried the materials gleamed with some beauty of decoration, lustre and detail, and the rags revealed themselves to be dresses in bright fashionable colours. Each item, from day dress to evening, was exquisitely made, heavy with laces, velvets and embellishments of the highest quality.

With difficulty they were loaded on to the barge, followed by the gentleman, who made his way towards the bows. The servant was turned away. Rocking in the filthy slime of the shallows, the gentleman looked as if he might fall, but then sat down in the boat with the dresses heaped about him. The craft was rowed out into the swift part of the river, where it was kept steady only by the kindness of the wind.

1

Once the vessel was still, and at a nod from the boatman, the gentleman began methodically to throw each dress into the moving filth, attempting to submerge them with an oar. But their voluminous skirts filled with air and the movement of the tide, and they floated, like so many bodies, away.

PART ONE

CHAPTER ONE

Mr William Cornford   High Trees School
Cornford House   Rochester, NY
Boston, Mass

March 10th, 1861

Dear Mr Cornford,

It is with regret that I begin the task of writing to you about your niece, Emily. Her recent behaviour, which I have outlined to you in previous letters—most specifically her unfortunate, extravagant friendship with a fellow pupil, Augusta Dean, and its unsettling effect on the other pupils, all girls entrusted to my care and to whom I owe a great duty—compels me to request that she be formally removed from the school and returned to your care with immediate effect. It is a sad request. I am aware that it comes before the completion of the school year, but we all believe that any shock felt by her abrupt departure would be less than that felt by her remaining.

For your consideration, her many faults are as follows: she is too vigorous, too quick to question, and her temper is variable. You will not find any consistency in her behaviour. She is by turns bewildered, good-humoured, angered, merry, pained and aloof. She always says what comes into her head, as if she has a right to her peculiar thoughts. She laughs

5

loudly. She is untidy. She almost expects to make an impression. She suffers from a lack of meekness, a lack of decorum, a lack of discipline. It is as if she is surprised that there are rules by which she must be controlled.

Yet for all her abundant defiant life, she can often be extremely solitary and remote. She can spend hours in drawing, if ever she is given an opportunity. On nature walks, she is always trailing behind the other girls, gathering keepsakes and talking to herself and the trees; at streams kneeling and plunging her fingers into the water, even when there is ice and the sky is dark and obscure and threatening rain and we really should be hurrying, going, turning for home.

And when she is laid up in bed shivering and burning—her health is never robust despite her ways—one or other of the servants will always take pity on her and come with beef tea or gruel and a hot brick and tell one another how she is the only one of the girls who will always say thank you and never complains.

During the holidays when she has remained at school, she has been notably self-contained, befriending the cat and looking out for its every comfort. She rambles in the woods for hours a day, returning to school with her thin hands sunburned because she swears she has not worn a bonnet in the glare. All these things she will not wear: gloves in summer—how many pairs dropped by the side of the road?—shawls, wraps, coats, hats. She has even boasted of taking her shoes off and paddling in the streams but I can neither countenance nor believe it. When questioned she looked right at me and asked directly if she were being accused of lying.

As a consequence of my affection for her, I admit that I may have been indulgent towards her these two years. But now my duty has been made especially clear to me because of this business with Augusta. Augusta is a girl of good family, one of the best families in the school. She has an acute understanding but a somewhat impressionable disposition, and it is this that I fear could influence her prospects. She and Emily became inseparable immediately she arrived and in a thousand ways. At first, I welcomed her influence. In her society, Emily became calmer, and Augusta, homesick to begin with and fretting, was devoted to her, steady as a sister. But as one term has passed and now another is nearly at its close, the girls have proved that together they are anything but steady.

The passion of their friendship—exclusive, possessive, overweening—is clearly developing into something that could become unhealthy. I take daily notes on conduct and I am afraid to inform you that your niece and Miss Dean have now accrued several black marks against their names. But it is not so much what they have done as how they are. Discipline has suffered, the very spirit of the school is being challenged; their studies have been compromised: I have no other choice but to take this course.

The reason I write to you at such length is so that you may attempt to understand the girl, having not seen her for two years. I should like to impress upon you that she is by no means a bad creature by nature, but that the death of her family, and the immediate separation she then suffered from the place of her birth and all that she held dear, I am convinced has contributed largely to the formation of her character.

As I trust you are aware, we are all deeply fond of Emily. On reflection I remain convinced that she would own that she has not been mistreated in any way—quite the opposite—although I imagine she might claim to have been misunderstood. Our task, which has been to show her that the world need not trouble to understand her, but that she should be at pains to understand the world, is one at which I fear we have failed, and I must admit my part in that. Perhaps a change of society, to be amongst thinking people of her own family in a home such as yours, could well be to her advantage; if her wildness continues, none of us can predict the consequences.

We shall miss her. We entrust her to your care with affection and regret.

Yours truly,

Miss Margaret Alice Miller

Miss Augusta Dean   A train carriage
High Trees School   Somewhere in
Rochester, NY   Upstate NY

March 12th, 1861

My dearest Augusta,

No journey has ever been so painful or felt so long. Here I am quite alone in this carriage, my paper lit only by the breaking of the day. It appears that I was warned and did ignore the warnings and so as a consequence my departure must needs be abrupt, almost nocturnal, and surrounded by the aura of disgrace. But not to be given the opportunity to say goodbye! I have taken it very hard, even though I believe Miss Miller to consider herself to be acting for the best.

Indeed my interview with the lady only this morning would have been comical if it had not been so scrambled and brief and clumsy—if it had not been such a painful and so acute a shock. I think she was embarrassed, or having made up her mind to despatch me, wanted it done as soon as possible. She promises that my uncle is expecting me.

I will not cry. I will write to you instead. I have to tell you—despite the noise and speed of this carriage—that I love you now and always. You are my dearest girl, and I intend to keep the memory of you alive. As you know full well, so many of the people I have loved exist now only in my mind. I believe I am developing a peculiar talent for it. I will not

9

wish for the parting we have been denied, but I will treasure these memories of you and hold them in my heart until we meet again, wherever and whenever that may be.

A pause while I lean my head against the window and recollect.

Item one: you sharing that immense plum cake your father sent you with me, housing it under your bed to supplement our meagre rations. It was not the cake (which was very good) but your generosity I loved you for.

Item two: you and I stamping in those puddles as they began to thaw in the woods, jumping with all our energy and slipping and sliding and falling and hurting our backs and soaking our clothes and making our hands all red and raw, even inside those foolish gloves. That tremendous snapping, to know we would hear running water again soon and the birds rejoicing with us and that there would be leaves on the interminable trees in another month or so because we had been fortunate enough to discover a bud. (I think to live in a clearing in the woods as we have for so long must be bad for the soul. The times I have dreamt of hacking my way through those trees, of wide rivers and pastures and slopes and flowers and sky.)

Next item: drawing you during that tedious Mathematics lesson—could it be only three days ago?—when you leant your chin on your hand and your hair fell heavy and your eyes gazed in concentration at the slate. If it had been me at the sum I would not have seen the chalk marks at all but some other thing entirely under my fingers; but you were thinking, that was the loveliness in your eyes. I love that drawing and wish they had not taken it away.

What were our other crimes? Let me think. Oh yes—laughing at prayers. I know that was very wrong, but it was such a bright morning and telling you all about my brother Charlie at breakfast had made your smile so irrepressible, and there was your beauty and then the frivolous, idle speculation that if he had lived you might have married him one day, and the children you might have had, and when I caught your eye as I thought of it again at prayers, you smiled and I laughed and you laughed too. It was not malicious, schoolgirl impious laughter; there was no mockery of people or of God. They did not understand that. The fact remains that we were meant to be praying and we were not, we were meant to be thoughtful but we were not, and our heads should have been bowed and they were not.

We deserved the scolding and the lines in our books, and perhaps even the hundred other petty slender separations, so harshly felt, but now, by comparison, so tiny and inconsequential. But *this* unnatural and sudden wrench, it seems unjust, very cruel. And to be going to my uncle, to a remote place I do not know, to a family I have not seen for several years— from my memory and my mother's tales I do not anticipate a single sympathetic soul. A very grave and serious thought.

11

I fear I will survive only in your letters.
Write to me soon.
Affectionately,

Emily

Miss Augusta Dean   Bluff House
High Trees School   Newport Beach
Rochester, NY

March 13th, 1861

My darling Augusta,
   Foolish to begin a new letter to you when I have yet to despatch the first, but I simply cannot blow out my candle without telling you that I am arrived.
   Mrs Bradley, the housekeeper, met me at the station in a hired conveyance. It appears the family do not keep a carriage here, as it is only a summer house. The lady was rather reserved—doubtless not relishing being out on a dark night, or is it better to say early morning, to meet a wayward orphan from so obscure a branch of the family—but she was civil enough.
   I could not help feeling the most enormous excitement as we left the little town behind and I could smell the ocean breeze, feel the largeness of it before me—and the stars as big as lanterns in the sky.
   I could not see very much of the house but it is clapboard, a seaside house, right on the beach, and so I must love it already. All the family were abed. I will meet them in the

12

morning: father, son and mother. The other brothers are at training for the war, and my cousin Mary is at present visiting in New York. It will be awkward as we were always so completely estranged from every member of my mother's family, and they were not even present at the funerals. The first and last I remember of them is my brief stay with my uncle and my aunt in Boston before he took me to school. All I can do is attempt to quell my nerves, remember my good manners and good grace, and that they are, after all, my flesh and blood.

I must try to sleep now. It will be time to wake again soon! I have already been to the window but it does not face the ocean.

Good night, my darling,
Your devoted,

Emily

CHAPTER TWO

'Come.'

Her uncle had chosen to receive Emily in his study as a visitor, even though he had greeted her formally at breakfast and pleasantries about the journey had been observed. Her cousin William had been working in his room. It was the same massive desk she remembered from the Boston house he lived in but this room held more dark and shiny furniture than she had ever seen and all its brightness had been dimmed: she could not make out the sea from the shrouded window.

'Uncle.'

He motioned for her to sit opposite him. She was not afraid. Indeed she did not want him to see how unafraid she was. The large dome of his forehead, the delicate spectacles, the roughness of his beard, the fineness of the manicure of his hands, all absorbed her.

'You have nothing to say?'

'Concerning what, Uncle?'

His voice remained quiet and dry, the loudest noise being the rustle of the letter he was holding, the one Miss Miller had written to him from her school. He looked up from the pages.

'It has come as no surprise to me that you are considered wild. Your mother was similarly . . . unthinking.'

Emily had expected to be lectured on her conduct but this sudden sharp mention of her mother caught her off-guard. Her mother had been anything but unthinking. In a sudden complete, absorbing vision, she saw her sitting by the fire, saw her now in bright colours against the greyness of this room, flushed with that intruder, that consumption, bending over her work, bravely talking, explaining to her daughter about the myth of the Fall, about how Eve and the apple was as much a fairy story as any of the tales she had read to them as children. She had always tried to pass on her knowledge quickly, as fast as she could; she had known perfectly well that there would not be sufficient time. In that piercing second Emily wished more than anything that he would not mention her darling mother. With this memory in her eyes, she would not flinch; she would not be

14

drawn on the subject. She would hold her mother close and not reply.

He continued as if he had not seen her hurt. 'Tell me, my dear, what are your thoughts concerning how you intend to spend your summer with us before we consider what is to be done with you?'

She answered swiftly, too swiftly, no doubt; he seemed surprised. 'I thought I might read extensively, and draw. It would not be a course of study as at school but I hope—'

'Are you not aware that too much thought is bad for the female nerves?'

And now this fierce quick anger that she could not control sprang up in her. 'Did you not only a moment ago say that it was wrong for women to be unthinking, Sir?' She saw the colour mount in his face and the red lips press together. 'Uncle, I did not mean to cause you annoyance. Your displeasure—'

But he was clever and wiser than she and she could see would not be addressed with such openness. His voice remained calm and even.

'It matters little to me what you mean. You are my ward, not my child. If you were my daughter I might consider sending you for the cure as I have sent my dear Mary. She has not been well, filling her days with reading, writing and study—it is bad for her mind. The doctor in New York prescribes no reading matter for six months, fancy work only, and plain sewing. And under his care she is being fed plenty of butter.' He sighed briefly before continuing, allowing his eyes to leave Emily's face. 'Butter is good for her. All fat is soothing. She must be soothed.' He repeated the words like a litany, and then, quite suddenly, stopped. After a

15

pause his voice gentled. 'What pretty needlework are you engaged with, my dear?'

'I have no sewing. I used to read at home, or draw.'

'At home was two long years ago. What did you sew at school?'

'I have left my sampler behind.'

When she looked at him now she saw a tremendous anger, far greater than her own. He took off his glasses and polished them, revealing the smallness of his milky blue eyes. But he was quiet. He did not burst out as she did.

'I am not used to being spoken to in this way.'

'I am sorry, Uncle. I do not know how it is that I should speak.' With difficulty she stayed still in her chair, resisting the urge to stamp and tap her foot, and walk briskly, pace, longing to shrug him aside, alter the line of her vision, go to the window and see the ocean.

'Emily, let me try to explain what I have in mind and then you will be in no danger of misunderstanding me.'

She had to look down at her hands in case she were to laugh or cry.

'You may walk, and exercise your body. You may read, no more than two hours a day, and I will see what it is that you are reading.'

'But I may draw?' Why had she sounded so eager, so pleading, why had she let so much of her voice come into her throat?

He did not force her to wait for a reply. 'I can see no objection. And you shall sew. Ask your aunt to guide you.'

A pause full of dry breathing. If it could be over she might go outside.

'My dear, there should be no need for me to remind you, you have no fortune. Your destiny will be to marry. If you cannot be accomplished, or rich, or beautiful, at least make yourself agreeable. Talk to my son, he is a sensible fellow, and he will walk with you when his health permits. You may go.'

She wanted to cry suddenly, when really he had not been so harsh. She admired him for speaking the truth.

Miss Augusta Dean   Newport
High Trees School
Rochester, NY

March 15th, 1861

My dearest Girl,

Only two days here and it is so complete a change that we could have been separated for a month. Let me hear from you. I long to know how you do.

In the meantime I will tell you as much as I can about my situation. This place, the house, is glorious, built close by the ocean—and what an ocean: a wild, wide salty shore, so much sky—always changing, and angry waves—so much light and dark.

I have met my cousin William—as quiet and watchful as my aunt and uncle, but with an air of profound interest in others—if not a lively one—and he has extended every kindness and politeness towards me. It appears he has periods of invalidism. He is a writer and not

17

expected to enlist against the South. He advises me that the shore will be calmer in summer and it is true, spring is always such an unpredictable time. Already I cannot decide which walk I love better: the cliffs, with their wind and open prospect, or the beach, with its contemplation of the waves.

The town itself, as befits its name, is fairly new, and feels extremely vigorous. Beach houses like ours line the shore, wooden with generous rooms and verandas—it is too cold to take the air on them now, but in the summer it will be open and wild. It is all so wide and open after the woods. The heart of the town itself is close by and there will be plenty of people who summer here. William assures me that there will be good society. I hope that this will be so, for I regret to say we are very quiet here at present.

I find my aunt a curiously lifeless person. I suppose because I did not know her as a child it is hard to imagine her nursing three boys and a girl, listening to tales of their blunders and dreams at her knee. I do not think it is a lack of devotion—she fusses over William and his supposed cough (I have not heard it once)—but she does not appear to feel, or see. She dresses in black; I would find it unbearable, day after dreary day. She appears not to notice me, but I fear she notices everything; while my uncle, shut up in his study reading his Theology and writing his many treatises, appears to be intentionally blind. He has not looked at me—not a glance—since our interview in his study yesterday morning.

18

It seems I am to do as I please, within his limits, but be watched closely. Yet how can I be watched if the people who are watching do not see? It is in every aspect peculiar and contradictory, and in every mouthful I take or chair I sit in I feel conscious of doing something wrong. In their eyes, I mean, not in my own. I must draw it all for I cannot write it. As for my cousin, he comes and goes infrequently: he too is mostly at study in the library.

I love my room. It is sober and plain and I can see plenty of sky from the window, even though my eyes are deprived of the ocean. How I long for you to be here to talk to, to grasp your hand and look at you and you to know all of this without having to be told. We could lie on the bed together and laugh at their owlish ways.

After supper this evening I was invited to play, and being at the piano again made me feel calmer and more hopeful. It is a beautiful piano, with a clear and resonant sound, and the rosewood is embellished with remarkable artistry. My playing was pronounced good with a raising of the eyebrows by my uncle; my aunt did not look up from her work, but cousin William professed himself 'transported' with a slightly comical expression of surprised appreciation, his head on one side like a bird's, his narrow face and penetrating eyes gazing as if at something invisible. I laughed and said it was hardly more than proficient, but he said I had a talent, or rather, 'A way of letting my soul speak through the music.' I could tell this irritated his mother, who began to bustle about the room turning down the lights. William's work has only recently begun to appear in the periodicals, but it appears grand things are expected of him. I have read nothing of his, or of my uncle's, of course.

It is late now, and no moon. I think it may be raining over the ocean.

I send you my fondest love.

Emily

They walked up the cliff path—Emily dancing ahead, William at a more gentle pace behind. It was not a beautiful day, the wind was too strong and the expanse of sky thick with cloud, but her spirits were soaring, as always on gaining higher ground. He was breathing heavily behind her and leaning on his stick; she had teased him about his comical stick, such a part of him at the tender age of twenty-nine. He had not laughed but she did not think he was displeased.

She did not hear him call her name but paused and turned, for he might have done so, and it was only polite to halt a minute, even though she fell short of offering him assistance. He was not an old man. She saw him looking carefully at the ground, picking his way as if through the treacherous undiscovered territory of their forefathers rather than a well-worn, if narrow, path sprinkled with long grasses and boulders. A little higher and the wind would whip her hair in earnest and she could already feel the longing to run and laugh. But she stayed.

Reaching her, he was breathing and panting and

20

stooped, beginning only slowly to straighten up. Looking at her, he smiled. It was a surprisingly beautiful smile, not least for being so rare. 'You are very quick.'

'I know the path.'

'And unusually tactful.'

She had to laugh. 'Perhaps.'

'If it were not for my back . . .' He put his hand upon an obviously tender spot and allowed his words to trail off.

'It is not broken, I assume?' She laughed again and this time he laughed too.

'An obscure hurt that cannot mar the beauty of this day.'

She looked about her at the headland still rising above, the beach below and the veiled sky. 'It is not so beautiful today.'

But he was looking at her only. 'I assure you, it is a beautiful day.' And it gave her an unexpected delight to be looked at as a source of pleasure, to feel that by standing beside him she was recognised as something good. She looked back at the light in his eyes and felt for the first time that here was another human being who might perhaps feel as she did, even if he seemed so unknowable.

'Are you sufficiently rested? Shall we go on?' And this time she smiled in a way that approached tenderness as he returned her gaze.

'You lead the way, my dear, you lead the way.'

Turning away from him into the wind and beginning almost to battle its full force, Emily began to fear it might be too much for him, but she did not want to turn and look behind her for fear of disconcerting him. She could tell he hated to be embarrassed. And so she went on blind to him at

21

her back, yet checking her pace and the briskness of her step. It was not far until the ground became a smoother turf, and the prospect was complete. In another minute he stood beside her, and although they were within touching distance they were obliged to call to one another to be heard because of the strength of the wind.

'Do you take this walk every day?' he said.

'I roam about here on the cliffs. Do you know it well?'

'I am not in the habit of walking far, and we have not been staying here long.'

'Further along I found a perilous place where the sea boils called the Devil's Punch Bowl. I have approached it, but my nerve has failed.'

He frowned. 'I am glad of it. You should not venture that far alone. I have heard of the spot, it is treacherous—promise me you will not attempt it.'

'Of course I promise.'

He gave her his arm, although she took care not to lean on it.

'I love it up here—it is wild and undisturbed and I can look over the ocean and imagine crossing it one day.' She was shouting. It was the wrong occasion to attempt a conversation, let alone a confidence, but she could not help it. She turned her attention from the ocean to his face. 'You have been to Europe, have you not?'

'Yes, travelling with my father, and brothers.'

'And was it everything you hoped?'

'More. If I am to be the man of letters, the man I mean to be, it is the only place.'

He, too—weak as he announced himself to be— would contend with the wind to voice his

22

ambitions. She felt he would not object if she were to ask him why he did not live and work there already, but it was not the right time. His desire for it seemed tinged with a sense of the impossible; but the confidence was inspiring. She longed to tell him how she and her father would go to look at the pictures in the gallery at Buffalo and how their physical presence was like being surrounded by creatures, friends who loved her and whom she might one day come to know; and how she longed to leave America also, to study in Europe and to learn. She wanted to tell him that for her the study of Art was everything, but it would have been a ridiculous thing to say. And besides, she was not sure it was the truth.

Instead she made the decision not to speak about her desires. They stood still side by side. Gulls wheeled in the sky and their far-off cry was the only sound. She studied his freckled cheek, the fineness of his profile and the intelligence of those far-seeing shortsighted eyes. He shivered slightly, though she herself was warm, desirous of the indefinable.

'Time to go back down, I think,' he said.

She was disappointed he did not want to walk further. The wind dropped and his words resounded clear to her. There was a kindness in his voice and look that left her not knowing how to feel.

*   *   *

They continued their talk at tea; he huddled in his favourite plaid blanket, she head bent over her fancy work, needlework clumsy in the extreme.

23

She had told herself an artist should be able to apply herself to anything, but could bring neither discipline nor passion to it. He recounted his experiences of Paris with its constant fervour over the latest thing (he said the French were very hysterical when it came to beauty), the fashions, the salons, the novels, the weather in the streets; Rome with its stench and its antiquities; the sheer dust and exhaustion of the travelling; the exhilaration in his soul. In the lamp and firelight and gathering dusk they were undisturbed.

'You would love it, my dear. In Europe they have quite done away with vulgarity.'

She laughed. 'Indeed? I am not convinced that that is possible.'

'Our country is—they say we are entering on the greatest conflict of our generation, this war with the South. I have visited the wounded and I have written stories of soldiers and their struggles and their lives. My health does not permit the battleground to be my field of endeavour, and fortunately my brothers uphold the banner in my place. I have a different path to follow. War is not my subject—the private wars between people are more appropriate to my gifts.'

'You are very sure of yourself,' she said. 'I wish I could be that sure.'

'Don't be deceitful; I have already decided that you are the truest person I have ever encountered in my life.' He looked at her and looked at her and she became still and could no longer sew. 'You have the gift of pure and unadulterated life, my dear; of vitality, of a great soul.'

'You hardly know me. And you are talking nonsense and you are making me blush.'

'That is your special gift—life. In movement, in speaking, the way you play the piano—the way you express yourself without fear.'

'You are mistaken. I am afraid of a great many things.'

'Do not think I am making love to you. I am not, although you are a girl with whom absolutely everybody will be in love. I am your devoted cousin, and your confessor. It would please me greatly if you would confide your impressions of everything you see and hear and feel to me—hold nothing back.'

Emily did not enjoy listening to his opinion of her, formed and phrased as if she were a picture he was required to study. It was true that she required a confidant, but that it should be him would have to depend on more than his command.

'Let us leave me aside for a moment. Tell me more about what you intend to do.'

'I will write. I will write a novel as great as any of that of Mrs Eliot, or of Flaubert, or of this Trollope with his flabby literal style that exhausts the readers of his brutish books. I will write. There will be no toil in it. It will be like a gilded web and I will catch my people in it.' He smiled. 'It is all to come. It is why I must travel. It strengthens the mind, the spirit. It hardens the talent. This New World is so full of self-congratulation: declarations of this and declarations of that. It is embarrassing. We did not invent the human. If anyone did it was Shakespeare, and I am not at all convinced he was human himself and not some visitation from another sphere. It is in the Old World we must seek for meaning.' He kept looking at her. 'You have read Shakespeare?'

'A little; not very much. *A Midsummer Night's Dream.*'

'I will fetch you some reading matter directly. Shakespeare, and Keats. You shall start with *Romeo and Juliet* and the Odes.'

'And will your father approve?'

'My father is of the opinion that the correct subject for both reading and writing is the exact will of God, something it appears only he and his cronies are entitled to construe.'

She laughed, left looking into the fire as he went into the library for the books. He had dropped the shawl on the floor by his chair. It must be a comfort to him to have something to stroke, she thought. The colours: tawny, russet, crimson, gold and green were beautiful too. And the way it had fallen with the shadows around it. She put her sewing aside in earnest and fetched her sketchbook from the window seat. She was at work when he returned.

'If you please—will you leave the shawl?'

'Certainly.'

He stepped over it, carrying the books and putting them on his lap. Pulling his chair closer to the fire he watched her work. She did not mind in the least. He had a way of observing her, she observed, that was both hungry and discreet. It did not take long. It was only a sketch.

'That, I presume, is your interest? Drawing.'

'It is just something I have always done.'

'May I see it?'

'Of course.' She held out the book and he passed her the Shakespeare. He glanced at her drawing while she admired the bindings with hands and eyes. 'These editions are very luxurious.'

'You are accustomed to the school library. I like my books to be beautiful.'

'And your father can afford to pay for them. I am sorry. I did not mean to say that. It was so vulgar, and I—'

'Don't apologise, my dear. It is not the first time I have heard you say exactly what comes into your head. That is how you must remain. It is part of your peculiar and considerable charm. But only part. The rest is ill-defined and requires work.'

'*I* require work?!'

'No. It is I who must work to capture you.'

Miss Augusta Dean   Newport Beach
High Trees School
Rochester, NY

April 3rd, 1861

My dearest Girl,

 First I must assure you that I have received your letter—and regret that I have not had the opportunity at least to dash off a line to thank you for being so faithful a correspondent. Do not for a moment imagine you have not been in my thoughts, it is only that I have been unexpectedly taken up with so many new impressions that I have not had the usual opportunity to brood over a letter.

 It does not come as a surprise to me to hear that nothing whatever is changed at the school. That you are resigned to my departure and that the other girls are proving kind in extending their friendship is welcome news to me. And yes, we shall continue to write—never fear. You are also quite correct in pointing out that I am fortunate to find myself amongst a family once more after so long, and that it should not be wasted in longing for you.

But let me say again that there is not an hour that passes when I do not think of you, still shut up in that dreary place amongst those dreary trees. It makes me angry that a creature of such warm and breathing energy as yours should be so confined—just as it made me angry for myself when I shared your confinement. But, my dear girl, without seeking to belittle your fate, I feel I must draw your attention to the future.

Either at the end of this semester or, Heaven forbid, after the completion of another year, your father, in his wisdom, will conclude that your education is complete, and you will be transported in all your golden and abundant beauty, all your tumbling hair and merry spirits and quick mind, to a place far more worthy of you. You will be finished in the civilised surroundings of a great city, and you will be provided for. You will marry well and you will be allowed, within reason, to choose.

I, on the other hand, fear that without independent means I cannot do anything in this world.

I remind you of this not to lecture you, nor to bemoan my own circumstances, but to urge you to take comfort in the notion—the solid idea—that what you endure will have a clean and definite end. The uncertainty of your life and destiny will of course continue, and it will

28

never be entirely in your hands, but its sphere will widen and become more receptive to you and your treasured gifts. Know that I desire an early release for you, but know also that I follow your career with a sense of confidence I fear I cannot attach to my own.

Darling girl, I must also remind you that, despite our separation, we are lucky in our friendship—truly blessed—and never let anyone persuade you to the contrary. I remember and treasure your cream and apricot solid flesh, that healthy complexion that is both delicate and robust—your firm step; your lovely voice and direct way of speaking and listening; your easy manners with any person, whether high or low—and others will love all these qualities with equal passion.

I am reminding myself of you too much and it is making me miss you unbearably. I shall cease singing your praises directly—you must be blushing—and embark on as lengthy a description of the events of the past few days as your patience can bear.

My cousin Mary returned from New York yesterday, her arrival so quiet and subdued it could hardly be called an event. But then she is like her mother, not only in the apparent calm of her demeanour, but in the constant watchfulness of her gaze. In her sideways appraisal of my face and figure I felt an intense dislike: the way I used to know Mrs Darkins disliked me at school, however much the Head Mistress protested that it was my poor attitude and performance that was to blame. She has been taking a cure in New York, where, poor thing, she was shut up in an upstairs room of some doctor's house, away from the light and given a great deal of butter to quieten her nerves. It has had the desired effect; she was certainly quiet but, I might also add, uncomfortably plump, for which she cannot be said to be at fault.

She has the same penetrating eyes as her brother, except, of course, only at close range, for she suffers from severe myopia and must wear spectacles. She is only twenty-five but looks and behaves like a widow. It makes me sad. She keeps to her room a great deal and when she does come down conversation falters as we cast around for subjects so suitably bland as not to cause her distress. My uncle warned me about this before her homecoming, saying extremely sourly, 'As everything you say comes out of your mouth as if it were an explosion, it might be better if you were to keep entirely silent.' I am sure in this case he is right. I would hate to be the cause of disturbing poor Mary's nerves.

I imagine you asking me how the arrival of so gloomy a person could have made me so occupied I have been unable to write, but in truth she has been only a small part of my life's jigsaw. I have found myself increasingly in the company of my cousin, William, whose opinions and objectives in many ways correspond to my own. We walk the beach with the gulls circling over our heads, continually contemplating his future across the ocean. I am increasingly convinced he might well be the great writer he believes he can be, although I am forbidden to read his stories because of their unsuitable subject matter. Just the little topic of the war and its painful accompaniments disease, death and loss, along with unorthodox opinions about such things. The fact that I share his convictions about the monstrousness of war and have seen more death in my short life than he will ever know appears to be neither here nor there. It is very galling, this veil of unsuitability.

But I must add that I am beginning to suspect that my uncle's displeasure and the question of what constitutes appropriate reading matter for young ladies might well obscure his real reason. I think at heart he is afraid to show me his work. So far he has had only minor attention and been published in a small way—he is choosing me as his intimate—someone so passionate and unformed, as he constantly reminds me—that he is excused for keeping me in ignorance. Yet I sense he fears my judgement. He fears my eyes on the pages he has written. And I suppose I fear it too—but oh, my dear, I am so curious! It is extraordinary, how curious I am.

There is so much time to think. It gives me an odd twist at the heart to be reminded that had my darling Charlie lived he would surely have enlisted and be facing this new mortal danger. You will be glad to know that I have refrained from engaging anyone on the subject of the cruelty of war; I would doubtless be reprimanded strongly. It seems mankind feels compelled to consume itself either from within or without. But I am losing my gaiety. William tells me he loves my gaiety.

So long a letter—I hope you are not bored.

My uncle remarked that I am looking less pale. It is the first time he has spoken to me for several days.

What I struggle to say is that for my uncle and my cousin it is the life of the mind that is their concern. All I know is that I have a horror of blood.

So very affectionately,

Emily

CHAPTER THREE

From his window William watched his cousin running towards the ocean. He had been up since six writing, finding that to move from dream to page often yielded an interesting if not always satisfactory result, and now, dressing and glancing out at the beach, there she was. Through the glass he could see but not smell the beauty of the morning, the very bright dancing light. It would be warm today. The colours were true, there was no mist or early cloud, it was all promise of summer ahead, and he saw her standing and looking about her and he knew she felt delight, alone and in possession of the purity of the shore. He watched her sit on the ground to take off her boots and stockings, then, abandoning them, she ran without hesitating into the ocean, lifting her skirts but wetting the hem of her blue dress.

He left his desk quite without deciding

consciously to do so, hurrying down the stairs to find his coat and muffler waiting for him in the dark hall, and went to join her, walking slowly for fear of interruption, glorying in the vision of her in the waves.

When she turned she seemed only momentarily surprised to see him standing there on the ragged dune grass at the edge of the beach. He did not want the sand in his shoes.

'Good morning, Cousin!' she called to him. 'We should breakfast on the veranda, we really should! Have you seen this beautiful day?'

Any reply would have been inadequate, so he stood still and observed her: the bare flesh of her legs red with cold, dark hair tangled, skirts held in her hand. How could it be that with her mouth too wide for beauty, her nose too definite and figure too slight and unbending, how could it be that this creature could catch at his heart because she was so exquisite? He did not feel his own joy, but he could feel hers.

'They will be calling for you soon.'

'Indeed?'

'Searching high and low.' He wanted to prolong the moment of looking at her and embracing her with his eyes.

She smiled as she tried to pull her hair out of her eyes with the hand that did not hold her skirts.

'It is time to come in now.'

'Is it really? What time is it? I lost my watch.'

'Quite eight o'clock. You were up early.'

For a second she hesitated as if to refuse, then waded towards him. 'I wonder you were not all up and out on this glorious day.'

'I was awake, but I was working.' He held out his

hand as she picked up her boots and stockings. 'I will carry your things.'

She appeared almost angry and yet she was laughing. 'Why should you carry them? They are my poor old things, after all.'

He touched her hand as she drew hers away from him, clutching at her belongings like a child with its plaything, and with bending head studied the veins that held so much life, wanting to seize that hand and wrist and kiss it, knowing he could not, would not, never should. Her playful glance seemed to understand and they approached the house together, its long gabled structure a grey-blue presence in this new sunlight, made somehow benign. To be by the side of such a creature on this morning held a grandeur for him.

And then she broke away, running ahead and up the steps, across the veranda and into the breakfast room and he followed, out of breath, catching at some indescribable feeling of unease.

He could hear her voice calling, 'Good morning, Uncle, Aunt, Mary,' but not their reply. Breakfast was a silent time when his father prepared his mind for the day, his mother her tasks and his sister her spirits. 'This day, have you seen it? It's—'

He gained the doorway and, to his horror, saw his cousin wheeling around the fine old table, still fluttering and running as he had seen her on the beach, more wildly even, racing past the backs of their chairs like something possessed.

'Emily, stop this at once.'

His father's words were spoken too late. She had already made herself giddy and collapsed, laughing, on to the floor.

'I do apologise,' she laughed. 'What could I have been thinking?'

Now that William's horror had subsided she was irresistible to him once more. But to his soberly clad family she was an aberration that they could scarcely raise their eyes to contemplate. His father, that fiery scandalous theologian, who could shout his doctrine from any podium in the country, could not suffer this little girl. Their faces began to turn angrily to her and frowning; it seemed to take more time for Emily to comprehend the extent of their distaste than the gasping breath that shook her and froze her smile.

'Truly, I am sorry, Aunt, Uncle. It is only that it is such a beautiful day.'

'Does this mean we must fear the beauty of every day this summer in case we should again be treated to such a scene?'

'Of course not, Uncle.'

William knew his father had not expected a reply, especially one so swift. 'You are not properly dressed, young woman. Go.'

In her beloved countenance William saw a flash of pain before the anger rose, and when he knew she was angry he was afraid of what she might say. He should intervene. But she said nothing, and neither did he speak, not one word, nor did she look at him as if she expected it. She turned to the door, showing the presence of mind to retrieve her boots and damp sandy stockings, leaving a faint mark on the dark polished floor with her bare feet as she walked away.

His father stood up, wiping his mouth with his napkin. 'Emily.'

She turned and looked at him, with no attempt

35

to hide her tears.

'Keep to your room today. You are obviously much excited and will benefit from the rest.'

Did she curtsey? Was there a suggestion of a bowing of the head? William could not be sure.

'Ah, William, I did not notice you were there. Come and sit with us.'

William sat. He drank his tea and ate a slice of toast. His sister's face bore a look of satisfaction that animated it and filled it with ugliness. He wondered to what degree Emily had already unconsciously become her enemy simply by existing. He understood, if he did not pity her her jealousy. His mother's face, implacable as ever, betrayed nothing.

His father, attempting to contain his agitation by clenching his teeth and rustling his newspaper, eventually spoke. 'My house is a temple to my work, to my ideas, and to the development of my thoughts. That young girl has no place in it.'

Miss Augusta Dean   Newport
High Trees School
Rochester, NY

April 10th   11 o'clock

My sweetest Friend,
    I have been in captivity today and am feeling very sorry for myself. I was sent to my room at breakfast this morning and have not had a bite to eat since waking. Despite your advice to me to make myself agreeable I have singularly failed to gain the family's good opinion. High spirits brought on by the beauty of the day

caused me to forget myself—that is I treated the breakfast table to a glimpse of my happiness, and I do believe there is nothing this family hates so much as happiness. Forgive my bitterness: but that they should have the good fortune to summer in such a place as this while young men prepare to die on the battlefield, while poverty destroys families such as my own—it makes me angry. Perhaps that is precisely why we should not be happy, but I cannot look at it that way. Every morning could be the last morning—the last—do they not see?

It has felt cruel to be locked up. I have watched the occasional walkers returning from the beach. There was a family, a little girl with fair hair had gathered some shells. Nothing happened downstairs. My uncle and cousin have been working; Mary keeps to her room on this floor, I can feel her uncomfortably close. (I sensed she took pleasure in my disgrace today.) If I could calm my fretfulness and self-pity I could pull my chair to the window and read the Shakespeare and Odes that William has lent me; at least then I would be improving my mind instead of longing and longing to be free.

3 o'clock

Unexpected news. A message came this afternoon from William's brothers' regiment— they are to call here to say farewell before their first engagement, which is expected shortly. I heard my aunt speaking of it to my uncle in the hall, and now there is some commotion in the kitchen and I believe the boy has been sent to the butcher. I wonder if I will be permitted to come down when they are expected.

I must restrain myself from walking the floor. It will only perturb them, for I am sure they would hear it.

Forgive my selfishness. If I do not continue this later, write to me with your news.

Yours in affectionate agitation,

Emily

CHAPTER FOUR

They rode their horses up to the house, which Emily felt was very thrilling. She could hear the sound of hooves from the stairs. She had never ridden a horse but had longed to all her life. The creatures were taken to the side of the house where the kitchen boy held them for the length of the entire visit.

Three cavalry officers with blue uniforms and clanking boots stepped out of the sunlight into the hall, where they became boys again.

The whole family was assembled to greet them, and Emily was introduced to her two cousins and their superior, Captain Lindsay.

'I am honoured to make your acquaintance,' he said, taking her hand.

She wanted to say, 'Do not trouble yourself to be charming. I am not the daughter of the house,' but her uncle interrupted before she could speak.

'My niece and ward, Emily, she is with us for a

38

short spell. And this is my daughter, Mary.'

Mary, dressed in black, her collar tight around her short neck, seemed more uncomfortable than Emily had ever seen her, her face emptying of colour in the way most young women might blush. The Captain spoke to Mary with a respectful seriousness that would have soothed her if it were possible for her to be soothed. His easy manners reminded Emily of Augusta's, that and his fair hair and colouring and his obvious rude health. She liked his smile.

William's brothers were a different matter. Brown-haired and slight, each echoed the other in pallor. They did not hold their bodies upright, as did their father, but stooped in the manner of their brother, and while William's dress, that of the intellectual invalid, gave him a certain gravity, their uniforms appeared to overwhelm them. They looked at Captain Lindsay with admiration and shyness.

After the bowing and the shaking of hands, there was luncheon: her aunt's finest, yet served somehow with an air of distaste for its own luxuriance. The jelly seemed frivolous, the sauces unlooked for, uncalled for, and the elaborate table decorations Emily had never before seen did not prevent the room from being austere. Her aunt enquired about life at the barracks, but not in the usual way of mothers, concerned for comfort and the quality of the food and linen—rather she wanted to know about the rigour and the discipline, the rules and routine of the day. Her uncle conducted himself as if his sons were not in uniform at all, but merely visiting from a distant and faintly eccentric college in whose teachings and ways he was not only ignorant but uninterested.

Emily saw Captain Lindsay observing this. The openness of his expression, his direct way of looking, listening and conversing, made it obvious to her that he was somewhat taken aback. In every household in the North the talk was of war and its ideals and objectives and the revulsion felt for the South. Williams elder and younger conversed about Theology and the correct response to Atheism, although Emily noticed that her cousin was careful not to contradict his father's views freely, as he would had he been alone with her.

With coffee they had candied fruit. The ladies were not obliged to withdraw—after all, it was a family visit, and the young men would within a week be at the Front. There was a momentary lull in the conversation, and William coughed. Despite being sharply aware that she should not speak unless spoken to, Emily could not resist exercising her curiosity.

'And how would you be employed now, Sir, were it not for this war?' she asked the Captain.

'You ask a peculiar question—at this moment there is only the war.'

'I ask it nonetheless.'

'You are impertinent, my dear,' said her uncle.

'Not at all, Sir, your niece's question is fair. I would be finishing my Law degree, preparing for my life as a gentleman of property, undecided about a career.' He paused, turning to her uncle. 'I can see your niece attempts to discover me in one question.'

'And have I?'

'Of course not. And even if it were true, how

could I say yes?'

There was a smile around the table, yet she pursued the subject. 'But Sir, you are not forced to fight—you were not conscripted—nor were my cousins. Is it necessary that anyone in this room should have to do so?'

William interrupted immediately. 'I apologise for my cousin. She is never content until she has caused a great quarrel.' He seemed amused, but Emily felt she had embarrassed him deeply.

'It is the question of our time,' she insisted.

'Perhaps,' Captain Lindsay replied, looking only at her.

'I have witnessed the deaths of people that I love and I know that if I could have done anything to prevent it, I would.' Eyes were being averted from her face once more.

'There is no reasoning with the South,' he answered. 'You must see that.'

'But there is with ourselves. Cousins, I have only lately made your acquaintance, and when I think I may never see you again after this day—'

'That is enough, Emily. Captain, please let me apologise for my niece's manners.'

Emily looked at her cousins in their uniforms, at the plates they had eaten from and the glasses from which they had drunk, and felt sobered and becalmed.

'I am sorry, Uncle. I did not mean to cause any embarrassment or pain.'

'You are too free in your reference to others' feelings, my dear.'

Emily felt a brief wild despair. He would oppose her. He would continue to oppose her. He was unyielding and would not tire as she did.

41

'Mr Cornford, might I request that you allow me to take a short walk with your niece on the beach?' Captain Lindsay was already rising from the table. 'Miss Emily, would you care to accompany me?'

She scraped her chair getting up, banged her knee on the arm of it, so great was the longing to get away.

*　　　*　　　*

He looked larger out of doors. 'You are bent on causing a scandal? These are my men you terrify with the idea of death.' They hurried down the worn and slender path among the grasses, as if pursued. Warm salt air was blowing, and the sun was on her face. He stopped sharply to look at her.

'Death is not an idea to me.' Stupid, angry tears.

'Please, accept my apologies. Your cousins have told me about the tragic history of your family. You are an orphan?'

'Yes.'

'You are fortunate to have been spared.' She was silent, knowing she was expected to say: Yes, fortunate indeed. 'They say that our loved ones are never so truly ours as in death.'

'I have heard it.' They were still looking at one another, the light on their faces.

'We are very morbid on this beautiful day.'

'Yes. Unexpectedly. I am in the habit of being scolded for being too happy.' He made no move to walk on but continued to give her his attention. 'May I ask you another question?' she said. 'Are you not afraid?'

'Of what is to come? Extremely. I only know that if I do not lead them it will be somebody else. That this great nation—'

'A nation cannot be great that fights itself.' She was fierce.

'It is only to achieve our ideals that we fight.' He was measured and sure.

'Fighting is the enemy of ideals.'

He kept his temper. 'Ah, now I see. You are a pacifist.'

'My brother used to fight with his friends when they were children. They did not pretend it was for the love of a better world.'

He laughed. 'My dear young lady, I can see you will not be subdued.'

'No. I will not.' She liked him immensely. He shared her passion for the day.

'Let us be friends. It is my cavalry at war on your behalf, after all, and I must say I find you most ungrateful. You modern girls.'

She realised, too slowly, that he was teasing her. Charlie had used to tease her, but not with such a smile, a smile she could only construe as admiring. It was a little like the way her cousin smiled at her, but it was more open and generous—she could feel a wholeness in him.

'Of course we must be friends.'

And she gave him her hand.

*   *   *

At eight o'clock Emily and Mary sewed together in the parlour, each holding their work close to the lamplight.

'I must say, Cousin, you have a passion in your conversation that I fear will work to your detriment in this house.'

43

Emily was surprised to be spoken to; they had been silent for an hour. William had gone into the town, her aunt had retired early and her uncle was at his desk. There was only the sound of the ocean waves.

'I don't consider your fears ill-founded.' She looked up but could see no expression save concentration on her cousin's face. 'And yet I cannot entertain them.' Bending, she continued with her work. There was quiet again for a while.

'Did you love them so very much?'

'Who, my dear?'

'Your brother and sisters, your parents.' Still Mary looked at her work.

Emily observed the face, half blind. 'I did. They were all my heart and soul to me.'

'I think that is what galls my father the most. It is obvious that you have been loved. He had no love to give us. None. He once told me that the best course for a parent to take in this sinful world would be to annihilate his children.'

'You cannot mean that? He did not say it.'

At last she looked up. 'This is a nest of vipers, my dear girl. You are not safe among us.'

'Mary, you are tired. The strain of the day—'

'He loved your mother, I think. Very much. But she made that unsuitable marriage, had to be cast out.'

Emily could not bear to hear her mother discussed in so dry a voice. 'My mother is my own memory—not yours.'

Mary, who had seemed all bitterness and envy, now confounded Emily with her concern and advice. Looking at the empty grey eyes, she felt a great sorrow and fear for this woman of shadows,

44

but no concern for herself.

*   *   *

They sat on the veranda, she and William, in the morning sunlight, her book on her knee. He had pulled his chair close to hers, 'So we can be *tête à tête*,' he had said.

'How do you get on with Mr Keats and Mr Shakespeare?'

'Very well. I like them very well.'

'*Like them*! I don't think I have ever heard you express so bland an opinion.'

'Very well, if you are set upon more detail: I find them beautiful and I love their beauty. They write about the yearning and the longing of the young heart and the exquisite nature of the universe and you chose them for me for exactly that reason.'

'And now you are too clever.'

'Indeed?'

'And very lovely. You are very lovely today.' He called her lovely but did not look at her as he did so.

'Shall we walk?' she said. 'It is not too warm for you?'

'You can hold your parasol over my head.'

'I detest parasols. Bring your hat.'

'Be patient while I fetch it.'

*   *   *

There was only a fluttering breeze. It was a glorious blue day. The sand looked almost white. They walked arm in arm studying the ocean, the shells beneath their feet. Unlike the Captain he

45

did not care to look into her face too often.

'You were impressed by Captain Lindsay?'

'I was. Even though I did not agree with him.'

'He is an old acquaintance of ours. Always forthright. He is the apotheosis of the brave gentleman soldier.'

'You describe him as if he were a type.'

'That is exactly what he is. He is heir to a considerable fortune and is therefore untroubled by doubts. He knows his place in the world.'

'You generalise far too much. You too have expectations—'

He adopted a superior expression. 'None so large.'

'But why should it be that the fact he has no financial concerns mean he does not give due attention to—'

'To what?'

'As you call it, his place in the world.' She said this as deliberately and calmly as she could.

'I don't know why you feel you must defend him. He is no relation of yours.'

Emily felt her irritation rise. 'You are accusing him of being somehow narrow.'

'Not at all. It is only that he is who he is, exactly who he is and he wastes no time or trouble contemplating it.'

'He is a man of action.' She laughed, forgetting her annoyance. 'This has made you horribly cross.'

'Nothing of the kind. I just don't see how you could admire him so much when there is so little to admire.'

'Did I say I admired him?'

'You didn't have to.'

'William, you are being ridiculous.' As these

46

words rang out of her little body she felt that if only she could have grasped them and forced them back into her lungs she might restore the temperate climate between them, that sense of ease.

He stopped. 'You have offended me.'

'I can't say I am glad of it. But the fact that I should enjoy the company and thoughts of anyone other than yourself cannot—surely—be so very loathsome.' She tried to speak coaxingly, but she had never coaxed in her life.

'My dear, the truth is I am too fond of you.'

'Nonsense. You are too fond of yourself.'

'I fear you must continue your walk alone.'

'If I must.'

He turned and walked away, leaving her angry and the morning spoiled.

Miss Augusta Dean   Newport
High Trees School
Rochester, NY

April 14th

Dearest Girl,

This afternoon I received a message from Captain Lindsay asking if he might call and accompany me on a drive. It is the kind of pleasant surprise I had not looked for. It seems the regiment is delayed at ——— for another few days. I asked my uncle's permission and was more than a little taken aback when he agreed, brushing me aside as if I were an

47

insect, of course.

Laugh if you will but it was nothing short of exciting to be bowling along in an open carriage away from the oppressive atmosphere of that house and in the company of someone who sought to enjoy himself with such obvious relish.

'First, let us have no talk of war or death,' he said, as soon as I was settled. 'Let us be carefree.' It was like an answer to a prayer to hear another human being say that. We clattered through the streets, and all the store fronts and people and houses looked so cheerful and bright. We turned off Main Street and explored the avenues where all the houses are new and, while modest, beautifully sited, and with generous space around them, big windows and flower-filled gardens. I felt a little envious of their inhabitants for having so much life around them: people walking, children, and babies in their perambulators, even cats and dogs. I miss the company of children. Then we took the road out of town along the shore: the country is wild and beautiful and as I had seen it only at night when I arrived, new to me. There is so very much horizon, so much of the ocean.

He told me about his family at Boston, his dear sister who is close to him in age and about to be married. He joked about what a poor student he had been at college, but I think he is too modest. We returned to the house for tea. I had such an appetite!

He asked me what would become of me when this delightful summer was over. I told him I imagined I would be sent to another school, but that there was a possibility I could visit Boston, perhaps at Christmas. I confided that I hoped to be able to continue with instruction in drawing, but did not mention the lack of my own funds or the goodwill of my uncle. Indeed I tried to appear light-hearted about the prospect of the future, and feared I might seem either brittle and frivolous or melancholy as a consequence. It always makes me feel that way—more than apprehensive—when I think of the Fall: darkness in the rooms and uncertainty, but I did not want him to see.

He asked me how old I was, and I said I was nearly nineteen and he pronounced me a very young girl. I teased him for speaking of it, when he must be all of twenty-four.

Then he said a strange thing that moved me. He said there was a tradition of New Year parties in his house in Boston and he very much hoped I would be able to attend. He said he thought the house would suit me. He dropped his voice then, although there was no danger of our being overheard. The parlour is very private. He said, 'I can see you against the portraits and chandeliers, as part of them, almost.' I felt peculiarly moved by his speech. But again, I did not want him to see that I was moved. I looked away. You know me, Augusta—I never look away.

I would not like him to be killed. I would like him to come back and I would like to see him again. Perhaps if I admitted I felt affection for him the fates would immediately conspire to annihilate him, so I will admit no such thing. I just pray earnestly that God keeps him safe, his horse is fast and his battles are mere skirmishes. For God knows he makes the world a brighter place by being in it.

I have forgotten to thank you for your letter. I cannot close without a promise to take your advice to heart and once again try to be more cautious in all things. I know you understand, my dearest, how I feel, but I also know your counsel to be both practical and wise. It pains me to hear that you have been in low spirits—but remember, your period of uncertainty will be at an end by the close of the summer. Remain strong until then.

Affectionately,

Emily

With the departure of the regiment there were only brief messages from the brothers, but for Emily, a letter:

Miss Emily Hudson   ———— Regiment
Bluff House, Newport Beach

April 16th, 1861

My dear Young Lady,

It seems melodramatic to be bidding you farewell on the eve of battle, so I will simply inform you that we are on the move at last. It is surely a nobler thing always to act than to wait, and the fewer thoughts I devote to the task ahead the better in my present frame of mind. I recall clearly your blue dress against the dark of the carriage, and the gaiety of our last meeting.

I hope that neither of us will be so very much older when next I grasp your hand.

Yours truly,

Captain James C H Lindsay,
———— Regiment, ————

'Such an expression at the breakfast table. Could it denote a proposal?' remarked William, *sotto voce*, but no less publicly for that.

'Do not be cruel, Cousin, it does not become you. And you know perfectly well it cannot.'

This exchange roused her uncle. 'Who is the letter from, my dear?'

'It is from Captain Lindsay, Sir. He says they are going away soon.'

'Indeed. Do not reply for the present, Emily.'

'May I be excused from the table, Sir?'

'You may.'

*　　　*　　　*

And she was alone again, walking along the beach and holding the letter. The sky was unexpectedly overcast but it was not cold.

It would not do for her to brood over this man and the extreme tenderness of what he had written, the charm of its light-hearted tone. She had never received such a letter before. She understood that if a person were about to enter circumstances of acute danger it would be quite understandable that they should attach undue importance to a drive through a town along a wild

51

and beautiful shore, and allow the company of the young girl who had—by an accident of fate—been accompanying him to somehow feel significant. It was quite understandable. That in itself was not what moved her; whether he saw her truly when he imagined her was of very little importance. How could it be compared to the hideousness of the ordeal he was about to face? A battle with killing and maiming and blood. It was quite terrible that her face should be streaked with tears; try as she might to convince herself that she did not cry for herself but for him.

The awful recollection came to her of holding Charlie's lifeless form in her arms the night he died, the girls sleeping in their beds, her father exhausted in his chair before the fire, and she, with Charlie, holding him, but so alone because he was no longer there. At least her mother had been spared that. It was not right a child should die before its parent, and yet nature had no respect for what was right. Of God she had long ceased to think, though she still prayed out of habit. Darling Charlie. She had closed his eyes, smoothed his hair and tucked him in before her father could be afforded a glimpse of him.

It was bad, this new pain for another human being. It laid her quite low. It would not do. It would not do at all. Her mother would chide her. She would tell her to make herself useful. And yet she could not bring herself to turn towards the house, reach for her sewing, for her books, even for her pencil. She must walk and arrange her thoughts.

*   *   *

It was a long walk, and as she made her way back and approached the house the cloud parted a little and a few shafts of light fell over the ocean. It moved and heaved as if some sleeping beast were stirring beneath the mirrored waves.

William was waiting for her, reading in the shade.

'You are sad, Cousin?'

It was hard to be on-guard after such thoughts and feelings as she had so recently endured. They had not spoken privately since their painful and trivial quarrel the day before. His eyes were gentle.

'Perhaps. A little.'

'Come and sit with me. We will discuss the Odes and if you consent I will fetch you something new to read.'

She said nothing, but brought her chair close to his, pressing the backs of her hands against her cheeks and eyes to ensure they were no longer wet.

Miss Augusta Dean   Newport Beach
High Trees School
Rochester, NY

May 2nd, 1861

My dear Friend,

   I am so glad to hear your spirits have lifted and that the summer promises such delights for you. It is hardly imaginable, picturing you borne off by your father to taste the delights of Italy. Do not concern yourself about the heat. Providing you guard against fatigue by frequent rests and make sure your clothes are not too restrictive, you drink water often and do not travel in the heat of the day, you will be quite safe and secure. In his youth my father travelled extensively and would always entertain us with his stories of the many precautions taken by female travellers against the rigours of their journeys. And now here I am, repeating his observations and sounding more like a maiden aunt than your rebellious friend! Remember, too, that your father is a most experienced traveller, having essayed most of these places before—and I do not imagine you will venture too far South.

How thrilling to have such a trip to plan for and to occupy your thoughts—but how extremely frustrating that he refuses to commit himself in either direction about whether you will return to school in the Fall. Perhaps he intends to test your company first while you are in Italy, so take my advice and take care not to anger or oppose him, but be an irreproachable travelling companion throughout the journey! Easier said than done in my opinion: if it were your devoted Emily I would cause some disturbance by an untoward remark before even setting sail. For his sake we must be thankful that he has sweet-tempered delightful you as his daughter and not this unfortunate girl.

Do I mean to describe myself as unfortunate? I confess I do not—for it is not the case—and yet my spirits have not been high these past few days. Perhaps it is all the novelty of making the Captain's acquaintance (as described in, I hope, not too tedious a length in my last letter!) and that very touching missive which I have now consigned to my locked bureau drawer. At my uncle's request I have not replied to the letter, and in this case perhaps it is for the best. I should not like to brood over it and become sentimental. I have heard nothing from him since, and am both relieved at it—because I do not wish my feelings to be brought to such a pitch of fearful anticipation on so slight and brief an acquaintance, and in so short a time—and disappointed because I would like to be assured at every hour and minute that he is alive and well. As, I hasten to add, I would all those foolish and brave young men who have undertaken this rash war so unthinkingly.

My uncle spends the breakfast hour in study of the newspaper, but I think he considers it unseemly to discuss its contents, or for anyone else in the family to know too much. It is not as if the lives of his two sons are bound up in it, or any such thing.

I have been troubled with a slight but persistent cough that I am sure I have caught from William and this unseasonably damp weather is doing nothing to subdue. It will not rain properly, but only denies us sunlight, and there is a fine mist, not even a drizzle, in the air. I have been taking my daily exercise regardless, but William does not approve. Relations with my cousin are now more secure, even though I did not apologise for daring to disagree with him. He treats me with a consistent affection and consideration that eases my spirits. We have progressed to that new and exciting novel of Mrs Eliot's, *The Mill on the Floss*. I must confess to being far more interested in Maggie than its description of the changes in rural society in that particular corner of England. Doubtless I am proving myself to be quite as young as William persists in telling me I am.

My aunt, uncle and cousin Mary appear to have settled into a routine of barely acknowledging my presence. We do not converse except in the most limited and expedient way, such as 'Could you pass the salt and pepper?' or 'I wonder, shall it finally rain in earnest today?' They do not like me. They wish I were not here. And it is wearing to know that my fate is in their hands. Before I continue in this self-pitying vein I will sign myself,

Your ever affectionate,

Emily

CHAPTER FIVE

A brilliant morning brought the end of Emily's days of low spirits. She went out early with her sketchbook, determined to attempt to catch some of the light on its paper, and settling in a sandy hollow in the dunes, fell asleep in the unexpected warmth of the sun. Its return had seemed to promise her less uncertainty. She felt she could work clearly in the light and, satisfied, she could sleep.

Only the sound of a little party of walkers passing close by woke her. Her face was hot and the glare considerable. A glance at the sky proved it was beyond midday. Luncheon. Tying up the ribbon of the sketchbook and walking rapidly back towards the house—she did not run in case her uncle should be watching from the window—she had that all too familiar feeling of distracted and vague guilt. She was in the wrong: unconsciously she had put herself there again.

Now she could see them, already eating in the dining room, a subdued tableau of soberly-clad shadowy figures. Determined not to burst in on them from the veranda and cause displeasure and annoyance by her lack of consideration, she decided to go around the house and enter at the front. The maid would come if she knocked quietly. But there was no need. The door had been left open and in the hall she put down her book and attempted to smooth her clothes and tidy her hair. It would take too long to go to her room and try to mend her appearance better. She must hurry. With a light step she crossed the morning room and parlour and approached the dining room door. Her uncle's voice boomed from within, easily penetrating its thickness and that of the walls.

'. . . her carelessness, her lack of decorum, her insulting ignorance of every subject including the manners of polite society—all these things I have come to accept, but your unaccountable affection for this troublesome girl, this I cannot countenance, William. I absolutely cannot. Do not exercise yourself to defend her. Who knows where she is now. She cannot come to her meals without being called, it seems—no better than a dog.'

Standing still and slight outside that tall dark door, Emily had never felt so mortified and alone. But in that quick, breathing second where her ears were noisy, her eyes full of tears, her face hot and every part of her body quivering, she did not think to turn away. She knocked, sudden and quick, and entered the room.

'I am afraid I am late for luncheon, Uncle.' She tried to speak as an honoured guest might. They all looked at her with eyes hollow and unreadable, except for William, whose expression was compassionate. He did not scold her or ask her where she had been.

'You are very pale, my dear, are you quite well?' enquired her aunt.

'Quite well, thank you, Ma'am.'

'Then you must take your place with us.' It was strange that it should be her aunt who should question her, that her aunt should decide, but no one appeared to think it strange. Her life was strange; these people were strange, floating around the shiny table, strange and unreal.

She found her place quietly and sat. Her uncle rang the bell for her to be served, then lifted his own knife and fork and recommenced eating, followed by his family. Emily took a sip of water. *No better than a dog, no better than a dog*, and now her heart was racing to the sound of the words. If she could gather her belongings and go—she suddenly had a picture of herself gathering her belongings into a reticule—if she could walk out of this house and along the cliffs and follow this shore to the end of her strength, in the hope of finding somewhere she would be welcome . . . But she was wild and desperate, and there was nowhere. She sipped her water again. Her uncle was saying something but she could not understand the words. She knew he did not require an answer from her.

She looked over Mary's shoulder to the window and to the moving ocean, but that was no good, her eyes were blurred. It seemed she would not be able to maintain her composure after all. She thought of Augusta, laughing in the woods on a summer day as they counted patches of sunlight. She thought of the Captain handing her into the carriage with a delicacy that indicated she was precious. Her lips and mouth were dry and she kept on thinking of these two friends, as her plate was put in front of her and she chewed the bitter bread.

When they stood up to leave the table she was forced to lift her eyes. William was studying her face, quiet and intent, begging for a look, which she gave him. He knew that she had heard, they all knew. His expression—she was not prepared for it—was all curiosity, an excited curiosity, and his face was quite flushed and damp as if from sudden exertion. She had anticipated sympathy, a sympathy she would have wanted hastily to push away. He was quite absorbed in her, looking in so acute a fashion, and even though she had offered him a glance he kept on looking, she could tell, as she put her napkin on the table and turned away. He wanted to stop her, she knew, and she did not know if she wanted to be stopped. The thought of the silence of her upstairs room oppressed her. Now that the days were becoming warmer her uncle encouraged the ladies to rest after lunch.

She hated rest.

'Cousin.' He put his hand on her arm as she moved towards the door. It was peculiar. He rarely touched her and the sensation was strange, adding to the strangeness of the day. 'My dear.'

She was very tired. Being compared to a dog had made her very tired. Her uncle had gone. The effect of his insult had not interested him sufficiently for him to seek an interview—or even a look. He did not appear to wish to admonish her. He had other things on his mind.

'Yes, William.' Her face was turned from him.

'My dear, I cannot help but be aware that you must have heard my father's outburst. He was much exercised. I hope you understand—'

She looked at him directly. 'Do you apologise for him?'

'I apologise for us all. I lack courage when it comes to my father. I fear I should have defended you. I was distinctly ungallant.'

'William, I have never believed you in the least gallant.'

'Might you smile then? You know him for an old rhinoceros.'

'It seems I am a dog.'

'Oh, my dear, I—' In their look he seemed at pains to assert their mutual bond. 'Are we serious, or do we laugh about it? Is it painful, or is he our little joke?'

'He is a joke for you who are not tied to him. You have the means to escape him whenever you choose.'

He allowed himself a smile, his expression turning inwards as if to examine himself, the same flush on his cheeks. Emily herself felt drained of colour. 'How little you know about me.'

'On the contrary, I feel I know rather a lot.'

It was still in the room and his hand remained on her arm. 'Tell me, Cousin, I long to know, tell me about your mother. Let us remember her together. My father will not speak of her, and yet I know that once she was his favourite little sister.'

This was an unexpected request and Emily was disarmed, raw from her uncle's anger. 'Why should you mention her now?' He had never referred to her family before.

'I do not know. It is just I think you must be very like her—I think she was very proud. I think my father sees her shadow in you, we all sense it.'

She felt a little faint and unsure what was for the best. 'Must I, William? Must I talk of her?'

His hand increased its pressure. 'Come. Come. Please. I would like to know her better. And it will distract you from this unpleasant scene. Tell me the story.' His hand guided her out on to the veranda, the reassuring heat of the afternoon tempered by the overhanging roof, the gentle breeze easing her. They sat on the steps, close together, like children sent outside to eat fruit. The backs of their hands were touching, their forms huddled together. It was a comfort. She did not look at him but down at the step.

'I thought her very beautiful. I adored her.'

'No. Start from the beginning,' he insisted. 'It is not enough that she was beautiful. You must start from the beginning of the story.'

'I doubt if I know it all.'

'No. The whole must be assembled. But your part is what interests me now.'

'Well. You know there were three of them.'

'My father was the eldest.'

'Then brother Ernest—'

'He lives in New York, and they do not speak. And then there was your mother.'

'She was the younger sister—they spoiled her and loved her,' said Emily in a low voice.

'That is not my understanding. Their upbringing was strict, but they held her in high esteem. She was their girl, their precious, beautiful girl. And when it came time for her to marry—'

'Our grandfather was very rich—land prospecting.'

'I know that they moved a great deal to remote places, and our grandmother pined for her family. He was always in pursuit of money to be made.'

'But eventually they settled in New York to find my mother a husband from their acquaintance among our grandmother's more respectable family. She had a large portion and competition was fierce. But she fell in love with my father, who was her drawing teacher. He had not a cent, nothing by way of land or even connections to bring to the match. She told me that her father wanted more than a respectable family for his daughter, but a grand and established one. I do not think they planned to elope, not in the beginning. My father did not want her to forsake her expectations or break her bond with her family all for him. He begged her to wait until he had made his way better in the world. But she was very young.'

'The same age as you are now, I think.'

'And eventually he let her persuade him. They were both terrified she would be married against her will if they delayed and then it would be too late. My uncle, your father, believed he had her trust and her confidence—and it was true, he did—but that did not prevent her from wresting her own destiny from his hands and from her father's hands, and leaving them all.'

'It was a most terrible outcome. Regrettable. Painful.'

'I do not think so.' She was still looking at the wooden step beneath her feet and fancying it very warm by now. 'They loved each other very much. They were happy.'

'She was ruined. She died young. They all perished.'

'All except me.'

'My father sees it as God's punishment.'

All before Emily's eyes was the home she had lived in with her mother, father, brother Charlie and the girls, and she could not speak.

'What were your sisters' names?'

'I was just thinking of them. Isabella and Helena. Very unfashionable in our age of plainness. She was a romantic. We lived at Buffalo; you probably know that. So much building going on. They kept a poor but respectable house. They taught us a great many things. Mother said a person must always think for themselves. I remember stories before the fire, and in the summer, excursions to the lakes—you should see them, Cousin. But the winters there are cruel and neither of my parents was particularly strong. The life is hard. She used to laugh and talk about the pioneer spirit but that was not how she had been raised. She had been cosseted. I think it grieved her deeply not to see or hear from her family. She did not say so, though. She remained a loyal, dear heart. She was fond of music. It was she who gave her time to teaching me to play; her touch was superior to mine. My father instructed me in drawing.'

'And yet they were cursed, cursed with the consumption.'

His voice tugged her back to this time, this place. And now she looked at him, at his pale profile drained of blood. 'It is not a curse, but an illness, it is an infection—bad air and—'

'I only describe it as my father described it to me.'

'My mother succumbed to the consumption. We nursed her as best we could. Then it came to the girls. But Charlie died first, of a fever. At the end there was only my father and me. We took care of one another.'

'You were sister and mother and wife.'

He provoked her with his quiet voice. 'I was not. I loved them, and I was myself. He could barely live without her, and after the girls had gone I think he would not stay just for me.'

At last he looked at her but she had bowed her head. There were too many tears. 'You are weeping.'

'How could I not weep for my darlings? How could I not weep? I wish I had not told you. I wish I had not.' And yet still she would not give herself up to passionate sobs, not before his eyes.

'And you were spared. You are fortunate.'

'So I am told.' She struggled to stop her tears with only the sound of the ocean in her ears.

'If you were known to suffer from consumption you could not marry.'

She lifted her head. 'Do you think I am ignorant of that?'

'My father feels it keenly.'

'That I must marry before it comes to claim me? I may be free of it, or if I am not, no one knows how long it could remain waiting after first I had— It might be nobler for me not to marry at all.'

His voice was urgent for the first time. 'But you *must* marry. You have no fortune. You must marry and well. And perhaps if Father approves your choice he will settle a reasonable sum on you.'

'I am weary of this conversation. I do not want to hear any more.' She got up, holding on to the railing with a damp hand.

'But surely, my dear Emily, you must be sensible from everything in your story that your choice is of the utmost importance. You must find a gentleman sufficiently placed to appreciate you without a significant fortune, someone who will protect you from the vicissitudes of the time, guide you through your struggles with your own passionate nature . . .' He stood very close to her now.

'You are very presumptuous, Sir.'

'Don't be angry with me now, Emily. You are too tired—and you must acknowledge the sense of what I am saying. You are too intelligent—'

'If you tell me anything further about what I am and who I shall be, I fear we will quarrel, Cousin.' And now she was standing, and looking down into his thin face. 'It is true that it is hot. It is true that I am tired, and thirsty, and full of the sorrows of the past. But if you were to ask me about my mother's destiny, I could only tell you of her happiness, of her radiance, of the things she would have us feel, experience and know. It is senseless to you, and yet if you were to ask me what animated me, what lights my way, it would be her tender love. And I will not hear you scorn her actions and the path she took.'

'You speak well. But tell me, Emily, precious Emily—would you choose such a path?'

And when he said that, the weariness came over her again, her spirit assailed by his clarity, by the dissection he applied to her mind.

'In truth, William, I cannot and do not know.'

Miss Augusta Dean   Newport Beach
High Trees School
Rochester, NY

June 10th, 1861

My dear Augusta,

Summer wears on and I fear I am not myself at present. But only for the present. Without telling you the details I must own that relations with my uncle have once more deteriorated and a distressing scene with my cousin has left me quite undone; and now he has gone to stay with some acquaintances in Boston I am left quite alone to brood on it. I lack vigour or my customary interest in my usual pursuits. Walking tires me and I am still troubled by this cough. I am advised to rest, but I will not keep to my room entirely—it is too solitary, although of course I must be solitary everywhere.

Forgive me. You must be in the midst of preparing for your journey—keep me apprised of your many plans.

Fondest love,

Emily

In truth, it was more than a slight cough, and Emily knew it. But even to Augusta she could not admit she was confined to her bed, or express the terror that clutched at her heart every time she coughed, and as the fits of coughing became more frequent she could no longer count them. Nor could she reassure herself sufficiently to lift her spirits, assailed by memories of her mother's bloodless face, the shadows that had claimed her sisters, extinguishing the light in her father's eyes. No loving hands tended her. She was entirely alone. To be brought low by any physical illness was to be intruded upon to an unacceptable degree. Her whole spirit fought it, while the animal in her suffered the invasion and could not resist.

On the third day the sound of William's return filled Emily with agitation and not a little dread. Confined to her room as she had been for a vague and seemingly endless period of time, prostrate, as she hated to be, with blinds drawn on the day: it was not the way any creature would like to be found. He made very little noise as was his habit, but she heard her aunt admonishing him to speak more quietly. 'She is quite ill with that cough, I think. She has not come downstairs yesterday or today.' Then their footsteps and murmuring voices died away.

It did not hurt to breathe. But it hurt so terribly when she coughed, and she could not help coughing. She was feverish, she knew, because everything was the wrong colour and to think on any subject made her want to cry. She took some water from the untouched tray of luncheon beside the bed, and allowed herself the luxury of ceasing to try.

He came to see her in the evening. She heard him tapping on the door. She did not know if she had been asleep.

'Cousin?' his voice said. 'Might I intrude, just for a few moments?' He brought a lamp, holding it up in the doorway. She raised herself on her pillows. 'You are still fully dressed.' He looked like a child, surprised.

'I intend to get up. I have been up. I—' She smiled at him, curious at herself for being so pleased to see him when their last interview had caused her so much pain. 'I am not really ill, you know. A little influenza, I fancy.'

'If you are not improved tomorrow, the doctor shall be called.' He seemed chastened.

'William, it is all right.'

He took a step closer to the bed. 'I—I'd be— what I mean to say is—at our last meeting—I am sorry for the way I pressed you to speak on a subject which—if you had had the choice—'

'You have misunderstood. You are not to blame yourself. It was the memories that undid me.' She held out her hand and he came and took it.

'You are too generous to me.'

'Possibly. You are too mournful, William. Come to me tomorrow and we will be friends once more.' She did not quite know how she could sound so decisive in this gloom.

'It is only that you are so pure, so wild and so pure, that I wanted to find out—I long to know—'

'Please, William. Enough. You are my dear friend and cousin. We will not speak of it. I will be well again directly.'

*   *   *

It was another day before the fever passed and the cough began to heal by degrees; a week before she could walk without being tired. She told no one of the terror she had had that she might find a speck of blood upon a handkerchief, just that one speck on the virgin white, on the lace. Her dreams of blood on the snow.

In the real world the sky was bleached with heat, the sand and dunes too and the ocean lazier as the summer reached its peak. When it waned and gentled, she felt, she knew, a change would come to her vast cramped world.

Miss Augusta Dean   Newport Beach
High Trees School
Rochester, NY

June 21st, 1861

My dear Friend,

Thank you very much for your sweet and loving letter. In truth there is little cause for concern. The fact of being alone in the world is that sometimes one has the occasion to feel it, but reading your words, with all their sweet concern and lively news, has benefited my spirits miraculously. And as for my cough—it has quite disappeared. Sea air and the

69

dampness can often encourage the most unseasonable ailments.

Now that I am feeling stronger the sun and light appear less unrelenting, and I have returned to my old ramblings and hauntings of the shores. I have discovered one or two spots where I am always quite alone, and yesterday I unpinned my hair just to feel the breeze in it. It became such a tangle that it was a ridiculous business trying to put it back together again. I do miss you. Do you remember how we used to dry our hair before the dormitory fire together, and brush it for one another? You were always so skilful and nimble at helping me with mine. That it should be so thick and heavy is such a trial—why can it not be fine and biddable like yours? My mother did not have such hair—I must have inherited it from my father.

See how small my world has become? Hair and a walk on the beach, while you assemble trunks and look for just the right ribbon! My dearest, I am simply so completely happy for you. I will direct the first of my letters to you to the Hotel at Como and continue to do so until I hear that you have moved on.

Bon voyage, my darling, and *bonne chance*.
Affectionately,

Emily

PS. Be sure to have comfortable walking shoes for the lakes—it would be a shame to miss a fine vista for the lack of them. xxx

Miss Emily Hudson   ———— Squadron,
                         ———— Regiment

Bluff House, Newport Beach

July 3rd

Dear Miss Hudson,
  Far be it for me to complain about my travails in the battlefield—but I will own to a disappointment in not having heard from you. I apologise for being abrupt, there is not very much time here.
  Tell me how you do.
  Yours truly,

  James Charles Lindsay

Captain J C H Lindsay   Newport
                         ———— Squadron,
                         ———— Regiment

July 5th

Dear Sir,

  Your letter has indeed found me in good health and spirits, and all the better for ascertaining that you too are well. Forgive me for not replying to your previous letter, but it was at my uncle's request. How formal and conventional I must sound! I must own that I am not in the habit of writing to captains serving at the Front. If I think about it too consistently I begin to bite my nails—a habit I

71

should not admit to a living soul.

We understand that loss of life has been heavy and the toll in bloodshed high. I flinch to picture you in such circumstances, and yet I also feel that your men are indeed fortunate to be led by a person of such clear-sighted confidence and resolve. But I would not have you dwell on your task, however, through any words of mine, nor question you too closely on your privations. Instead, I shall simply attempt to amuse you with other things.

My uncle is deep into a treatise on The Blasphemy of Thought.

My aunt has ordered the parlour to be swept and cleaned, and so we cannot sit in it and have invaded William's library.

William, therefore, has discovered urgent business in town and has been away for two days. He must stay at his club for the house is shut up.

Cousin Mary has completed three samplers and is beginning a tablecloth.

As for your friend, I continue my literary education. My cousin is, I think, intent on whipping me into a ferment of Romanticism— from Keats we have progressed to Shelley, Lord Byron and Wordsworth. He has rejected my demands for the great American authors. First things first, he says. And I continue with Shakespeare, which I own is a world in itself so glorious and great and yet still half-submerged that I feel on occasion altogether weak about addressing myself to it. Weak, but enthralled at the same time.

I continue my drawing but long for

instruction. No one in this family has the slightest interest in Art. But I am unfair. William likes to pronounce things good or bad.

I play and I love my playing.

The country blooms and becomes more beautiful every day. I know spring is exciting and to be admired, but the glorious bounty of summer, its abundance—I cannot describe it— it is just so beautiful the way the flowers throw themselves away. And there is also my constant companion, the ocean.

So you can imagine how it is with me. Beautiful, but very quiet.

You are in all our thoughts. Please remember me to my dear cousins.

Yours truly,

Emily Hudson

*   *   *

'I see that you have received another letter from our Captain Lindsay, my dear.'

Emily and her uncle stood in his study again, his desk between them, amongst the many dark things. She began to imagine the objects being taken out of the room by removal men one by one, and the thought was pleasing. She waited for him to speak, shrinking from the next encroachment on her feelings, on her world, yet curious at the same time.

Her uncle's expression was as severe as ever, but she heard in his voice an attempt to moderate the usual coldness of his tone. Emily did not like it, just as she could not bear for him to call her 'My

73

dear'.

'Yes, I have, Sir.' If he asked to see it, she would produce it, but she would not volunteer it.

'He appears to have formed some sort of attachment to you, Emily.'

'He has written me two letters, Uncle.'

'I have always held Captain Lindsay in very high esteem.' He said this with an air of self-satisfaction. She said nothing in reply. 'You are unusually reserved, my dear.'

'He is a kind and sensible gentleman.'

He sat down and began to adjust his cuffs. 'I hope it will come as a pleasant surprise to you, my dear, that I intend after all to bring you with us to Boston in the Fall. The season will be subdued because of the war, obviously, but I wish you to participate in all the usual events. William will chaperone you. There will be a dress allowance. You shall share a maid with Mary. It will all be taken care of.'

She had not expected to feel glad. But she felt glad. Thanksgiving in the warmth of someone's house instead of at school, a wider glimpse of the world, of people and of places—how could she not be glad?

'I hope I do not have to remind you that your behaviour will be closely judged. Unaccustomed as she is to a great deal of society, your aunt is willing to accompany you to remind you of the appropriate niceties. Outbursts of any kind will not be tolerated. Opinions will be held in check. You will put your considerable strength of will into appearing and being pleasant, cheerful and amiable at all times. If you disobey these words the penalty will be an immediate and complete

74

retirement from society. Do you comprehend what I am saying?'

'Yes.'

'You must marry, Emily. You may encourage the attentions of suitable young men. But if I hear that you have been in any way forward or flirtatious, or have encouraged addresses from any inappropriate persons—'

'What can you think of me, Sir?'

'Do you mock me, my dear?'

'I assure you I do not. I am more than sensible of your generosity.' And it was true, she was.

*   *   *

They sat on a picnic rug on the dunes: Emily had persuaded William to lunch outside and he had occupied himself with creating an elaborate system of interlocking umbrellas for shade. Summer being at its zenith he considered Emily wholly unreasonable, especially as she had at first sat apart from him in the full force of the sun. Now she joined him under their protection, sitting upright while he reclined upon an elbow with his back to the ocean.

'I don't know why you insisted upon this—the view is exactly the same from the veranda,' said William.

'You are perfectly wrong again. It is altogether different.' She delighted in pretending to scold him, sensible that it gave him comfort and pleasure while bestowing on her an illusion of her own power.

'Let us argue it.'

'Then you must turn and look.'

75

'Very well.' He waved his hand. 'Grasses. Sand. Ocean. Sky. Cliffs.'

'Let us not argue it. Believe me, it is different in every respect, and I shall only win and annoy you.'

'How?'

'Would you truly like me to tell you?'

'When am I not perfectly attuned to the sound of your voice?'

'William, if you make me laugh I cannot concentrate on my argument.'

'You mean your point of view. Your mind is too unformed to fashion an argument.'

'Then why do you so delight in hearing me speak?' The laughter that had grown between them stopped. 'There is no need for you to answer that,' she said, too swiftly. 'Simply listen to what I have to say.'

'Very well.'

'The curve of the dunes and all these little hummocks here, they are close to our faces and bodies and we can observe each grain of sand if we wish, and all the creatures busy among them.'

He sighed. 'Unfortunately that is true.'

'And we can touch and stroke and smell the grass and sand if we so wish—'

'Also true.'

'Then the light as it blazes on the beach nonetheless forms a pattern of brilliance and shadow, and the ocean as it moves has an energy we cannot discern from the safety of our little wooden house. Lastly, we can look up into the sky.'

'And be burned by the sun and have our skin roughened by the salty wind.'

'But look—you have on your hat and you are

buried beneath umbrellas.' He said nothing, averting his eyes. 'Are you comfortable?'

'Reasonably.'

'Then I shall draw you. Turn your back to it and you shall dominate the view, and the elements will merely frame you. I hope that will satisfy you and stop you from being so cantankerous.'

He smiled. 'When will you ever stop teasing me?'

'Do you give permission to be drawn?'

'Freely, though I have no idea why.'

She looked at him firmly. 'Perhaps because it is a fair exchange.' She seized her sketchbook, settled it on her lap and began to work. 'You are an excellent subject—you know how to remain still.'

'You are very kind.'

His reclining form in the shade of the umbrellas and the glare of the beach took rapid shape beneath her hand, and the quiet between them was deeply satisfying to her young soul. 'Don't look at me work—for then I cannot concentrate.'

'What should I do?'

'Look over my shoulder. Think about your latest story while I strive to capture the loftiness of your expression.'

'All I see is dry grass and a hot sky. We shall have to seek shelter by and by.'

She continued to work and then, pausing, looked about her. 'Do you know what I would like to do before we leave here? I should like to go out in a boat.'

'And you expect *me* to take you?'

'I do not think I could trust you to captain the vessel quite alone. Perhaps a fisherman would take pity on us.'

'Probably. If we paid him sufficiently.'

She could not stop looking at the bright ocean and the reach of the sky. 'I am so happy. And I want to remember it—remember it by being on the water, and the sky and the glory of this place.'

'You are happy because you are coming home with us next month.'

'What other reason could there be?'

He sighed, fidgeting slightly, looking away. 'You are so unspoiled now. They will all admire you in Boston and what will happen to your quality of innocence then?'

'I wish you would not describe me and pinpoint me so continually. Besides, in my belief, a person is always essentially themselves. That cannot be changed or altered.'

He gave her his amused smile. 'Whatever gave you that idea?'

She finished the sketch and turned it to look at him. 'I'm rather pleased with that,' she said.

Miss Augusta Dean   Newport Beach
c/o Hotel du Lac, Como

August 20th, 1861

Dearest Augusta,

How exceptional the lakes sound! I can only begin to picture them in my mind. I am so gratified to hear that you and your father are enjoying them in such harmony and are so companionable together. If your mother had lived I am sure she would be enormously proud of you both (although, as I have said before, you were fortunate that you never knew her and cannot feel the lack).

I must own that a slight loneliness is preying on my spirits, so you must forgive me for that sudden burst of morbid thought. It is all because my few belongings are packed once again and despite their scarcity my bedchamber looks much the poorer without them. It is extraordinary how one becomes accustomed to the look of a room one has inhabited and is forced to see it with new eyes after it has been stripped. It is not so very much different—it is only that the heart and soul of it—and my time here—has gone. I feel sad and cannot help but mourn it.

I do not know when I shall ever see this house again after tomorrow.

I will write to you directly from Boston.

Continue to enjoy your adventures and do not forget to direct your next letter to the Boston address.

Affectionately,

Emily

CHAPTER SIX

The town house at Boston was larger, grander, more imposing than Emily remembered from her brief sojourn there two years before, a grief-stricken child. From the flight of steps up to the black front door and the hard bright brick, to the elaborate classical mouldings over the windows, the feeling of magnificence, colour and wealth overcame her. She could not love such a place as she had come to love the weather-beaten boards of the seaside house. She doubted one could even inhabit it. Merely crossing the threshold alarmed her, and the feeling was new. The hall was dark red and sombre despite marble and mirrors. How could her uncle, a man of such mental austerity and fastidiousness, live in such a place? But after all, it was where he had been born.

Her aunt, who had ordered the house to be opened up in advance of their coming, began quickly to inspect all the rooms. Mary went to her modest chamber on the top floor, leaving Emily with her uncle, William and the luggage, looking about her and unsure of what to do. Her uncle called for the housekeeper, a gaunt and efficient-looking woman, who introduced herself as Mrs Beadle and took Emily up the stairs. She turned to look at William as she followed her, but he did not glance in her direction, remaining below in conversation with his father.

Emily's room was similarly dark and austere but with every comfort, looking out on to the square rather than the garden. Immediately, she went to the window to take in the life. Trees were already turning blazing red at the edge of each leaf, she saw a brilliant blue afternoon sky: people, perambulators, dogs, messenger boys, carriages, sound, energy, noise—no more mysterious ocean to study, bringing weather from far away.

A knock at the door announced her aunt. 'We have returned well in advance of the season in order that we may have dresses made up for you. You cannot be seen in that blue cotton, and the lavender dress is severely faded from the beach. Neither is suitable in any event. Country clothes.' It was extraordinary how she could speak and still have so little expression on her face, not in her eyes, nor in the corner of her white mouth. 'Do not expect richness of dress—I disapprove of it in young girls—nor embellishment—'

'Believe me, Aunt, I would not look for it,' she said, but the lady went on speaking and Emily remembered that her opinion was not important and she should not give it. Had she not been told?

'My dressmaker will come directly. Expect her tomorrow. And we shall have to teach you better how to arrange your hair. I will leave you now.'

'Ma'am, excuse me, how should I occupy myself for today? If I could go out walking—'

'You must understand that that is out of the question in town. William may accompany you later if his time permits. If you care to play I will show you the piano in the music room.'

Her heart leapt. The music room. She had not expected to be allowed to draw immediately—but to play! If she could fill these strange rooms with music it would be almost as good as opening the shutters and blinds. This only appeared to have

81

been done at certain windows.

'Where is my cousin?' she asked as they descended the stairs.

'Why, he has gone out, of course. He has considerable acquaintance in town.'

'Of course,' replied Emily. 'Of course.'

*   *   *

It was the colours of those first Fall days she would remember most and which she longed to paint, but having only charcoal and pencil and rough paper at her disposal the sketches were fleeting chiaroscuro—sometimes soft, sometimes fine-lined—but never rich and glowing like the paintings in her mind. In her imagination canvases accumulated of the house and its dark interior, the furniture that shone in sun or lamplight, the rich velvets, all reds and purples, the trees in the street. Apart from the sky her world held no more blue and no more grey. The colours of her dresses surprised her. She had been used to feeling like a sea-shadow in her faded cotton. Her neck was encircled constantly by white starched collars, and she was obliged to wear ribbons and tortoiseshell combs in her hair to keep it in place. She had young ladies' shoes and stockings and bewilderingly painful undergarments, and became accustomed to closely examining herself in a looking glass with three sides.

She could not but think of the vast cold woods and tracts of land her grandfather had toiled through, and bought and sold to make this fortune that led to her muffled interior world. She could not help but think of her mother as a child in this house, and then as her mother in Buffalo, and she groped to understand it all, waiting before the fire in the morning room, reading the books in her uncle's library unobserved and dreaming, resting her chin upon her hand.

Society was a blur of colour and movement at times so confusing she could not swallow or direct her smile in the correct direction. When first she entered a stranger's drawing room it was to a peculiar combination of trembling terror and the wild excitement she used to feel running along a shore. In this unknown country there was so much to look at but—she quickly discovered—very little to say. Nobody wanted to know what she thought and felt about anything, even while they were admiring her with their eyes. Any hopes she had entertained of finding another bosom friend such as Augusta were quickly dashed. The young ladies rarely addressed one another: it was to the gentlemen that all conversation was aimed. They were the prize. On the rare occasions when her cousin Mary was considered well enough to accompany them, Emily noticed how she contrived to make herself invisible; sitting with the matrons and the elderly aunts, and avoiding any appraising youthful gaze. Emily could understand why.

What surprised her was that—as her cousin had predicted—gentlemen admired her. The words 'fresh' and 'unspoiled' were pronounced to her face as if she were a piece of fruit. It was remarkable, she thought, that they did not assess her with their hands as well as eyes. The alarming aspect of this was how much pleasure it gave her to be admired, however nonsensical and continually embarrassing it could be.

'Well, Cousin,' said William, drawing her aside towards the close of their first dinner party. 'You are now formally introduced to the best Boston society. Unthinking patriots are engaged elsewhere. Is it as I described it?'

'Unfailingly.' She smiled at him.

'Don't be enigmatic. Remember your promise? To give me all your impressions—always?'

'I do not recall a promise; a request, yes. And we must not whisper in a corner, William. You know as well as I.'

'Tomorrow we will sit and gossip and drink tea together and you will tell me what you thought of them all.'

'If you insist.'

The truth was, she was relieved that he should ask her for an interview. She had barely seen her cousin since coming to town. He had embarked upon a new piece of fiction that kept him much occupied and which he was wary of discussing, as well as promising his work to several periodicals. He hurried from his study to luncheons, to meetings, to his club, and Emily adopted the music room as her parlour, with its long view of the garden alive with Virginia creeper spilling over the walls to the damp and dying grass. Mary kept to her room and did not essay her companionship. Emily waited all that day and he did not come.

When she passed him on the staircase after dinner that evening he merely smiled as if he had no memory of his own request.

Miss Augusta Dean Cornford House
c/o Hotel du Lac, Como ——— Square,
Boston

September 14th, 1861

My dear Girl,

First let me apologise for the gloom of my last letter. The tenderness and calm of your reply was gratefully received and I heartily regret intruding on the pleasure of the lakes with my woes.

For my part I hardly know how to begin to confide my myriad impressions of life in Boston, except to say that we are very busy without being occupied. Perhaps that is what social life is, I do not know. I never thought I would miss the continual solitude and uncertainty that accompanied me at Newport, but I must admit—and feel I can freely to you—that I do.

Boston is a fine place: its inhabitants are sensible of this fact and very proud of being at the cradle of the New World. And there is no sense of doubt about embarking on this war, although its cost is continually debated. Fear, both of the act and its consequences, is not entertained. Neither is there a lack of gaiety at the evening parties I have attended, although my aunt is quick to remind me that they are not frivolous. Conversation frequently touches on matters I have very little knowledge of: History, Literature, ideas of which I do not grasp the fundamentals, let alone feel equal to debate. I notice the other young ladies appear very forthright when expressing their views, although these views do not differ one to another in any way that I can discern. As for me—you would not know me I am so still and quiet. There has been no dancing.

And what news of your travels? To head South now that the weather is to turn cold seems a most appropriate course. Christmas in Rome—the very words hold unimaginable delight to your devoted friend. Do not allow it to pass by without experiencing every impression you can grasp. Do not waste your time in writing it if you are not inclined, but a postcard of something beautiful would lift my heart.

Not that there is no beauty here.

I long to work on it, be out in it. I have discovered that there is a drawing class, life class and watercolour class held here at several places in the city, but I have not even dared ask if I might attend.

Observe how this family has succeeded in instilling fear in me where the school entirely failed?! It is only that I do not want to break the fragile bonds that keep me here. Exile would be far worse.

With fondest love,

Emily

'Niece, you are aware we will be holding a Thanksgiving party in this house?'

They were in the breakfast room that overlooked the blazing reds of the garden, and was used for no other purpose.

'Yes, Uncle. My aunt has told me.'

'It is to be the largest party we have ever given.'

Mary spoke, deliberate and slow. 'There will be flowers.'

Her father continued as if she had not. 'There will be a great deal of preparation.'

'The floors will be waxed and polished, and the silver. There will be musicians,' said her aunt.

Emily looked at William, who allowed a faint amusement to come into his eyes.

Her uncle remained concentrated on her face. 'You are sensible that this is a great honour, young lady?'

'You shall have a dress for the occasion,' said her aunt.

She did not know how to reply. Did they think her so frivolous that the idea of a new dress would make her squeak? Instead, she felt uncharacteristically ashamed.

Her uncle went on. 'Fifty will dine with us.' He stood up, folding his napkin carefully. 'I have spoken with Captain Lindsay's father.' His voice reminded her of paper, it was so dry. 'He has been granted leave for Thanksgiving so he will be among us.'

Emily was unaccustomed to blushing but she felt the stain climb her throat and flood her face. She could not speak or look into anyone's face but felt the look, almost of disgust, her cousin Mary immediately gave her.

'So. Your admirer will return,' said William lightly, and she felt how odious he could be in that second.

'I will be glad to see such a friend.'

*　　　*　　　*

In her room Emily looked at the clothes in her wardrobe: the shiny stuffs, the damasks and occasional silks, they hung there like so many uninhabited bodies. These different costumes she tried on were beautiful, burdensome, distant. Now there was to be another: alluring in intention she had no doubt; modest yet alluring; decorous yet alluring, and she clenched her little fists in a kind of anguish. She longed to see Captain Lindsay again, the warmth and confidence in his eyes, to hear him speak and feel he listened to what she had to say. She longed to know about the battlefield—how it was with him, whether he was afraid. She knew he was strong, but she feared he had changed. Above all she feared so public a meeting, the theatricality of the event. Would it not be better on the beach they had walked together, beneath the clearness of the sky?

*　　　*　　　*

Nervousness and irritability took her appetite, and she could not help but spend the day of the party restlessly pacing the house until her aunt ordered her to take up her sewing in the music room and confine herself there until tea. Her cousin took himself away for most of the day but knocked on her bedchamber door in the afternoon when she was pretending to rest. The blinds were drawn. She came to open it and with the light came the clattering and the footsteps from below, and the sound of voices.

'Are you indisposed, Cousin?' His smile invited a confidence, as ever.

'Not in the least. But foolishly I think I may be suffering a little from nerves.'

'They are only people. It is only a party.'

'William, you know precisely what it is.'

He was holding a rosewood box. 'I have something for you. Do not be concerned, it is with my father's permission. Would you like to open it, or shall I?'

She felt a nervous clutching at her throat, an anticipation. 'I am afraid.'

'It is not Pandora's box, you know. Merely a jewellery case. And you are never afraid.'

She felt awkward, standing on the landing, the light from the long window staining his pale cheek and shadowed face.

'You look tired, William.'

'I wear the night out with working.'

She felt a sudden tenderness. 'A far from sensible habit.'

'Open the box.'

She touched the lovely surface and lifted the lid. Inside, on a bed of black velvet, lay an exquisite garnet necklace of simple and old-fashioned design: very delicate, the necklace of a young girl.

'It was your mother's.'

'She never spoke of it. But of course, she left all her belongings behind.'

'We would like you to wear it this evening, to receive the company.'

Her dress was russet, in some lights inclining to olive green. It would be a perfect complement, both in colour and ornament. Her head drooped, looking at the gold and garnet and the exceptional

89

promise its richness held.

'You are certain my uncle would like me to wear it?'

'He asked me to bring it to you.'

She couldn't quite touch it, but closed the lid. 'Then I will,' she said, and he gave it into her hands.

* * *

Emily was unable to look at the necklace again until the moment after she had been dressed and her hair almost elaborately arranged. The maid, Betsey, gently helped her to fasten it, smiling.

'You are beautiful, Miss. Look.'

There was a kind of splendour in her reflection. The necklace embraced her, its delicate teardrop pendant sitting flat beneath her collarbones like an amulet. *Mother*, she said silently to her reflection. *Mother*.

Betsey hurried away to attend to Mary and she was left alone in the lamplight.

There was a knock on the door and it was William. He was beautifully dressed in evening clothes. He looked comical. 'I wondered if you would like me to accompany you downstairs?' he said. She felt that the actors on stage at the play must behave like this. He took a step back to look at her and smiled.

'Don't you dare pronounce on me,' she said.

'I would not presume,' he replied, making way for her. She closed the door.

* * *

After that it was all waiting for Captain Lindsay to come to her. At first she stood in the marble hall among the strangers: some whom she knew, some she had never encountered before. The candlelight was very beautiful and the shadows made it no less so. Soft light brought mystery to the most prosaic face, glamour to the blandness of any grouping. At the beginning it was difficult to breathe, standing beneath the chandelier.

'Smile, my dear,' whispered her uncle. 'Smile.'

He did not come while they received the guests cold from their carriages and wrapped against the night, and after that she began to forget she had been waiting for him, because her uncle remained at her elbow, guiding her through the rooms amongst the throng of distinguished young and distinguished old.

She found herself beside William's godfather. He had white hair. 'I have never known your uncle give such a reception,' he said. 'This house has not held such a party since your dear mother lived here. What an entrancing young lady she was.'

'I am sure.'

'She had a great deal more than beauty. They do not speak of her?'

'No.'

'Then neither should we.'

Had her mother's presence been so fleeting that it had left no imprint on the richness of these rooms? But Emily knew fiercely as she thought this that she *was* present, and not only to herself, in every form save the substantial.

Captain Lindsay came into the room as the guests were beginning to go in to dinner, the noise of the party disguising his arrival until Emily

91

glimpsed him moving towards her with a smile that was not quite his accustomed easy expression.

'My dear girl, it has been too long. I am delighted to see you.'

He grasped her hands and she looked up into his face. 'I too am delighted.'

He looked sunburned, or rather weathered, as if he had been to sea, and larger than she remembered, and his eyes were a darker blue.

'And how is Boston treating you, my dear?' He still held her hands. She knew he should not.

She could think of nothing. 'It is a fine place. It is . . .' She searched for a word.

'Aah. I see. Worse than I feared.' He smiled. 'Tell me, have you been out walking?' The firmness of his hands transmitted something of his energy to her. She did not want to let go.

'No.'

'To the play?'

'No. My uncle does not approve of the play.'

'Then your cousin must take you.'

'I do not think he cares to. He has many occupations, you understand, beyond my amusement.' She tried to sound light-hearted.

'You do not complain.'

'Why should I complain? This is a splendid party.' She felt conspicuous; William was looking at them—they were at the very centre of the room.

Captain Lindsay seemed unaware of this. 'Do you pursue your drawing?'

'Sometimes. My resources are limited: I have no colours. I play. Why so many questions?'

'I seek to imagine your life here, all at once, and it cannot be done. I— Forgive me for interrogating you.' His voice gentled. 'I only mean to see how you do.'

'And how do you do? I take it *your* time is not spent at the play?' She laughed and it did not sound to her as her laugh should. 'Forgive me. It is my turn to apologise. I am awkward when I try to apply myself with any decorum to the danger in which you put yourself.' The room was emptying around them as the company went in to dinner. She knew—standing so still—that they were the object of glances but she could not look away from him.

'What a formal speech,' he said.

'I wish you would not go to war.' She spoke in more like her accustomed tone and in a lower voice, and at last he let go of her hands and they turned to follow the others. She felt a little tremor as the bond was broken.

Velvet curtains hung at the room's long windows. 'Which is your favourite window seat?' he asked.

'The one to the left.'

'Of course,' he said, 'of course it would be.'

In his smile he was still holding her hands. She knew he should not have held them for so long and she knew she did not care.

        *   *   *

At dinner he sat down the table and across from her at a diagonal. She tried not to look at him. He was speaking with great vigour on the subject of the arming of the South and he looked so definite and solid and alive it was as though he could never be killed. His evening dress, his cufflinks, the shape of his hands, it was as if their very existence denied that they could ever be extinguished.

Perhaps there was no need to be afraid. Perhaps he could not be killed. And yet she knew her reasoning was entirely flawed. Had not Charlie looked that way, and her mother, and her sisters, and her dear Papa? It seemed so peculiar to be sitting at this long shiny table heavy with silver and crystal and candles and be eating so opulent a supper and be thinking such thoughts.

An unending interval divided dinner and their next words. It was not as if he were the only gentleman to whom she was expected to speak. But after the pouring of the coffee he came to her where she sat on a little sofa in conversation with William, who moved away, murmuring something in an irritatingly insinuating tone.

'I regret that my sister could not be present this evening,' he said. 'She is on her wedding trip, and I would so like for you to have met her.'

'You are very kind.' She had never sat so close beside him before. It felt absolutely natural. She had the extravagance of minutes in which to examine his face so she could try to remember it before the next time.

'And you are very changed now you find yourself in these surroundings,' he said. 'Do you know that? So quiet, you see.'

Was he disappointed in her? She hoped not. 'Is it so apparent?' She looked into his face and was relieved he should know her.

He smiled. 'I hope I do not presume.'

'Not at all. But I have been warned not to disgrace my family with my opinions.' She said it lightly.

'Is that indeed true?' He lowered his voice. 'Your family's behaviour towards you has always . . .

94

surprised me, but—'

She smiled as if it did not matter. 'Yes. It is true.'

'But Emily, you could only ever adorn it. Forgive me, but you are very beautiful tonight.'

She wanted to laugh but the laughter died. He began to speak more quickly as if anticipating an interruption and in an urgent tone. 'There has been no opportunity to converse—in private— about anything important, but please know you are constantly in my thoughts.' They were silent but continued to look at one another. And then he smiled. 'I promise to survive until Christmas so that I shall be able to continue to court you.'

'You are far too frivolous, Sir.'

'But not mistaken, I hope, in my expectations.'

'No. Never mistaken.' She could not look at him. Glancing up she saw her aunt beginning to approach from across the room.

He continued to speak rapidly, almost in a whisper. 'Will you not take my hand again and smile and say there will be time, at Christmas, time then? Just one word?'

She looked up quickly and his eyes held all the fervent energy she felt she now lacked—that her stay in this house had sapped—but all the interest and feeling she shared. 'Yes,' she said, revived, clasping his hand briefly. 'There will be time.'

Her aunt was before them and he got to his feet. 'We are not in the habit of keeping late hours, Niece. Have you not noticed that the party is beginning to disperse?'

Emily nodded, murmuring something about bidding farewell to the guests.

'You are an angel,' he whispered, as he said goodbye.

*   *   *

'Death can be such an aphrodisiac, don't you find?' said William, as they parted with their candles outside her bedroom door.

*   *   *

All the next morning Emily felt choked and heavy and thirsty. The house had been overheated the night before, thick with candles and fires in every room. It was emptier than ever after so many footsteps, voices and so much laughter. She was at her sewing when her uncle's servant came into the music room with a substantial package wrapped in brown paper. It was addressed to her. She waited until he was gone to open it. It was a large and beautiful wooden box with a shining clasp. A series of delightful cubby holes and drawers contained paper, oil paints and brushes of the highest quality.

The small card attached read: *Paint me a portrait. Respectfully, Captain J C H Lindsay.*

It was then that she cried and longed to have spoken her heart to him when he had first held her hands.

Miss Augusta Dean   Boston
Hotel d'Angleterre, Rome

November 30th

My dearest Friend,

How I long and long to see you again. If only

96

you were beside me in this room, close to this piano, this mantelpiece, this fire and this friend who so fervently desires to confide in you. I fear I am becoming a stranger to myself.

But forgive me, and allow me to explain, if you have the patience. The Thanksgiving party of which I wrote was pronounced a great success by this family—not in so many words, you understand, because that would indicate too deep an engagement with worldly things, but my uncle said it had been 'Most satisfactory', my aunt that she was 'gratified', and William that it had been 'particularly interesting and diverting'. Mary did not express an opinion but I feel she had no cause to shrink from the company as she might have feared—it was indeed entirely convivial.

As for your girl—it was like being at sea in a storm! So many people, it seemed unreal, and I could not remember their names. I was trembling because I so longed to see Captain Lindsay, and trembling because I so feared it. When he did come, he was very—I struggle for the words—solicitous about my welfare, without abandoning his customary energetic air. He brought the feeling of being outside with him, beyond these rooms and this self-regarding city. He carried with him that delightful air of conviction I have always so admired, and he remarked on a change in my spirits that I must admit I had not observed in myself, but has been encroaching by degrees. There could never be bare feet here.

He said he would return. He said he intends to court me: such a very serious word. I must

97

admit that I was immediately filled with delight, and that I also do admit to a profound affection for and interest in him.

Yet my first thoughts regarding his attentions were that they were an answer to my uncle's prayer: he could have me out of his house easily within a twelve-month. He would be satisfied and tell us all it is God's will. But then what would my future existence be? I lay in the dark last night terrified of looking into the future—but it must be done—it preys on my mind even if I decide it must not. If I were to be married I would have the Captain by my side, and he is a companion to whom I believe I could become devoted.

But—you must be shrieking as you read this—if he were not all he is in the world, with his income and property and the sum of independence that that implies, would he still be the seemingly limitless possibility he is to me now? In short, do I truly, deeply, love him, devotedly as a wife should? Could I? Does this excitement, this delight at the thought of him and his presence, does it presage the strength of a life-long bond? I am sensible I should not even be debating these things within myself, especially as he has not yet made an offer, but I believe him to be a man of honour whose affections are truly engaged and therefore there is scant reason to expect that he will not.

I do so long to be free of this place.

And then there is the other matter, to which I have shut my eyes throughout this long and contorted letter: what would be my fate if he were to make the ultimate sacrifice and not return from this war? Could I bear to be promised to him and fretting every minute that he could be wounded or killed—could I be his wife with the same terror clutching at my heart? Should we not wait until the war is over? Or would my uncle banish me well before such a time could ever come?

If only you were here for me to unburden this to and hear your sensible counsel. You have always had a wiser head than mine.

Here I am in the panic of my thoughts and feelings, scribbling so fast that I have forgotten that I had planned to write to you of all the things I have been reading about Rome in my uncle's library—and dazzle you—and convince you that you have another (invisible) companion on your journey.

I long for your return to Boston and apologise for my own selfishness in so doing.

Your ever loving,

Emily xxxxx

Miss Emily Hudson ——— Battalion
Boston, Mass

December 5th, 1861

My dear Miss Hudson,

I trust that you have received my respectful present in good order and that you are beginning to make good use of it. When I remember you it is always with an impression of vivid colours and it gives me happiness to imagine them at your disposal.

I feel I cannot write with any clarity about how it was for me to see you while the impression remains so strong, and yet it is like another world compared to this place.

Be occupied, my dear girl. Try to persuade that languid cousin of yours to take you for a walk.

Yours truly,

Captain J C H Lindsay

Captain J C H Lindsay   Boston

December 6th, 1861

Dear Sir,

I must take this opportunity to thank you for your recent letter and—once more, as I sit beside them—for the oil paints. (My previous letter of thanks must have crossed with your own.) I have never owned anything so luxurious in my life. They are such a joy.

I promise to go out walking.

Yours truly,

Emily Hudson

Miss Emily Hudson ———— Battalion
———— House
———— Square

December 10th, 1861

My dear Miss Emily,

   Two such brief letters! But then I admit I am
a poor correspondent myself. I lack the knack
of letter writing; or skill, or talent, what you
will.
   Shortly you should receive an invitation to
my family's New Year's Eve party in town. I
cannot write adequately of my longing to see
you at our Boston house. God willing, it will be
soon.
   I will write no further until then.
   Yours ever,

J C H L

CHAPTER SEVEN

'I hope you have a pair of galoshes, Cousin—it is
cold out of doors.'
   'Of course I have. I went to school in the woods,
you know.'
   William and Emily emerged from the house on
to snow-covered steps and snow lay in abundance
in every direction.
   'This is not merely a stroll along city streets,' he
said, attempting to guide her by the arm as they

descended. 'It is an expedition to the harbour.'

'Let me go—you will trip me up.'

He was avoiding her eyes. 'I planned it, for I know how you love the water.'

'Cousin, I am glad of it.'

* * *

The carriage made its muffled way through the snow.

'Fresh snow,' he said, 'fresh snow has a glory in it. Not slushy and brown and melting—I can't abide it then, but now, when it is all clean and thick and deep. Full of promises. Unsullied.'

She tried to smile at him but he was not looking at her, but contemplating the snow. 'Yes. Now it is at its best.' They had made snowmen in the yard as children while their mother baked biscuits. 'Is the snow this heavy where they are fighting?'

At last he turned to her and gave her a quizzical look, as if she amused him with her ignorance and girlishness. 'I believe so, my dear, yes. It is best not to think of it,' he said slowly. But now, of course, she could think of nothing else.

When he handed her out into the *mêlée* of the docks—the shouting and the coming and the going—for a second the world tilted as if her senses could not inform her brain fast enough of what it was they absorbed. Then the world righted itself and she welcomed it: people about their business; the trading, unloading, buying and selling, the glistening fish, the churned up snow, the great ships and little tugs and the sun on her face again and the blue blue sky.

'William, I fear we are in the way,' she called

above the noise.

'Just pick your path gently, my dear. Take my arm if you wish. The carriage will wait.'

They had not been in such close proximity to one another in the open air for a very long time. It came to her that she remained fond of her cousin and that they had become in some way estranged since their coming to Boston.

'Does this please you, Emily?' He was forced to shout to be heard over the din and she was reminded of the cliffs at Newport.

She smiled broadly. 'Most definitely.'

They walked carefully along the docks, past ropes and crates and all manner of obstacle; he with his stick, she with her skirts to contend with, her eyes moving from ground to ocean, to horizon to sky, biting cold on her cheeks. In a quiet and more sheltered spot towards the end of the semi-circle, he paused. She felt elated merely to look and to freely breathe.

After some silent reflection, he said, 'Partly I brought you here to tell you I mean to go away.'

She stopped gazing at the water and looked at him. 'Indeed? Where?'

'To England. I must go to London and begin this literary endeavour of mine without wasting any more time. I had meant to go before this but . . . there has been someone close by whom I have been privileged to observe and did not feel as if I could be parted from.' He held her gaze now.

She had a sudden feeling of sickness, a contraction in her throat. 'And is your observation concluded?'

His voice sharpened. 'I don't believe it ever shall be. But it is suspended for the present. I believe this person is about to embark on a most conventional course—quite beneath her, I am convinced—and I do not care to see any further for the present.'

His lips looked white, tinged with blue. She swallowed. There was no point in pretending she did not know what he meant.

'But you *said* that I should marry! In so many words, you said that!'

His reply was quick. 'I do not recall recommending so—*limited* a gentleman for the purpose.' She saw he was on a sudden truly angry, even more pale, and hoarse. 'There are so many literary, well-versed, thinking young men—'

'And you have taken such pains to introduce me to them!'

'Now it is *I* who am at fault.'

She was shaking at this sudden emotion between them and there were tears in her eyes. 'I did not say that, William. Let us get our breath. You brought me here to explain that you are going away and that it is entirely on account of the narrowness of the choice I may be about to make? Did it ever occur to you that I would like to travel also—to improve myself—in fact that I long to do so?'

He spat out, 'You may not go to the corner of the street without a chaperone!'

'Here I cannot! But if we were abroad—you are my cousin—you would be chaperone enough!'

'You want too much, Emily. Not content with Boston, now it is London you would like me to give you.' His words hurried over her senses.

Her face burned and there were tears in her eyes. She knew now he was determined to quarrel and would not be stayed.

'It was my uncle who brought me to Boston.'

'Only at my persuasion. Do you think he would have done so otherwise? You yourself know the slight regard he has for you. He, too, did not wish to see me go abroad.'

'I see.' She dropped her head. She had been the subject of a simple bargain: a trade.

'But we are neglecting our subject. Captain Lindsay. What a charming, easy-mannered, sociable, conventional choice for a girl of intelligence, wit, beauty such as yours—for the possessor of so much life.' He was still in a fury. She had never heard such malice in his voice.

She looked up and directly at him. 'You have never praised me so highly until now.'

On a sudden he gentled. 'Do not lie to yourself. For pity's sake, Emily, you are exceptional.'

'I am sure everyone in Boston agrees,' she said bitterly, turning her face from him.

'You are entrancing, if reserved, in company. It may take time. Not everyone who has met you has the advantage of seeing what I see.'

'And what Captain Lindsay sees!'

'You would be bored and suffocated for the rest of your life. If you did not die in childbirth.'

'Sometimes I think you are an extremely wicked person, William. You would not have me marry a man who is earnestly attached to me, but you would have me wait for the ideal match, a person of whom you could approve before I could venture on any step! I am not your creature.'

'You are entitled to your opinion on that, as on many other matters, of course.' He spoke as if he had written the words beforehand.

105

Turning her back on him, she began to walk as quickly as she could towards the carriage, aware he was watching her slipping and sliding awkwardly on the snow-deep, uneven ground. Her anger was so great that she did not care: it was as if her true self was returning. Who was he to tell her what it was that she should do? Who was anybody? This intricate path she trod, this way among the cables with the gulls screaming overhead and the cold salt air in her lungs, this heady oxygen, this freedom, she must grasp it somehow, and not let it go.

*   *   *

The silent journey back to her uncle's house—cold glass, hot cheek, blurred eyes—this could not be prevented. Just as the silence that grew between them after that could not be curtailed. It was not so much the silence of estrangement as that of complete understanding: she could see clearly how he meant to involve himself in her destiny, and she perceived in some fashion that it was connected to his feeling for her. That the feeling was not disinterested, she knew keenly, but the pain of it was the tenderness she felt for him. He, who would never present himself as a lover, who could not— she deeply understood—ever do so, nonetheless claimed a stake in her that she resisted with her whole self. And yet, apart from the Captain, and her darling Augusta, he was the only creature in the world that cared two figs what her destiny might be. That he could be cruel she now no longer doubted; how cruel remained to be seen. She did not want to see it. She wanted him to be as he had been at Newport, with his teasing and his books and his tender gentleness. She could not bear the hardening in him that came with this snow, this winter.

*　　　*　　　*

As time and days passed she found herself dreaming of Captain Lindsay, but in an increasingly distracted, peculiar way, like a child's dream of an angel or of God. Her idleness and restlessness returned—and her uncle had to remind her on many an occasion to make herself agreeable.

Miss Augusta Dean   Boston
Hotel d'Angleterre, Rome

December 28th, 1861

My dearest Augusta,

Your Christmas at Rome sounds as if it has been a splendid one, for not only does it appear pleasingly opulent, but you have the gift of making friends wherever you go. I do not even have to close my eyes to imagine a plentiful quantity of crimson and gold—more specifically velvet and brocade—and your bright laughing face.

I also begin to understand that to picture an event or place in advance and respond to it accordingly can be a very ill-advised exercise: misconceived, I think William would say. We have quarrelled terribly over my possible acceptance of Captain Lindsay. I am brooding over the concerns nearest to me: how to regain the goodwill and confidence of William (which at present I am too proud and angry to attempt, even if I secretly desire it) and how to answer the proposal, should it come.

We have kept a stern Christmas, solitary and cold, despite the presence of William's two brothers returned from the war. They are treated more as embarrassments than heroes. I cannot think of my beloved family and all the merry times we had together, or even of the peace and solitude of Christmases at school when I could be alone with my dreams. These are long slow days between Christmas and New Year. I am increasingly of the opinion that if the Captain were to make a declaration it will come before he returns to the Front early in the New Year.

My spirit is weary with the pain of my cousin's disapproval—and to be at table with him and in constant contact I find at times unimaginably painful. He keeps close to the house because of the season and does not busy himself with his usual many visits. In what society there has been I have become more practised at the art of manners and the correct small talk, of seeming to be present while being elsewhere, but it is not my natural way of being. I have never before achieved such tiny stitches in my sewing.

Later, before bed

I have pondered alone and I have made my decision. If Captain Lindsay were to propose to me at the party I shall accept him and it will grant me safe passage from this house for ever.

I think it the only wise decision I could make. And do I love him? I surprise myself by believing that I must—as my deliverer, as the best friend I have in the world apart from your dear self, and beyond that, for the joy in life I always feel in his presence.

I shall write to you when I am no longer poring over the obscure map of the future. When I can decipher it, you shall hear.

Affectionately,

Emily

*   *   *

'Forgive me for disturbing your family during this Christmas season.'

It was the unexpected voice of Captain Lindsay in the hall below, conversing with her uncle. It was New Year's Eve and Emily was upstairs, laying out her evening dress upon her bed: restless, she had decided to sketch it.

'But I wonder, if it is convenient, if I may have a few minutes' conversation with Miss Emily.' His voice sounded loud, as if he had been shouting out of doors, and it was full of eager confidence and delight. 'Perhaps just briefly, Sir?'

'I will send for her directly,' said her uncle.

But Emily could not pretend she had not heard. She came running down the cold stairs without hesitating.

He wore a greatcoat and muffler but was bareheaded. Spots of snow were melting on his shoulders. After glancing at him, she looked at his hands, embarrassed. They were red-raw with cold.

'Niece, you have a visitor.' And her uncle withdrew without ceremony.

'I apologise for coming here unannounced. I could not wait until tonight.' He was out of breath and he looked at her beautifully.

'There is no need. I am very pleased.' She could think of nothing and had to look away again, as if nothing had happened in past or future or ever would—just his presence, the height of him so cold close to her, his eyes. She forced herself to look at him. He appeared uncharacteristically serious, but only for a second.

'It is only that I am returned and we have been walking in the snow—playing, I must admit—and I thought of you as we were close by. I have been with my sister, who desires me to convey her impatience to meet you this evening. She hopes that her sudden recent transformation into a matron will not prejudice you against her quite.' He laughed as if it were all easy.

'I would be delighted to make her acquaintance.' She was aware of sounding very monotonous and withdrawn. He was so alive, so vital always, and she, despite her quickened heartbeat and trembling hands, felt like a shade.

'I do apologise. You seem out of spirits. Perhaps this has not been the right thing to do. My sister did warn me—'

Emily tried to smile, aware that she was looking at him strangely. This creature she had fretted over as if he were a problem in Latin grammar had now become a solid, joyous friend who had come to claim her. She was alert yet quiet in her soul, but the house surrounded her. Perhaps he might offer to take her for a walk, as he had once done.

'I am perfectly well. It is only the lack of air.'

He smiled at her simply. 'I am so happy to see you again,' he said. 'Are you sure you do not mind?'

'On the contrary, I . . .'

They were utterly alone. She could whisper any words to him freely, but could think of nothing. Part of her longed to confide in him about her quarrel with William, but she knew it would be quite wrong. She took a breath as if to begin.

'Emily, has something happened?'

It was not her uncle but William who came almost noiselessly into the hall.

'Captain Lindsay. How do you do?' he said, with an imitation of surprise.

'How do you do, William,' said Captain Lindsay, shaking hands in his open, gracious way.

'Will you not take tea with us? We could light the fire.' Her cousin spoke languidly and without interest. Emily could not look at him but only at Captain Lindsay.

'You are very kind, Sir, but I must return home to offer my assistance in this evening's preparations. This was merely a quick call, a little ill-advised, I fear.'

Emily saw William smile, slightly, raising his eyebrows. 'Indeed. Quicksilver speed.'

The Captain shook hands again with her cousin, then with Emily, glancing at her with a little hint of uncertainty in his manner, and was gone as quickly as he had appeared, banging the door and clattering down the steps as if in a great hurry. There was no backward glance.

Emily turned on William. 'That was very rude of you, Cousin.'

'I merely asked the gentleman if he would take tea. You make it sound as if I offered to shoot him.'

'As usual, you exaggerate. It was in your manner—your manner of asking.'

'I am sure he will recover. He does not strike me as a man particularly attuned to the nuances of things.' He smiled at her and left her standing, shaking in the cold hall.

*   *   *

'Your pallor has quite returned,' said her uncle, as they gathered on the steps that evening while the carriage was brought round. 'How regrettable.'

And he turned from her. They all did.

Emily wore her mother's necklace even though he had not requested it. She required the charm of its protection. William noticed it but pretended not to. It was the same dress; she would look precisely as she had at Thanksgiving and all of a sudden she longed to appear seeming altogether new. During the journey she suffered the floating feeling of unreality that had begun that evening when the Captain had begged for a word, as if she were a jewel. And now, crowded in the shadows opposite her uncle, beside William, she felt almost invisible.

There had been a fresh fall of snow and the Lindsays' white house, generous and classical in proportion, boasted flickering tapers on each of the steps, while lights blazed from every window, flooding the snow. The splendour made her chest ache, breathing in the cold night air. In the vestibule, standing between his parents, Captain

Lindsay looked so very different from the way he had appeared that afternoon: all formal and dressed and restrained. She could not tell whether he was pleased to see her, perhaps he thought she did not care for him. In the formal, patrician looks and cordial greeting she received from his mother and father she glimpsed the possibility of her future family, yet she sensed that they were ignorant of any significance she might one day have for them.

William shook hands with the Lindsays with an air of studied lack of interest, and guided Emily quickly into the ballroom, where she had no choice but to allow him to introduce her to the company while the Captain continued to receive his guests. He seemed to command her in so arch and superior a way that it angered her, taking care rarely to leave her side, following her, clasping her elbow firmly, allowing his hands to hold her by the waist. The rooms were beautiful, decorated, and brimming with hothouse flowers, the Christmas tree covered with gold and white ribbons. There was an ebullience and youth in the company, a feeling of vigour in the house that began to thrill her. The young men of the Captain's set were open and generous in their manners, many enlisted and in dress uniform, and the young women had a similar lack of reserve she found charming. These might one day be my friends, she thought, feverishly.

She did not dance. She did not want to dance with anybody but Captain Lindsay, but first she had to explain to him that she had not said the right thing that afternoon, that she had not shown—but she felt a little confused about how this was to be conveyed and what she should say. When he came to her it was arm in arm with a young woman, undoubtedly his sister. She looked pretty and kind, as if nothing bad had ever happened to her in her life, nor ever would.

'I am Margaret,' she said. 'But you must call me Meg.'

'I am Emily.'

'I will not embarrass you by telling you that you are very much as he described you.'

If the lovely young creature that might be her sister had wanted to set her at her ease, it had been a good beginning. As Emily laughed and blushed, an acquaintance came to claim the Captain's attention, and he excused himself for a moment. She felt a little giddy. She had not eaten or taken any refreshment all day. The importance of the occasion must be telling on her nerves. She tried to close her throat but the laughter she could hear coming from inside her began to catch at her as she breathed and became a gasp, and the gasping, rasping, choking cough, at first unnoticed, mingled with the music and dancing, all at once echoed loud as the musicians paused before commencing the next dance.

Her handkerchief was in her reticule on a chair in the next room, so she could only press her hand to her mouth to stifle herself.

'Come,' said Meg, 'we shall find you a glass of water,' and she escorted Emily, whose head was bowed, fighting to contain herself, fighting to breathe, with all gentleness into the dining room where servants attended to the table and only one or two couples conversed. 'Wait there but a minute, Miss Emily—' and she hurried to the table for water. But Emily could not sip it because the cough would not stop, until with all her strength, she swallowed it down. At last she took the glass from Meg, seeing the Captain come into the room; he was visible approaching behind her in the huge gilt mirror, a golden reflection.

He put his hand upon her shoulder and touched her. It was an intimacy acutely gentle but she did not turn to face him.

'I saw you leave the ballroom. Are you indisposed?'

She could not reply but shook her head. The coughing was easing but her eyes streamed. It was galling to be quivering like a sick animal before him. The truth was that she was quite outside and above everything: the splendour of the rooms, the conviviality of the party, the sweetness of his sister, who still stood close by, attempting to comfort her—all the colours, sounds and lights seemed to rush at her and retreat just as the pounding in her ears reminded her of the ocean.

'Let us have a breath of fresh air. I shall fetch your cloak.'

While he did so she stood and looked around her, still struggling, desperate for calm. The peacock-blue of the walls made the room more cavernous than the ballroom with all its pale gaiety, and the vast portraits looming above her made her feel very small. He and his sister wrapped her up carefully and then Meg excused herself while her brother led Emily through the doors at the back of the hall and down the steps into the garden. It was extremely cold. She was still gasping.

'Hold on to my arm, and breathe,' he said.

'It is nothing, I assure you.'

'Do not try to speak. I will be quite all right with silence.' There were tapers in the snow along the garden paths and lanterns strung among the trees. They walked slowly, like dreamers. 'The truth is, I think I merely wanted an excuse to show you this.'

She stopped and smiled at him. 'It is beautiful. But I could see it equally well from the house.'

He laughed a little. 'I do not think I have ever heard you so prosaic.'

She pressed her hands to her eyes. How must she look to him? So flushed and strange.

'It can be stuffy in these ballrooms,' he said. 'And they are not your natural element, I fancy.'

'No.'

He turned towards her now and she looked clearly at him, knowing that if there were to be a moment for his declaration, this should be it, all the light in his eyes and softness in his face making her feel excited and afraid. But he said nothing, only lifting his hand to lightly touch her throat and jaw, as if to make sure they were real.

On a sudden there was an explosion of fireworks in the sky, a *rat-a-tat* that at first seemed like gunfire and the smoke of canon. It was a terrifying noise, but her sensation swung from fear to delight as sparks shot through the firmament, puncturing the dark night with explosions of light. Their joyfulness seemed to Emily immensely brave and when they faded, leaving only smoke on the night breeze, her heart longed for more. The sound of voices came to her, murmured pleasure, exclamations, footsteps, as the assembled company came out of the house to observe it also, to laugh and clap and ooh and aah as the New Year's bells

116

were ringing. The joy and clarity of the bells—the hope in them—made her want to cry. Captain Lindsay touched her hand but turned away from her to his guests. They had approached too quickly. The moment had passed.

Emily caught sight of William making his way through the crowd to her side. She did not want to speak to him; she did not want him near her, overwhelmed by the violence of the feeling. But she had nowhere to retreat to, and besides she was not in the habit of running away. He advanced with his usual slow step, leaning on his cane. She did not look away, but watched him watching her, the time stretching out, forcing her to shiver, as if at the encroachment of an unnameable horror.

He took her hand and, pressing it to his lips, he said, 'Forgive me, Cousin, if I am at fault and have hurt you recently. Forgive me. And happy New Year.' The gesture and look was humble, but he was not.

She could say nothing in reply; only smile a strained smile. Captain Lindsay was still at her side, but his attention was occupied in speaking to someone else, and with the increasing seconds she felt less and less under his protection. Her cousin began to press her to come away from the party: midnight had struck, his parents were tired and the carriage had been called.

Captain Lindsay accompanied them to the door of the carriage and closed it himself. He lowered his head and said to her in a quiet tone, 'I shall come and call on you directly,' but she had felt unable to look into his face. Her heart had trembled with inexplicable fear. She had not felt

117

radiant to him, not as she had done, not any longer.

Captain J C H Lindsay   Cornford House
Ashburton Place, Boston   Boston

January 1st, 1862

Dear Sir,

I write to you on a very delicate and personal matter, and I hope that in so doing you will forgive me my presumption and see only my intentions, which I assure you are of the highest.

It cannot have escaped your notice that my beloved cousin and your esteemed friend was indisposed on the occasion of last night's New Year's Eve ball at your house. Indeed, you were kind enough to go to her aid with great speed. What I believe you do not know, unless another hand than mine has made you aware of it, is that my cousin is very likely suffering from the early stages of the consumption.

It is a painful and unavoidable truth that this terrible disease was responsible for extinguishing her dear mother, and that the rest of her family also suffered from it, although I understand that fever was also present in that unhappy household towards the end and contributed to the tragic demise of her father.

Much as I treasure my cousin, and I do treasure her, I have come to the unavoidable if agonising conclusion that any gentleman who

118

may be contemplating the irreversible step of marriage to her must be, and should be, aware of this fact in advance. My dear cousin, for all her undoubted charm, is in my opinion—and that of the world were it more widely known—unmarriageable.

I believe that my father—who has yet to see any evidence of the disease in the young lady—is of the opinion that she has remained miraculously untouched by this tragic stain, and therefore has allowed her to Boston for the season, believing, for private reasons, that marriage is the appropriate course for her. Much as I respect and defer to his judgement, however, I think it was plain to those who have eyes to see it that she was more than temporarily indisposed last evening.

I write this to you because I believe concealment to be a dishonourable and impractical course. While it may cause you pain to acquire this knowledge, it nonetheless allows you to retain your freedom and your honour, as I understand no promise has been made between you that any gentleman could consider binding.

I beg you, my dear Sir, not to reply to this letter or to refer to it again. Emily's path must needs be a lonely one, but rest assured that I—her devoted cousin—will remain at her side to offer her my protection until her last breath.

Once again I ask you to forgive me for being the bearer of this intelligence, and entreat you to have the delicacy not to speak of it to another living soul—including, of course, the dear young lady herself.

Sir, I remain your true, etc., etc.,

William Cornford

Miss Augusta Dean   Boston
Hotel d'Angleterre, Rome

January 3rd 1862

My dear Augusta,

I understood from Captain Lindsay that he is
to quit Boston within the next day or, at most,
two—and yet he has not called as he promised
when we parted on New Year's Eve. Now that I
am decided, does he waver?
    Forgive me.

Your devoted Emily

CHAPTER EIGHT

'Miss Emily.'
 'Captain Lindsay.'
The moment had come. He had been shown into
the music room. She had stood up. He looked very
tired and very solemn and she felt afraid. She had
never seen him so pale.
'I trust I find you—well.'
'Of course. And I you?'
'Indeed.'
'Will you not sit down, Captain Lindsay?'
'Thank you, but I prefer to stand.'

This was not as she had imagined it, or as any conversation between them had yet been.

'You have come to bid me goodbye?' It was a nervous question, the words bubbling up without thought.

'I would like to. I find I can't.' He did not smile.

'Forgive me if I am stupid but I cannot understand you.' She did not like the way they were standing still and looking at one another in so frozen a way.

'I have something to say.'

She tried to smile. 'I must say it does not look as if it is to be very agreeable—'

'It is not.'

'Forgive me, Sir—is there bad news, a sickness in your family?'

'Yes. You have said it right.' He made an almost imperceptible movement towards her. 'There is a sickness in my family. I find the girl I love is ill—forgive me, I am not at liberty to say how I know this, but she is ill—and all sense and reason tells me I should not ask her to be my bride. And yet I find that I must.'

'I do not understand.'

'Your mother died of the consumption, did she not?'

Emily's hand came up to her mouth and she bit down on the flesh while a wave of sea-cold engulfed her.

'My precious girl—I am so sorry.' He took her hand and pulled it free, grasping it in both of his. 'I cannot bear to cause you pain.'

'I should have told you.'

'No. But if you are unwell . . .' He was standing very close now.

121

'Indeed I am not. There has never been so much as one speck of blood—' and saying this her throat closed and she began to cough again.

Keeping hold of her hand he pressed her to sit down. 'Is there water in the room? Is there?'

She shook her head and he immediately rang for it while she struggled to breathe. 'I am quite recovered.' There was a silence. 'But, Sir, I feel ashamed.'

'It is your uncle who should be ashamed.'

'I am always hoping that I will remain free of it— it is my constant prayer.' She was speaking rapidly, wildly, to his heart, reckless and relieved to be free of the secrecy, the burden of it.

'Listen to me, Emily. I meant to tell you in this interview that I could not ask for your hand and why—because it would have been dishonourable merely to have shrunk away without a word of explanation. I owe you—'

'You owe me nothing.'

'But as the knowledge settled with me, I came to understand its unimportance. Do you not see? You have my heart. Will you marry me?'

He sat beside her, holding both her hands in the safety of his grasp. She touched her forehead to his as if in submission and then drew back a little, looking at him, and thinking of the fear she had caused him, ringing for the water, the struggle with his heart he had already endured. She closed her eyes as if to blot him out and distinctly saw the row of new-made graves in the cemetery at Buffalo.

Looking at him, she said, 'I cannot say yes now, with sickness between us.'

He did not move, but stayed close to her. 'It is I who could make you a widow.' He smiled with great tenderness and solemnity, pressing his cheek to hers, and she felt all the satisfied longing that belongs to a comforted child. For a long minute there was no talking as she closed her eyes again. She saw herself in her wedding dress, delicate fine-spun lace. She saw the graves again.

'No, I cannot,' she whispered. 'I know now I cannot.'

The servant came into the room and he stood up in some confusion while the water was placed carefully on the table beside her. Then he held out the glass for her to drink but she refused it, shaking her head.

'Emily?'

'I cannot. I am sorry. I cannot marry you. I cannot marry.' She buried her head in her hands.

He took her wrists and shook them with some wildness. 'Do not hide from me. Show me your face.'

She dropped her hands and looked at him, his eyes so full of the promises in his heart. 'You have discharged all your duty, Sir—you have made me the offer in full possession of my shameful history. Your honour is unblemished. It is mine that concerns me now.' There was a pause as he seemed to grope to understand. 'Leave me, please.'

'Emily—I am your friend. You do not need to—'

'You must give way to me in this.' It was an odd whisper.

'My dear girl—'

'Go.' With her lifted head and blazing eyes she gave him the command like a queen.

When he had gone and she had heard his footsteps in the hall and the firm closing of the outside door, she went blindly to her sewing box and took out her cutting scissors. Then she went directly to her room and, without looking in the glass, cut off all her hair.

*   *   *

Waking in the night as if from a nightmare—but one she could not remember—there was a second's ignorance before the knowledge came to her: she had sent him away and he was gone. She put her hand up to her bare neck. She had been wrong. He would love her, he had promised, despite her shame.

Trembling, and as if to distract herself from the realisation, she climbed out of bed and went to the window, which, unveiled, revealed a terrifying glimpse of the moon. It was bigger and brighter, whiter than she had ever seen it, appeared nearer, illuminating the square outside and thickening it with shadow.

I have been wrong, she thought. He promised to love me, for myself, for ever, and I have said no. He would love me as his own family, as I loved my mother, as— And at the thought of her mother— the nursing, the coughing, the despair, the wild unfounded hope, the pain she and her father and Charlie had undergone—she felt in a flood of moonlight that she could not wish such a travail upon any living soul, particularly one she held so dear.

Her instinct—her memory, her pride, her rash blazing anger—had defended him as well as herself. This she must remember if ever she felt weakened again.

Miss Emily Hudson   Boston
Cornford House
Boston

January 3rd, 1862

My dear Emily,

Please forgive this somewhat ill-advised scrawl and give my words consideration nonetheless. Our interview of this morning repeats itself in my recollection and I long for a different answer.

On reflection—might you have another to give me?

Believe I am dedicated to you and you only.

Yours truly,

J C H Lindsay

PS. Kindly reply to this care of my regiment. I shall depart tomorrow.

Captain J C H Lindsay   Cornford House
—— Squadron,   Boston
—— Regiment

January 4th, 1862

Dear Captain Lindsay,

I must admit to feeling not a little pain at the contemplation of your handwriting—but that is merely for myself.

For your part I am most truly sorry to have caused you grief.

Circumstances decree that I must decline your kind offer.

You may yet have the opportunity to love another girl, and I do not think you should deprive yourself of it.

Yours truly,

Emily Hudson

Miss Emily Hudson   —— Squadron,
Cornford House   —— Regiment
Boston

January 6th, 1862

Dear Miss Emily,

I quite fail to understand why both you and I should be made to suffer because of 'circumstances', as you so describe them. If—as I flatter myself you do—you own to a wish to accept my proposal, I earnestly beg that you consider carefully once more before breaking both our hearts.

Yours truly,

J C H Lindsay

Miss Emily Hudson ——— Squadron
Boston

January 20th, 1862

Dear Miss Emily,

Why this silence?
I entreat you to write just one word to me,
and that word to be 'Yes.'
If it cannot be that, do not leave me with
nothing.
Yours,

J C H Lindsay

Captain Lindsay   Boston
——— Squadron

January 25th, 1862

Dear Captain Lindsay,

I entreat you to write no further letters to
me. My uncle declares it improper, as we are
not promised to one another, or likely to be.
Despite our interview and our recent
correspondence, you appear unable to respect
the decision I have made. Perhaps it would be
easier if I were to tell you that I am fully
resolved never to marry.
I cannot express to you how deeply I regret
what has taken place between us. I have always
regarded you as a true friend, and I hope that

you will allow me to continue to regard you as such. Know that I will always be your true friend if you allow it. I am so sorry and so ashamed of the pain I have caused.

Please also allow me the dignity of ending our correspondence. I beg you to understand my reasons for this; also that you remain in my thoughts.

Yours truly,

Emily Hudson

Miss Augusta Dean   Boston
Hotel d'Angleterre, Rome

January 27th, 1862

My dear Augusta,

He has not made an offer.
It seems I was mistaken in his feeling for me.
I shall remain as I am—quite inviolate.
I cannot write further.
Yours truly,

Emily

CHAPTER NINE

January days, February days. It did not feel as if there was anything new about the year, merely old snow and the birds still asleep. In a painful scene her uncle berated Emily for what she had done: for disfiguring herself, he forbade her to leave the house. If William were sympathetic he remained silent and did not take her part. Only Mary appeared to regard her with a new gentleness. Emily did not cry or storm or sulk. She did not pine. She bowed her head and sewed, barely lifting it to notice the comings and goings of William as he prepared to wind up his affairs in advance of his sailing. The watchfulness in the house made her tired. She knew that his mother did not want William to go, and that Mary's spirits were low, although she could not guess the cause; and that her uncle, always so patently oblivious, chose to look away.

She dared not ask about her future—whether she would go back to school; if she would be asked to get her own living. She tried to imagine being a governess. She could not. She did not know enough, and besides she would undoubtedly romp with the children and be dismissed.

She worried about Captain Lindsay: how he did, if he fared better than she. She was glad that he was occupied, if gladness could be found anywhere in war. The music room became her refuge. Rarely did any member of the family disturb her there.

William came to her one afternoon too dull for tears. He knocked upon the door.

'You wish to speak to me, Cousin?'

'I come to enquire how you do.'

'Is this to be a farewell scene?'

'You know I will not sail until the spring is properly advanced.'

'Of course. I forgot. You are so precise in everything you do.'

He pursed his lips. 'There is no sense in taking

an unnecessary risk.'

'No.' Emily bowed her head and continued to sew.

'You are recovering, I trust?' He spoke in a low and insinuating tone that she found unbearable.

'My cough is quite healed, thank you.'

'You know very well I refer to your heart and not your lungs in this context.'

She laughed bitterly. 'Oh, William, you have missed your calling. You should have been a doctor. All this talk of hearts and lungs.'

He said nothing but merely waited.

'Do you know what happened? Would you like to? I refused him.'

William blushed. 'I did not realise. I had understood that he did not make an offer after all. That can be quite . . . galling, I understand.'

'He did not deny me, William. He offered me his hand and heart.'

He took a step towards her and she tried to avoid his eyes. 'And you refused?'

They were in almost the same positions in the room that she and Captain Lindsay had occupied that painful day: her seated, he standing before her, but it was all different. William offered her nothing but his curiosity.

She stood up and went to the window, her back to him, and began to pull down the blind.

'Why did you refuse him?' He spoke with the old eagerness, the determination to know her.

She was tired. Why not tell him? He could put it into a story. 'He told me he had become aware of an illness in my family. He did not divulge how he came to know—'

'People talk . . .' interrupted William.

130

'He offered me his hand despite this. But I was ashamed. I do not wish to bring him trouble.'

'I see.'

She could not see his face because she could not bear to turn around and read his eyes.

'You are on a sudden noble then, my dear.'

'And foolish. I have little to look forward to now. I shall not marry.'

Emily was minutely examining the brocade of the drapes and observing how much care and effort had gone into making objects in every particular so hideous.

'What shall you do?' He sounded blank. 'You will not marry, you say? Even if the right match could be found?'

And now she turned on him. 'There is no right match, William. There is only what we find!' Did he have some defect of the heart? Could he not see how she suffered?

She tried to search his face but was blinded by her own tears. 'We are not pieces on a chessboard, William—' And then she sat down, altogether cold and weak. 'I cannot put together in my mind how he came to know. That is the nub of it. I cannot ask him now. But I would never have told him. When I refused him I thought that to have kept it from him would have been a wickedness, but now I am quite well I am no longer convinced. I am no longer sure of anything, the way I used to be.'

'As I have said,' repeated William, very self-possessed, 'people talk. It is a great human activity.' Emily did not reply. 'I do not like to see you brought to this. I do not like to see you brought so low. You used to have such excessive joy.' This last was spoken in an undertone.

131

'Could you leave me now? I am tired out.'
'Certainly I shall. I bid you good afternoon.'
'Good afternoon, Cousin.'

Miss Emily Hudson
Cornford House
Boston, Mass

February 28th, 1862

My dear Emily,
  Although it may seem somewhat peculiar to you to receive a letter from me when we are living beneath the same roof, nonetheless I feel, for the sake of clarity, that only the written word will do in this respect.
  I have been acutely troubled by your situation ever since our last interview. I can think of no other course than to ask you to accompany me to Europe. As you are aware, London is to be my initial destination.
  I can make this offer under the following conditions:

  – Neither you nor I shall mention Captain Lindsay's name.
  – You will abandon your determination never to marry, but will once more be open to your fate.
  – We shall reside independently of one another and you shall pursue your interest in art on a course of study.
  – While you shall accept my financial protection this shall not be alluded to between us.

132

I hope you can understand from the above that I entertain no greater wish than that you should continue to experience the world. Your qualities are rare and should not be denied a larger stage.

For the purposes of adventure and all that we used to ponder together (in a summer that seems so long ago, but is ever-present in my mind), rest assured that I will always remain your devoted friend.

Yours etc.,

William Cornford

Mr William Cornford   Boston

February 28th, 1862

Dear William,
I am moved. Beyond words.
I accept.
You are my very dear, very true friend.

Emily

*   *   *

'Why can we not sail next week?' Emily was pacing the floor of the music room. It had become a habit. With her frown and her pallor and her cropped hair she was like a different girl.

'The sea air will be good for your lungs,' William said. 'But we must not attempt to cross the

133

Atlantic until later in the year when the damp is not so pervasive.'

'William, we will be aboard ship—of course it will be damp! And I am quite well. It is March now and I have not coughed in weeks. In any event, my health is my own affair.'

'I have promised to take you with me; and this is how you express your gratitude?'

She turned her face to the window but did not disguise the storm of tears.

'Come, come. Sssh.' He approached her, but did not touch. 'You are young. Your heart will mend.'

'What do you know about it?' She looked up at him, her eyes narrowed and streaming and bright with pain. She felt ugly to him.

'We shall wait until the weather is milder. Besides, you must grow your hair. I am not taking a boy with me to London.'

She bent her head to wipe her eyes and he saw the nape of her neck exposed, the bones. It was a pretty neck. He felt a peculiar distance from her, from himself, almost giddy.

'Prepare your mind by reading about England. Turn to books. Books are the best cure,' he said, and left her.

*   *   *

Emily sat before her uncle in the chair of judgement. The scene was changed from that of their first encounter; it was now altogether larger and grander, but it had become familiar, the feeling of blindfold fear and disgust. The bright hopes of Newport had faded, and this new journey she contemplated was merely an exhausted escape.

134

'I cannot disguise the fact that I remain bewildered by your conduct,' he said. 'To refuse such a gentleman—but let us not dwell on that. William assures me you will not change your mind.'

'No, Uncle. I will not.'

He appeared to be waiting for her to speak further, then continued. 'What baffles me equally is my son's affection for you: to settle upon taking you to London is well beyond any familial duty I would have expected him to perform.'

'Yes.'

His hooded eyes blinked at her. His hands were still. He looked at her as at an old adversary but one aware his enemy was changing: fragile and yet stronger.

'You are determined to go away?'

'Yes.'

'What shall you do?' He had never asked her such a question before without being in control of the answer.

'If William agrees I will enrol at Art School.'

He pressed his lips together. 'I see. Allow me then to explain the arrangements that have been made for you. Up to the present time, I have supported you from my purse, believing you were soon to marry. As you have chosen to refuse the offer made to you, and appear to have no interest in securing another, I consider my obligation to you to be at an end.'

'Yes, Uncle.'

'Your cousin, William, however, sees fit to extend his bounty to you, which is independent of my own. He will cover your expenses from now on from his own fortune, while also providing you

135

with a small allowance for what I believe is known as sundries.'

'Thank you.'

'I give you nothing, child.'

'No, Uncle.'

'You are like your mother, driving yourself to your own destruction. Go now. I do not want to look at you.'

Leaving the room she encountered Mary in the hall.

'I understand you are to be saved once again, Emily,' she said. Her voice betrayed sympathy and envy both. As always with Mary, Emily was taken aback by the power of her cousin's feelings towards her.

'It is true I am to go away.'

'However did you persuade my brother to take you? He has always travelled alone.'

'I did not. It was his own idea. After my recent— trouble, I imagine he thinks it might revive me. He is very good.'

Mary smiled slightly at that, as if the concept of William's goodness was amusing. 'Better my brother's intervention than to be left to my mother's tender mercies,' she said, with her fierce, quiet bitterness. 'Think of me as you journey to your new country. And remember, like my father, William always has reasons of his own.'

Emily was moved by her cousin's sympathy, closely touched by her advice, and for the first time she was struck by a new affinity with Mary's bondage and the clarity of her vision, her honesty. She realised she had paid Mary very little attention during their time together, nor tried to seek her out or understand her, and for that she felt ashamed.

She answered warmly, 'Believe me, I will.' Thinking of the silence of the house after she and William had gone, she took a step closer. 'And I will write to you, if you will allow me.'

Her cousin, at one with the shadows of the house, reached out and took her hands. Holding them, she said, 'I would like that very much,' and gave Emily the bare suggestion of a kiss.

Emily had had few treasures to pack: her mother's necklace (she had not asked for permission), her box of colours, her letters. She left her sewing things behind. Her aunt did not trouble to supervise her packing. She felt herself as a ghost in the house before she had left it. She saw little of William, who was busy concluding business in the city, working, visiting his acquaintance. The solitude was unbearable, but she bore it. She found she could not write to Augusta.

But on the last morning, a letter in Captain Lindsay's hand:

Miss Emily Hudson ——— Squadron,
——— House, Boston ——— Regiment

April ——, 1862

My dear Miss Emily,

Please do not trouble yourself by taking this as a resumption in our correspondence; it is only that I have heard you are to quit Boston and journey overseas. Allow me to wish you *Bon Voyage*, a good sailing and—above all—

safe passage.

I hope you will find in the Old World what you could not in the New.

Sincerest good wishes,

Captain J C H Lindsay

138

PART TWO

CHAPTER TEN

'Nothing I can say will prepare you for London, so I shall not attempt it.' William was looking at her with all the old charm and warmth. They were on the deck, in powerful wind; Emily was in good heart and strong spirits. Her cousin, in all the detail of substantial colour and eyes bright with reflected light, appeared more present to her than he had been in a long while. For the first time she realised he would now be her only companion.

'But we land at Dover?'

The old quizzical smile. 'Indeed.'

'Look—I contrived to force my hair into a bun!' She turned her head to show him the small coil firmly in place beneath her bonnet. 'Admire it! You must. I am a young lady again.'

'Barely.' The light shone on his face. 'We will have to spend so much time explaining to every creature we encounter that you are not my bride.'

She smiled at him, gentle, as if he were a child. 'I am no one's bride, William.'

They stood, the sun falling on the backs of their hands as they gripped the rail, the sky wider, rounder, more infinite than ever; the sea swell a powerful promise of distance to be ploughed through, wakes to be made.

'I love it. I love the water,' she said.

Miss Augusta Dean   34 —— Square
Hotel d'Angleterre, Rome   Mayfair,
London

April ——, 1862

My dear Augusta,

After all this time, I am arrived! Look, I have
an address, a room of my own—more than a
room, in fact, two—and my own key. It is all
highly irregular: my extremely respectable
landlady made it more than clear to William
that I should not be by myself in this great and
wicked city without a chaperone, and his
response was uncharacteristically bland. Bright
things to their own destruction, he must have
thought.

It is raw and cold. Damp. Pale light. I do not
know how to describe it. I am still so full of
journey and being shaken in carriages. But it is
not as I would have expected springtime to
feel. No real warmth. William said it was
poised on the edge, and I will see by and by.

My lodgings are in a house in a square not
unlike my uncle's in Boston: the landlady—if I
can call her that without sounding
impertinent—a widow of late middle age, has
been forced to let her 'drawing room floor', as
they call it, through straitened circumstances.
Having nursed her husband in some retirement
for many years, she appears not a little
frightened by the world and, according to
William, rarely ventures out, so I should feel
quite safe. She and her servants occupy all the

142

other floors of the house, so I am to be the only stranger. William assured me that her severity and reserve were the English way and will lessen once she becomes aware of my good character.

I have a window box with flowers in it, and a view over the backs of houses that is all jumbled and irregular and new. Everything is new. I couldn't believe it when my cousin made to go after depositing me here and I found myself saying, 'So I am to live alone?' and he said, 'Remember, it is what you wanted,' in an extremely serious voice, the one that makes me want to laugh. But he is right. It is merely that I did not intend to cause a scandal purely by breathing.

William is to stay at his club in St James's Street so he will be nearby, and I am to register at the Women's Art School in South Kensington as soon as I please. All bills are to be sent to him. And I am to explore! He will give me my pocket allowance at the beginning of each week (he does not want me to carry too much ready money), but he says I am to go to the bank at Pall Mall St James's and ask for Mr Sinclair if there is ever an emergency and I am in need of funds.

This district is beautifully laid out and quite modern, close to Park Lane and the Hyde Park, although I understand it is no longer the height of fashion and abuts an insalubrious place called Shepherds Market that I am to avoid. And—he stipulates—there is to be no walking after dark. It seems places change their character quickly here and I have no desire to test the truth of his advice. I have bought myself a little map with the street names on it (for daylight hours!) from a man in a street kiosk who could not understand what I was saying.

The birds are wild with delight outside my window and my cousin will return shortly to take me to dine. Oh, my dear girl!—I am landed and in a passion of new hope and so much closer to you, my darling.

I am resolved to put all my energies into the present and thus forget the past.

I embrace you in your Italy, *cara mia*.

Emily xxx

Miss Augusta Dean   Mayfair
Hotel d'Angleterre, Rome

April ——, 1862

My dearest Friend,

My first letter—and from you! A thousand thanks. I look at it here beside me as I write.

You are perfectly right, nothing prepares one for the shock, or the distance of the crossing, and everything appears very small and very bright, like a miniature. What surprises me is how much building is going on in the city— such tremendous noise and upheaval—and the size of it, I can feel it like a living thing. And I have never seen so many houses in my life! I had thought because it was the Old World it would be like a living museum: Pompeii with crinolines in it, not this seething jumble on such an enormous scale. I am obviously far more ignorant and foolish than even I realised.

It is also so extraordinary the way the people seem to take it for granted that they live here and do not stand and gawp as I do. But in truth, I find I can do anything on the streets of this city and it feels as if no one would notice: there is so much speed of life and I am joyously inconspicuous.

William and I have taken the first of what are intended to be our weekly dinners together. I was wild to visit the Café Royal or Simpsons, but it is not considered respectable for a lady to sit in a public room, so I could only observe as much as I could of the dining room he took me to, quickly, before being led into a separate chamber at the back of the establishment. We talked all about the city: he took great pains to advise me to see Old London—the Tower and the Inns of Court, and especially St Paul's Cathedral—and to oblige him, and please myself, I did. I have to admit that its majesty is quite beyond anything I could have imagined, the curve of space so different from the narrow arches of the city's churches and even the grandeur of the Abbey. It bred in me the absolute conviction of my insignificance, which, I am sure, is exactly its intention.

It cannot approach your St Paul's at Rome, I don't doubt, but I was moved, and begin to understand that these English are explorers, setting forth and stealing what they can over the centuries to adorn their little island and make it prosperous. I have a great liking and admiration for that spirit—our own grows from it—the endeavour, or greed, call it what you will. Of course, I see the marble monument to it all and not the bloodshed. But that is culture, is it not—built on blood?

Today is my birthday. Like you, I am all of twenty. I spent the morning wandering along the corridors and through the rooms of the National Gallery, attracting not a little notice for being quite alone. I am becoming quite practised in pretending I am unaware of this. This visit has become quite a habit of mine every morning for the last week, partly for the pleasure of it but also to impose order on my empty days. I feel I can safely confide in you that I had had no idea William would leave me quite so free. But I suppose it is what I wanted. It is not that I am lonesome; it is merely that I am alone, without anybody to fight against. He has made it clear that while we inhabit the same city we do not travel together. There is so much he seeks to accomplish here, and when he is not pursuing his business he is at his work.

It is Easter and the schools are closed, so my resolution to do nothing but absorb myself in work from the moment of my arrival has been disappointed. I could walk into the Ritz and take a glass of champagne in the middle of the day, if I chose, eat a soufflé and look at the Green Park. You know I am being nonsensical, and I understand full well it would be scandalous, but who need care should I provoke a scandal? I am unknown here. I suppose it would not do for William to be

146

associated with so wild a young lady, but then he knows full well what I am. I do not seek to marry and neither, I think, does he. And in any case he has left me very much to my own devices, which I suppose I should be accustomed to. He was much the same in Boston. And I think his determination that we should not share an establishment in London means that he closely guards his habits and the careful arrangement of his day. He certainly does not intend to allow me to spoil them!

For my part, I merely wish to pursue my studies and feel this city. I do not pursue happiness. I have quite given it up. It is a specific yet vague end, and I am sometimes frightened. I haunt bookshops and coffee houses and walk long distances with the park to one side and the streets on the other. In my short time here I have neither been robbed nor accosted, but I have already seen sights my uncle would be appalled to have me know about: women with painted faces and gaudy clothes and too many children in rags.

But to return to the scene in the Gallery. All these pictures crowded my head, so I decided to make it my business to make a study of just one, as a present to myself. Also, because I have noticed crowds of young ladies making fair copies of masterpieces—albeit under watchful female eyes—I felt I might be less conspicuous while happily absorbed as they were. It is the perfect way to learn what I can— indeed, what I must. The light is not good and I think many of the pictures need cleaning. But they do overwhelm me so, Augusta, you can only imagine.

It felt irreverent to sit before such greatness, so I was standing, copying a Giorgione 'Madonna and Child'. The tenderness—but you must have seen many similar, my dear, I keep forgetting.

I was finding it hard to concentrate in so public a place because my efforts felt so poor and sometimes it is impossible to leave myself aside as I would wish, when I noticed a tall person regarding me from some distance away. He was dressed as a gentleman, in a distinguished manner—so exquisitely, in fact, that it was evident he took pride in his appearance. He must be of the fashionable world. He looked at me quite pointedly, and while I noticed this I turned my head away and did not meet his eye, continuing my study of the Giorgione. He must have known as well as I that I could no longer draw, and found myself blushing. Such pointed attention in a public place is extremely impolite. Then I heard footsteps and felt he had left the room, and then it was only myself and two elderly whispering ladies remaining. After an anxious glance about me I felt more equipped to work. Gentlemen should not stare so at ladies. (I fear I sound very prudish!)

As I was quitting the room, passing through another gallery crammed with the work of the Renaissance Masters, I saw him standing in front of the glorious Titian 'Bacchus and Ariadne'. If that blue sky is the colour of the air in the Mediterranean I must see it for myself before I die—and the leopards: such vitality and grace, yet I wanted to stroke them the way I used to make a fuss of the cat at school. I paused, because of the picture, and he turned quite deliberately to meet me and said slowly and distinctly, 'How do you do?', as if we had just been introduced. I was so startled that I replied, 'How do you do?' His eyes were a kind of golden-brown, a russet, most unusual colour, but his hair and moustache were dark. I blushed horribly and said, 'Are you in the habit of addressing strange young women in public places?', wondering why I had not merely nodded and passed on or ignored him altogether. 'Only when they are as unusual and beautiful as you are,' he said. Can you believe that is what he said, Augusta? To me?! And I smiled, I could not help it—it all seemed like the most enormous joke. 'You are very frivolous,' I replied. 'Not in the least,' he said. 'I am utterly sincere. Might I introduce myself?' But he did not come any closer. 'No, you had better not,' I said, and moved away, very heart-beating, very breathless.

It was all of little consequence, but I remember his face quite clearly: good cheekbones, fine brows, an intelligent, amused face—very English—a portrait face. Am I so starved of company that a few ill-judged words with a stranger appear significant? I fear the answer is yes. It was just it being today of all days—that stranger talking to me on my birthday, looking at *me*—I was charmed, while still feeling not a little afraid.

My dear friend, I ache to see you and come to know your little salon and circle and I have

taken your invitation to heart and in the spirit
that it is meant. But I cannot conceive of
another journey at present, and especially not
alone. I must content myself with imagining
your sweet face, this Mr Harper you so fondly
describe to me and your now-doting papa, and
be glad for you. Please write to me as soon as
he proposes! I do not think it will be long now.
If he delays, he does not deserve you!

    Love always.

    Emily

*   *   *

Their third weekly dinner and precisely the third
time Emily had seen her cousin. The formality of
the occasion had already been established and was
entirely English: the same private room, the same
elaborate service, William's restrained air of
patient interest. At the end of the evening he was
already in the habit of handing her weekly
allowance to her silently, as if in payment for her
company.

    Conversation faltered; she had something on her
mind to say, and was distracted. It was difficult to
approach, her subject: this sense of lack between
them—habitual, but broken a sufficient number of
times in the past; a gleam of light in the clouds, to
make her hope for a more permanent change in
the weather.

    They had finished their first course and the
plates had been cleared away. 'William, I had
hoped . . . to have enjoyed a little more of your
company here in London. In the spirit of our joint

150

adventure.' She tried to make the remark sound light, based on an intellectual idea, the thing most beloved to him, and not a feeling, never the shame of a lonely feeling. And she smiled.

If it betrayed anything his face showed only mild surprise. 'You are my kite—I have to let you fly into the sky so that I can observe you.'

And tug me back to you on a whim, she wanted to say, but did not.

He put his head slightly to one side. It made him look like a maiden aunt. 'Don't tell me the winds are proving too unpredictable for you?'

Again words bubbled up that she had to swallow. She wanted to say that the joy of flying a kite was both precise and chaotic, a partnership only partly dependent on the touch of the hand on the string.

'I see no need to prolong the analogy, William,' she said, more sharply than she had intended, for she was hurt. 'I have understood you perfectly.'

He smiled without a hint of malice, then added in a lower, more disarming tone, 'The social climate of this country is not all that conducive, even for your . . . faithful cousin.' (He appeared almost to fumble for a word to describe himself and she was relieved he did not pronounce himself humble. Humble was the last thing he would ever be.) 'Besides, the wheels here turn slowly, and I have my own way to make. I have always worked alone.' He looked directly into her eyes but she did not feel an exchange of feeling, rather the sense of exclusion increased.

'Please. Let us forget this,' she said hurriedly, embarrassed. 'I merely expressed surprise not to have seen you more often or made any acquaintance.'

But he would not leave it. He insisted himself upon her weakness. 'Only very lately have I begun to gain entry into proper society. Americans begin here always by being purely an oddity—the first time I came to this country I was passed from hand to hand like a performing animal—and only more recently has my reputation grown, my discretion found to be reliable, and people are beginning to suspect I might indeed be a man of—gravity.'

'And such a man does not arrive on the doorstep of the aristocracy with a young, ignorant, tactless girl—' she burst out, because her heart had begun to ache despite the pressure she put upon herself to disguise it.

He said nothing.

'But what about other artists? The Bohemians? Do you not share their society?' She knew she was pushing too hard, wanting too much, even if it were only understanding.

'Emily, so-called Bohemians do not interest me. Why should I trouble to record the lives of the second-rate and self-aggrandising? Nor should you concern yourself with them. I will not have you sink to any form of squalor.'

Emily laughed. And how can you talk of self-aggrandisement, she wanted to say, quickly, in temper, but did not have the stomach for it. He would quarrel with her for it, it was a certainty.

'I'm sorry, William, I—' Why did she always end up apologising, feeling in the wrong?

'Besides,' he continued in a reasonable, compassionate voice, 'you will do well. You will work hard. I understand term has commenced. I shall take you to register at the School by and by. You are not afraid of a little loneliness, I imagine?

152

Life cannot always be parties and necklaces and soldiers longing to marry you.'

'That was unkind of you, William.'

'Beware vanity, my dear. That is all I meant.'

The waiter brought her main course, but she was no longer hungry. She craved the quiet of her rooms.

Miss Emily Hudson   Carlton Club, SW
c/o Mrs C Denham
—— Square, SW

April 27th, 1862

My dear Emily,

Please be so good as to pack a reticule for a two nights' stay at the house of some friends of mine outside the city.

I shall call for you at two o'clock on Friday.

Let us hope that the company proves satisfactory to you.

Yours truly,

William

CHAPTER ELEVEN

'I am going to give you the benefit of your first taste of fresh air, Cousin,' said William as they bowled along beneath the blossoming trees. 'This city has the most unspeakable stench to it.'

Emily laughed. 'I am beginning to become

accustomed to it. I see now why a lady must carry a handkerchief and smelling salts wherever she goes.'

'Are you not curious as to our destination?'

'Always. But I know you will tell me when you see fit.'

'We shall stay with some acquaintances who keep a country house on the river at Richmond, convenient for Saturday to Mondays. It is not true, deep countryside, with gamekeepers and foxes and all things to delight the Anglophile, but it is pretty and picturesque. Very pleasant river walks are to be had.'

'I am suddenly rather nervous.'

'My dear, I know them only slightly, but they are good people and their manners are perfect.'

*   *   *

Emily exclaimed with delight at the house: like a dolls' house of mellow brick with a double staircase to the front in the Italianate style—formal, gentle, weathered, welcoming; in detail and proportion so unlike the imitations built back home which she now understood to be considerably coarser.

They were shown into the corner drawing room that had long windows in two walls giving on to the gardens at the side and back of the house. She had an impression of faded colours, velvets, tapestries, colours brown and gold and rose. It was a deliciously high room; she could not help tilting her head to examine the painted ceiling.

'Miss Trelawney—Caroline—this is my cousin, Miss Emily Hudson,' said William, surprising her with his pride.

'I am delighted to make your acquaintance.' Miss Trelawney was a tall young woman with upright posture and easy manners. 'I have been beginning to drown in intellectual gentlemen.' Her cool, ironic tone was nonetheless cordial, a particularly English characteristic, Emily thought. 'Allow me to introduce you to my brother, Mr Thomas Trelawney.'

He too came towards her, a brown-haired young gentleman, pleasant, distracted, kind. 'I have the misfortune also to call myself a man of letters,' he said, 'but I am merely a dabbler, not a great man in the making, as I am certain your cousin is.'

'You flatter me, Trelawney,' said William, looking gratified, and a look almost of affection passed between them.

'And allow me to present my editor, Mr Fowler,' said William, and an older, rather ferret-faced gentleman approached, smiling and bowing.

'Only one of your editors,' he replied. 'You spread yourself alarmingly thin.'

'That shall not always be the case. I must concentrate on more than stories or I shall not be satisfied,' said William.

'Indeed, you must, my dear fellow, or neither shall your readers,' said Trelawney. 'We positively require a novel.'

'Thank you for having me in your home.' Emily spoke to Miss Trelawney, smiling and extending her hand.

Mr Fowler said, 'Why do Americans always do that? Thank one before they have taken so much as a glass of water?'

'Do not be so impolite, George,' said Caroline

155

Trelawney in a manner that pleased Emily for being forthright and in charge. 'There are two of our American guests with us now.' A look of sympathy passed between the women.

'We were about to take tea, Miss Hudson,' she continued, and as the trolley came in, Emily glanced across the room and saw a tall figure standing at the far window who had not turned around at their arrival. 'That appallingly ill-mannered fellow over there,' Miss Trelawney said, 'is our dear friend Lord Firle—like all aristocrats born without manners.' This last remark was directed pointedly at the gentleman and was easy and teasing, as if born of long friendship.

Emily did not need to see his face before recognising him immediately as the gentleman from the Gallery. She felt a stain of acute embarrassment suffuse her face and neck.

Turning, he smiled and came towards her at a leisurely pace. 'I believe I have had the pleasure before,' he said, looking only at Emily, who could say nothing.

William glanced at his cousin sharply as she nodded slightly in acknowledgement, observing the look with awakened concentration. 'Indeed?' he said.

'Oh, quite by chance,' continued Firle, without glancing at William. 'It is good of you to remember.' And he came forward out of the light. He seemed paler than she had remembered, equally at ease, while she was clammy with discomfort and the feeling of having been caught in some unspecified guilty act.

Looking from one to another, William smiled.

Indeed all the comfort and grandeur of the

drawing room, the convivial company, the feeling of alert, refreshed calm at being given a reprieve from the loneliness of the city, had given way abruptly to the same sensations Emily had felt among the pictures: heat, thudding heart, a noise of blood in her ears. The great works of art in the Gallery had held a charisma, an almost animal quality that made real people shadows by comparison. But for all his pallor, this gentleman's grace, beauty and energy made her remember why he had stood out among them. As they took tea, and Emily fumbled to manage her cup and saucer, her plate and fork, he remained a little detached from the group, leafing through some periodical or other, but also taking the opportunity to look at Emily and study her quite openly. She did not look back. Neither did William, occupied with Mr Trelawney, offer her a diversion by speaking to her.

She began to converse with Miss Trelawney, who was asking her if she rode and what her interests and accomplishments were, why she had come to England. She was so charming and appeared so genuinely interested and kind that Emily began to become a little less conscious of being watched, and felt engaged. Her cousin and Mr Trelawney were debating the merits of a new book she had not read with a good humour that comforted her, and soft light fell from the windows, brushing their hair and hands and making long patches of bright soft-butter light on the faded rugs.

On a sudden Lord Firle said, 'I shall see you all at dinner,' and abruptly left the room. She heard him go outside, calling to his dogs, followed by his footsteps on the gravel.

157

'It is true, you have met Lord Firle before?' said her companion.

'I do not know him. I only saw him at the National Gallery—it is quite unimportant.'

'He spoke to you without having been introduced?' said Miss Trelawney, half smiling, half shocked. 'He is quite abominable with young women; I am not at all surprised. How disgraceful. And he keeps a wife at home, though nobody ever sees her.'

'Why on earth did you invite him then, Sister, if you disapprove of him so profoundly?' enquired Mr Trelawney.

Miss Trelawney blushed. 'He is clever, and he makes us laugh. It wouldn't do to be bored to death by all this literary gossip, would it?' she said.

At dinner, the abominable gentleman made no attempt to engage Emily in conversation; indeed expressed not the slightest interest in anything, or any person present, and she felt ashamed to feel so disappointed. All Emily knew was that she was curious about this gentleman, fiercely curious, and she wanted him to be curious about her. He was the first person who had truly interested her in a long time. His obvious lack of belief in anything banished the memory of the hopeful part of her heart that Captain Lindsay had taken with him. Yet she could not prevent herself from wondering how he could have behaved in quite such a brazen manner to her when he was a married gentleman, and she was shocked that Miss Trelawney should have referred to the fact so carelessly. Perhaps this was merely the way of the Old World. A gentleman who openly accosted a strange young lady in a public place could hardly be expected to entertain any qualms about his married state; he would no doubt expect any young lady daring enough to reply to be equally without scruple.

She tried to concentrate on the general conversation, which seemed to her lazy and somewhat self-satisfied. Unlike in Boston, where the habit of enquiry was endemic, the party preferred to refer to things they already knew: a shared history, an unarticulated bond. They also seemed to find things frequently amusing, and she had no idea why.

They took their coffee in the drawing room, listening to the hoot of an owl and discussing country birds and the preponderance of bats.

'I do not like bats,' Emily said.

'Nor does any woman,' said Lord Firle, 'but they are very friendly animals. Rather shy, I believe.' Looking at Emily, he seemed to convey a meaning in his words that was teasing, unfathomable, as if his brain was saying something else.

'Sir, are we to understand that you have become a champion of these creatures of the night?' said William, his remark striking Emily as awkward, neither witty nor clever.

'Every creature deserves its place in God's universe,' said Lord Firle, seeming rather bored.

'We must publish a treatise on the subject,' laughed Mr Fowler.

*   *   *

Miss Trelawney and Emily retired early.

'Travelling is so tiring, is it not, my dear?' her hostess said at her bedroom door. Emily's corner room was vast, with the same air of comfort, grandeur and age as the rest of the house. It felt as if she was being encircled by welcoming arms, and she walked into it with a feeling of calm.

'You have a beautiful home. You must love it here.'

'I do. Our father left it us. It was built by our family. I must admit it still feels strange without him. I nursed him in his last illness, you see.'

Emily could see. She could see clearly. 'Indeed. How long ago was that?'

Miss Trelawney looked taken aback and Emily was forced to remind herself that the English did not appear to deal in questions. 'Forgive me. I can be very inquisitive.'

'Not so very long ago, my dear.'

Miss Trelawney began to move about the room, turning down the bed, smoothing the covers and adjusting the curtains. There was an air of familiarity about her preparation of the room; Emily felt as if she had seen her perform these duties many times before.

'But I forget—we are both orphans, are we not? Although, of course, you are so very young.'

Emily smiled. 'That is a matter of debate.'

Caroline Trelawney stopped in her supervision of the room and looked at Emily. Her eyes were brown and intelligent but were small and lacked brilliance, her nose long and patrician, her mouth thin-lipped and pale. It was a face not inclined to beauty.

'My brother urges me to marry and busy myself with children. I have to keep reminding him that I am twenty-seven and no one has ever asked me. And I think I am content keeping house for him. I am always occupied. And I have my dogs, the greyhounds—I find they take up more of my heart, and I must admit to a great delight in having them run beside my carriage in the park. But these are confidences—and we have only met one another today.'

'I promise I will keep them,' said Emily. 'I will keep any confidence for a friend.'

'I am sure you would, Miss Hudson. If there is anything you require in the night, simply knock upon my door. I am just along the passage,' said Miss Trelawney, 'and I shall not be disturbed. I sleep lightly. Breakfast at eight. Good night, little American.'

She rustled away along the corridor before Emily could take the opportunity of thanking her again.

*   *   *

The morning, excessively bright and almost balmy for May, was spent with the whole party exploring the grounds and gardens, following the walks through rougher ground to the Thames. They stopped at the riverbank to admire the view of Richmond Hill beyond and above. Lord Firle walked by himself, always a little ahead and apart. Mr Trelawney knew a great deal about the history of the place and the origins of Richmond Palace, and Emily quizzed him about it.

'You are such a tourist, my dear,' said William, as if apologising for her. And when the others moved on ahead, he said in her ear, 'It is hardly the Atlantic at Newport, is it, Cousin?'

'No, but it is so delightful—so green. However does it come to be so green?' Emily made no attempt to lower her voice in response. She hated soft conspiratorial muttering.

'You know as well as I, persistent rain and damp—appalling for the constitution, perfect for the aesthetic appreciation of the summer months.'

'Don't pay any attention to him, it rains in summer, too,' said Mr Trelawney, at her cousin's side. 'Particularly in June. And everyone is always very surprised.'

'Oh, look at the darling ducks!' cried Emily, to general laughter.

'Do they not have ducks in Boston?' enquired Miss Trelawney; Emily could not tell whether she was in earnest.

'Yes, but they speak a different language,' she replied.

Mr Fowler snorted appreciatively. 'That is really rather good, Miss Hudson.'

'Please,' she interrupted. 'Call me Emily.'

*   *   *

'That was quite wrong of you,' said William as they turned for the house at the conclusion of the walk. 'Let *us* address you by your first name, but not Mr Fowler. He is a publisher, not a gentleman.'

'Oh, don't be so absurd, William—we are all here together as equals, thinking people—'

'Do not express an opinion upon a subject about which you know absolutely nothing!' he whispered, quite viciously. 'English society is a complex and delicate mechanism and far beyond your scope.'

'Snobbery is simply snobbery, William. It is not mysterious or sacred, as you seem to imply.'

'For pity's sake, Emily, when will you ever leave anything alone? Whatever you encounter has to be

162

altered to fit your sensibility! Have you ever considered how much of a toll that takes on other people?' He was shaking with rage and still keeping his voice low. 'I have worked hard to be included here. I am nowhere close to approaching the circles I wish to move in, the— Oh, I waste my breath.'

'Don't say that to me, William!' she cried. 'You are not the one who is entirely alone and without occupation!' Now it was she who was shaking.

'That was your choice. I shall say what I please.' And he left her, breathing hard, alone upon the gravel path.

'Miss Hudson.' It was Lord Firle.

'You must have a very light step. I did not hear you come near.'

'I think because you were absorbed in quarrelling so energetically with your cousin. You look rather flushed, young lady.'

'We did not quarrel. We have a lively discourse.'

'It sounded like a quarrel to me.' He smiled. It was a charming smile, very slight.

'Perhaps it was.' And she smiled back at him, valuing his interest, his directness, that he was not afraid to speak his mind about her without offering a criticism.

'Allow me to show you the rose garden. I believe some of the shrub roses have come into bud.' These were the words he used but he spoke them as if he were humorously commenting on them; she had never known it before.

She followed him across the lawn and through the wrought-iron gate in a wall to the side of the house. The paths surrounded beds of thorny shrub roses, barely in leaf or bud, like skeletons clutching

163

at the air. The old walls covered with climbers showed brighter new leaves. But it was beautiful. It would be very beautiful. And the sky over their heads was blue. Grey and green lavender lined the squares, divided the shrubs, and she knew there would be softer summer flowers too.

'I love walled gardens.' Emily was suddenly conscious that they were separated from the others and tried, she did not know why, to appear careless of it.

He gave her his arm easily, as if they had been friends for years, and she allowed herself the luxury of taking it. Perhaps her uncle and cousin were right. She had no notion of how to behave.

'Roses are the quintessential English flower,' he said.

They stopped so she could examine a pale serrated leaf. 'Why do you say that?'

'Because they are so tough. They are enduring.'

She looked from the leaf to his face. 'That is not what people usually say about roses.'

'No.'

'Their exquisite delicacy and beauty, and how short-lived they are—is not that part of their charm?'

'I did not remark upon their charm. I merely said that they were quintessentially English.'

'Of course.' She felt quite stupid, making ready to turn and walk on.

He bent his head to examine her face. 'You should be forgiven for making that mistake. So few people listen and think at the same time, don't you find? Particularly in the presence of beauty.'

He looked at her with great concentration, and his voice had a teasing, almost tender quality. On a sudden she did not feel stupid any longer.

'I do.'

'Caroline says you are studying to be an artist?'

'Yes. Although I find myself quite left to my own devices at present—I have not yet begun. I am waiting for my cousin to enrol me at the school.'

'Does William indeed approve of this desire?'

'He encourages me in every respect. He knows how much I want to see the world.'

'It seems to me he guards you jealously, as I would should I have such a prize. He looks at you all the time.'

When she failed to answer, at a loss, he said, 'A peculiar profession for a woman, is it not? Art.'

He was beginning to overwhelm her, so that she was forced to look away. Taking his arm again she moved and he kept pace with her.

'Yes. But it is not unknown. The pursuit of beauty, perfection, it cannot only be confined to men. The truth is, I do not know if I have the ability to make Art a profession. But I am determined to find out.'

'Good,' he said. 'Good. It is essential always to find out.'

*   *   *

The entire party came out to the front of the house when Emily and William departed. Miss Trelawney begged Emily to call her Caroline and promised to visit her in town.

'I am afraid I am rather out of the way. I have but two rooms—it is only—'

'How charming,' said her new friend. 'I do so like going somewhere altogether new.'

165

Mr Trelawney laughed. 'You talk as if Miss Hudson's rooms were a pleasure garden, Caroline.'

'Now *that* I have no desire to see, brother.'

'Whyever not?' enquired Mr Fowler, rather impertinently, Emily felt. Even she knew full well that the sight of everyday people desporting themselves in the open air would be quite inappropriate for Miss Trelawney's eyes.

Lord Firle handed her into the carriage. She could not see how this could be avoided as he moved to do so.

'A word, Miss Hudson,' he muttered conspiratorially, and she drew back, as if in fear of something improper.

His hand was very warm, his clasp surprisingly firm. It was a finer hand than Captain Lindsay's, she thought erroneously, more elegant, and she was suddenly flooded by the memory of the carriage ride at Rhode Island in the spring of another year. Closing her eyes against it, she opened them again to see Firle smiling at her, his eyes cool.

'I beg you not to make poor Caroline travel by omnibus. It is not Bohemian. It is merely squalid.'

'There is no need. I invariably walk.'

'Quite the adventurer, aren't you?' said Mr Fowler.

Emily felt embarrassed—too prominent, too loud. Ever since William's galling words the day before she had felt her cousin's reproach, her own obviousness.

'It is merely that cabs are so expensive, and one can see so much better on foot.'

William gave her a sharp look. She had done the

unforgivable: she had mentioned money. He had told her when they first arrived that this must never be done. While back home they talked of money and prices with almost every breath; here it was unspeakable. How had she forgotten? She stumbled and stopped.

'I think what Miss Emily means is that anyone with an ounce of gumption explores a new city according to his own lights,' said Lord Firle in his easy, superior tone.

'Indeed they do,' agreed Mr Trelawney, and he smiled.

'Let us leave you now,' muttered William, and the carriage pulled away. He did not speak a word to Emily all the way back to town.

Miss Augusta Dean   Mayfair, London
Hotel d'Angleterre, Rome

May 8th, 1862

My dearest Girl,

It seems William has withdrawn not only his approval but his attentions from me.

Since we went away to Richmond he has honoured our weekly appointment to dine, but has said barely a word to me and seemed irritated by my presence—which is something I have never felt before.

Perhaps I am turning out to be a disappointment to him after all, limited in scope compared to his Europe.

If he does not take me to the college by the end of the week I shall present myself there without him. I tend to forget that he is merely busy and must write and live. When I have begun to study I will not brood so over the uncertainty that has accompanied the loss of his attention.

With love,

Emily

*   *   *

Without reference to or hint of their former quarrel, William at last took Emily to register at the Art School, introducing her to the principal, Miss Norton, with an air of gravity and ostentation she could not help but find uncomfortable. She felt aware immediately that it was his own importance he wished to impress upon the lady, beyond the suitability of his cousin for the school.

Miss Norton was a large, prepossessing woman with abundant red hair and a suitably hawk-like expression. She looked on her cousin coolly, Emily felt, as at a necessary evil: a rich American client. But she expressed interest in Emily's portfolio, and a genuine willingness to engage with the work and its author.

'Which classes would you like to partake in, Miss Hudson? There is no proper life class, we are not permitted nude models, but we draw hands, feet, faces. We offer Still Life, Watercolour, Oil Painting and Drawing.'

'I would like to take all the classes, if you please.'

Miss Norton smiled in a somewhat superior fashion. 'Most of our young ladies only undertake one or two. We are in many ways seen as a finishing school; you should be aware of this.'

'My cousin's interest in Art is that of a professional,' said William. 'She is not a frivolous young lady. Neither are her wishes dependent on financial considerations. And all bills will, of course, be sent to me, care of my club.'

Emily blushed that he should be so obvious about these arrangements, when he usually advocated such delicacy. Could he not have put it more nicely?

Miss Norton replied, 'If you give the details to my secretary, they shall be recorded.' He nodded. 'And you, my dear, are most welcome to our school.'

*   *   *

The lady recommended an establishment in the Burlington Arcade where they could purchase suitable materials, as only the most basic were provided by the School. Emily and William strolled in the dappled sunlight along the streets of South Kensington before catching a cab for the short journey, and Emily felt a great surge of happiness and desire for the future.

'I do so hate feeling exhausted,' William said.

Emily was elated, not only that her studies were settled upon at last but because of her cousin's expansive mood.

Arm in arm at the Arcade they stopped outside one of the jewellery shop windows. The display was crowded, brilliant with heavily set gems, old and new, of such grandeur and magnificence that Emily could not imagine ever wearing them.

'Do they not hurt your eyes, William?' she

169

laughed.

'I think the sapphires would be your stone,' he said, ignoring the question, and indicating a necklace and earrings glowing and glittering with dark marine-blue and encrusted with diamonds. 'I should love to see you— But I could never buy you jewellery: that is for a father, brother or lover only.'

'None of which I have or am likely to have,' said Emily, lightly. Pausing to observe, she continued, 'I must admit to a weakness for jewellery—or is it only for the beauty of the display? And I love imagining all the stories of all the women who have worn these pieces, and shall wear them, alive or dead.'

'They tell of a history of wealth, the safety and security of riches.'

She could see William was comforted by that, their part in the edifice of money. 'But is it not more their beauty that is to be treasured and celebrated?'

'Beauty caught—that is how I would prefer to see it. Beauty caught and, more than that, for ever enshrined.'

They walked on.

*   *   *

In the artists' shop William bought thick paper and fine brushes, oozing colours and clear solutions, with an extravagance she had never seen in him before, so far exceeding Emily's expectations that he had to order the items to be wrapped and sent to her address.

'William, stop! I will not be able to carry it all to

170

school!' She had never been so spoiled and indulged and was surprised by how uncomfortable it made her feel.

'It is of no consequence. I desire you to have the best, and never want for anything. You must have every means at your disposal necessary for your work. If there is no room for it at the school you shall keep a small studio in your rooms, and then you shall have no cause to feel alone.'

Miss Bridget Norton   Carlton Club, SW
South Kensington Art School
SW

May ——, 1862

Dear Miss Norton,

I write to confirm the arrangement made today between us, namely that you shall undertake the instruction of my young cousin, Miss Hudson, in any class she might care to attend at your establishment.

My other purpose is to state, as delicately as possible, for I have no intention of causing alarm, that her health has not always been strong, and so I would urge you not to tax her nor to expect too high a standard of work from her. Your emphasis should be on the enjoyment of her work: criticism would come as a severe blow to her. She requires a diverting occupation, nothing more; I shall take it amiss if I see any sign of strain or exhaustion in her face.

This letter is written without my cousin's

knowledge, for reasons I am sure you will understand. I am her protector and, as such, must also defend her pride.

With all good wishes
Yours etc.,

William Cornford

Miss Augusta Dean   Mayfair, London
Hotel d'Angleterre, Rome

May 30th, 1862

Darling Augusta,

Your Rome sounds splendidly easy and full of pleasure—beautiful at this time of year! But still no news of a proposal. You are very patient, dear girl, far more patient than I should be!

Here, in the Anglo-Saxon world, I work hard and apply myself.

I have started in earnest at my new school: it is hard work, very hard work and solitary. Although I am continually among people, I feel set apart, dressed in my sombre Boston colours, speaking in my alien voice. Most young ladies attend classes as a form of finishing school, and they giggle and chat and gossip about parties and balls and entertainment and where to get the correct lace, and their hair is invariably elaborately dressed. I wonder if you and I behaved in that silly way when we were at school! Surely we had more passion, more life in us, less frivolity.

172

It is baffling. I do not know.

But the work is a joy. Applying myself, learning, stumbling, and very occasionally approaching what I am attempting is infinitely satisfying. I think of my father and his beautiful work, so sadly lost when our house was sold, and hope he would be proud.

I find I adore Miss Norton. There can be no other word for it. She teaches many of the classes herself; she is emotional and disciplined and intelligent and utterly frightening with her loud voice and her unsmiling, concentrated air. And she is beautiful as well as stern. I long for her either to criticise or praise something I have done, but to date she has only looked on in silence. The girls say they think she was once married, but no one knows for certain. It is impossible to discern her age.

I work at the school every morning. In the afternoons I frequently stay to finish a piece in the studio on the top floor, a comforting room and sunny. Sometimes I continue my street wanderings, or occasionally copy a masterpiece from the Wallace Collection. I avoid the National Gallery: it is so noisy always, and full.

Occasionally in the evenings I dine with William, away from his club, which he never ceases to remind me is an inconvenience for him, for they will not allow ladies—as if it were my fault! He is frequently waspish and tired and, although eager to hear entertaining stories of my adventures about town, shows little curiosity or sympathy. I have come to recognise it in him when he is absorbed with his work, and he is under particular strain because he has started his first novel and feels he has much to prove. His stories have been so well-received here that he feels a public weight of expectation that has never troubled him before.

And so we rub along, and it is altogether rather strange.

Please write to me with some very mundane news of your life in Rome (if that is all there is), because I own that sometimes the peculiarities of this country—and indeed my cousin—threaten to overwhelm me.

Looking forward to your news and gossip.

With all love,

Emily

CHAPTER TWELVE

Lord Firle was waiting for her on the steps of her lodgings. He was standing, head down, stroking his whiskers as if uncertain how to proceed. She felt a shudder of recognition somehow guilty, as if in thinking of him so often she had willed him to appear. It was definitely he. Quickly she debated with herself whether to turn and run away. If she were to hesitate a moment he might go and she could breathe more easily. Instead, he looked up and directly at her across the road.

She broke into a sudden wide smile, unexpected for them both, and almost ran across the street to meet him.

'This is most improper,' he said, as if it did not matter in the least.

'Yes.'

'Will you take tea with me?'

'Yes.'

'Or do you have another engagement?' He was teasing and she laughed, both terrified and elated at her own daring.

'No, I most certainly do not,' she exclaimed.

'Let me take your things.' He relieved her of her portfolio and small reticule. It made her feel curiously bereft. 'We shall go to Brown's. I think it might rain.'

She looked into his face so closed and sure, but he did not glance back, concentrating on avoiding pitfalls and the mud splatter from carriage wheels. They hurried along, past the blur of other people and their lives. She was with someone at last and had somewhere to go. She felt some tired part of her fall away.

*   *   *

The hotel was a warren of low-ceilinged rooms, plush and warm with fires that reflected off the silver. His was one of those presences that a waiter could never ignore, and they were instantly attended to.

He sat quite appallingly close to her, their knees almost touching, and he rubbed his hands. 'Tea cakes, I think.' He looked at her. 'And sandwiches. You do not look as if you have eaten a thing since I last set eyes on you and that was at least—'

'A month ago,' she replied.

'Indeed.'

She removed her gloves, cloak and bonnet: she must not think of how she must look, all rain-stained and bedraggled. The tea was hot, scented, delicious, the china exquisite and she was hungry, if a little throat-closingly sick at the same time.

'That's better,' he said, when she started to eat.

'I am not a starved London sparrow, you know.'

He laughed. 'You seek to quarrel with me, as well as your cousin?'

'Of course not.'

'How is dear William, by the way? I hear he works hard.'

'He does. And his stories are appearing everywhere. He says there is nothing so stimulating as travel for a writer.'

'I wonder he doesn't tire of it.'

'Might you, if you were in his place?'

'Certainly. But that is my misfortune. I tire remarkably easily.'

She looked up at his smile and intense gaze and decided he was teasing; he was the most energetic gentleman she had ever encountered.

'Being descended from a long line of idlers, I find time weighs on me, and no especial responsibility or imperative has ever held any weight with me. But you interest me. You—like myself—are entirely alone.'

This was not what she should be doing. He was talking to her in the worst way, quite intimately. She must show him that it would not do, but she was at a loss as to how to reply, how to attempt to take the subject away from the personal. She said at last, 'Do you have business that keeps you in town?'

'Nothing in especial. I will stay for the season, if

176

it is not too dull. After that I shall go into Northamptonshire to my estates. Perhaps travel a little. I do not know.' He leaned closer towards her. 'I would like to take you to the play.'

Emily felt that everybody must be looking at them. Such a *tête à tête* in so public and respectable a place could not pass unnoticed.

'I think I should like that,' she said, without thinking. 'But not—alone.'

'Of course not. Whatever gave you that idea? That would not do at all. I shall call on my dear Caroline. She sends her regards by the way. She and her brother would make up the party. Eat a little seedcake, my dear. Then tell me about this Art School of yours.'

'It is beautiful. Very demanding.'

'Schools are not beautiful, Miss Hudson. Go on.'

'I work hard and I am learning.'

'May I see?' He began to untie the ribbon on her portfolio.

'No.'

'You are very decided.'

'Nothing is ready. Nothing is—right.'

'Very well.' He yawned. 'I think you are becoming altogether too serious. What do they call it? Bluestocking. I want a return of the pretty young thing in the rose garden with the dew still on her I remember so vividly.'

'Was that more amusing?'

'Infinitely.'

He wore a heavy gold signet ring on his arched and elegant finger. She studied it, feeling she should be annoyed, angered that he should refer to her in that way. But instead it made her want to laugh.

'It is not that you are amusing,' he said. 'That is not your quality. It is all the passion you have in that slight young frame, in your mind and heart, and—who knows—you could even have talent. In addition you have the courage of your convictions. There is very little of that in the world.'

He looked at her, her naked throat and wrists and hands that were smudged, and she looked back. 'You are lovely. A little American bird.'

On a sudden it was very serious, their look, and overwhelming to her blood. Then he smiled. 'Will you have a glass of champagne?'

'No. I most certainly will not.' But she laughed.

'No matter. Another time.'

*   *   *

He hailed a cab and bundled her into it.

'I do not want you walking in the dark,' he said, pressing coins into the driver's hand. 'Oh, I nearly forgot,' and he passed her the portfolio through the window, 'I will make sure Caroline sends to you about the theatre.'

And before the cab could drive away he was gone.

Miss Augusta Dean   Mayfair, SW
Hotel d'Angleterre, Rome

June 2nd, 1862

My dear Friend,

You may remember I mentioned a gentleman to you whom I became acquainted with at

Richmond. It is of no consequence if you do not recall. It is only that I—I have been entertained by him in private and altogether intimate circumstances that I fear I should not have allowed. Indeed I know I should not. My darling girl—do not distress yourself—it was merely the taking of tea—and yet we were quite alone.

You—more than anyone—have always known how little I care about the opinion of the world. Equally you know that all my misdemeanours have been of a most minor kind. It seems my uncle has entrusted me with more of his conscience than I care to admit.

My mother would always advise me to judge according to my own standards, but that is what I am struggling with—understanding them, coming to appreciate what they are.

Since I have come to this country I have felt remarkably confused. The steady things are the school—the work, which I am thankful for— but the luxury of solitude can transmute into— not exactly a curse—but a burden—a burden of varying weights.

I write myself into a corner.

This gentleman interests me. He is intelligent and his view of the world is unusual, might I say. He also holds an attraction for me that I cannot describe, but feel you might understand if you were to see him. I fear he flatters me. I have always prided myself on being unique. People of unique sensibility are naturally inclined to one another—are they not? But we all know what comes after pride.

Forgive me, my dear friend.
I will write in more favourable mood anon.
Fondest love,

Emily

[Letter unsent]

*   *   *

Miss Trelawney waited in the carriage while her
brother climbed the front steps. Emily had seen
them draw up from her window and felt
unaccountably moved that they had come
expressly for her. She ran down on hearing the
bell, without waiting for the servant to come up.
Important things must be accomplished at speed,
she felt. Passing the open door of the parlour she
glimpsed Mrs Denham sewing in the lamplight,
but was unsure whether it would be better
manners to acknowledge her or pretend she had
not seen her. Full of vigour and excitement, she
did not much care and hurried past the door with a
barely perceptible nod.

Mr Trelawney's greeting was agreeable, formal,
full of his peculiar charm of reserve and cordiality
combined, and Emily felt a gaiety sweep her even
before she had pressed Miss Trelawney's hand.
Her friend was looking altogether handsome in
some richness of dress, the brightness of the new
fashionable colours contrasting with Emily's dull
green stuff.

The crowd was thick on the steps, in the bar,
every possible part of the theatre—'All preening
and plumage,' Mary would call it, she thought. But

the splendour and the brightness of the people against the theatre's red plush and pale blue and gold was a delight to her eyes.

'You have gone very quiet, Miss Emily,' said Mr Trelawney as they took their seats in the box: ladies in front, gentlemen perched behind.

'Poor creatures,' murmured Miss Trelawney, indicating them, as she guided Emily to sit down.

'I am a little overwhelmed, that is all.'

'Firle will be along shortly,' said Mr Trelawney as the lights were dimmed. 'He is invariably late, you know.'

Emily felt a pounding in her ears, a foolish panic. She had already decided not to say a word to anyone about their last encounter, sensing that he would know exactly what to do and say, but now that the moment approached her, the feeling of wrongdoing and excitement entwined overwhelmed her breathing. She must not think of then: the charm of the rose garden, the dark glow of their last interview, or of the encounter to come. She must think only of this moment, the box, keep it in her memory with her letters and her box of paints.

The curtain went up and her first thought was of the quantity of face paint in the flickering gas light—beautiful yet grotesque, the words booming out over the noise in the pit and the chatter of the boxes. She suddenly thought it extraordinary that she should be doing something of such enormity without William.

'Why do they not hush?' she whispered.

'We are not in church, my dear,' said Miss Trelawney, and Emily felt the absurdity in the idea that she should be thought staid by anybody,

181

especially at this moment. She was becoming acutely conscious of how she held herself, her quick breathing and the beating of her heart—and yet equally she felt invisible in the darkness compared to the jewel-like silk Miss Trelawney wore, giving off its soft lustre, the cool gleam of riches all about her, the top hats—all black play of light like the furry heads of animals—the gas lights flickering, the noise of the boards, the heat and the collective smell of perfume and of sweat and the softness of the powder upon the ladies' cheeks; and all the time she waited, suspended before the stage, above the stalls, free to study all the occupants of the other boxes, free to look only at the stage, but bound by the darkness behind her.

When Lord Firle opened the door to the box he let in a blaze of light and then fumbled in the dimness to close the door. 'Confound this infernal thing!' he said, quite loudly.

'Good evening, my dear fellow,' said Mr Trelawney, and the ladies, turning, politely inclined their heads.

Emily felt a wave of pleasure at the sight of his singularly fine face, and his air of naughtiness that on a sudden spoke to her of Charlie. But Charlie had never been elegant. Charlie had never had a fine suit of clothes.

Pushing that thought aside, where it could join the many others she did not want to think, she turned and glanced at Lord Firle again, desiring him to see the brilliance and gaiety in her eyes. And he smiled, once more in that disarmingly tender way he had, while his eyes remained amused, as if to promise all the things they would say to one another if an altogether different time and place existed. She took pleasure in believing they communicated with such ease in this imaginary sphere, holding herself very straight until the curtain fell on the first Act, because she would not want him to see her as anything but entirely graceful. And there had been too much stooping over her work at the school.

During the interval the gentlemen fetched refreshments and Emily, in such close proximity to Caroline Trelawney, felt suddenly overwhelmed by the desire to say something to her of meaning, exchange a perception that would somehow unite them in intimacy, as if they were true friends.

But Miss Trelawney began with, 'And how do you find the play, my dear?'

And so she replied in great deference to the conventional, 'It is very amusing. I did not expect that.'

'That is because it is a comedy,' laughed her companion. 'Do they not have comedies in Boston?'

'This is my first visit to the theatre. My uncle did not approve of any lady of his acquaintance, let alone of his family, venturing out in search of pleasure.'

'And what is his opinion of their crossing oceans?'

'As you may imagine, not high.' On a sudden it felt very trivial and nonsensical to Emily, the struggle she had had. Laughter caught in her throat, the breath in her chest. Miss Trelawney smiled, but remained reserved. She did not appear to share the giddy aerial view of her travails that Emily had so swiftly attained. When the gentlemen returned to the box her giddiness only grew.

On the foggy steps outside the theatre Mr Trelawney shook Lord Firle's hand. 'Most enjoyable. Shall you say goodnight or come back to Grosvenor Square with us and take a little supper?'

'Very kind of you. But I shall see Miss Hudson home.'

'That is for us to do,' said Caroline quickly.

'Do not trouble yourselves. Allow me the pleasure,' said Lord Firle, as if it were the most natural thing in the world. 'It is of no consequence. And you would have to go out of your way.'

'My dear, I think you had better not,' whispered Miss Trelawney when Emily failed to reply, looking only at Lord Firle. She put a hand on Emily's arm, quite firmly.

'Miss Emily?' said Firle. When she remained silent he laughed, then continued easily, but with an air of irritation, 'If you must be so conventional, go with Thomas. I simply seek to make it easier for us all to find our beds as quickly as possible.'

'My dear fellow,' said Trelawney in warning, as if 'bed' were somehow an appalling word, thought Emily. It was foolish and made her angry. Besides, she could not bear to say goodnight to Lord Firle.

'I will go with his Lordship,' she said, avoiding everyone's eyes. 'It is far simpler.' And rapidly she turned to bid the Trelawneys goodnight. Their manners remained perfectly pleasant and polite but she knew that they were displeased.

'Goodnight to you both,' said Firle briskly, and they walked away.

Emily began to laugh without gaiety. 'I am not sure that I have acted wisely,' she said.

'One must "act" in one's own best interest,' he replied. At once she knew for a certainty that she had done wrong.

After some silence he said, 'I shall take you to the perfect place for a late supper. It is just a moment's walk from here.'

'I thought you were only to escort me home.'

'So you are truly not hungry?' He turned and smiled.

'Supper would be delightful,' she replied.

*   *   *

'You would do well to allow me to order for you,' said Lord Firle.

As he studied the menu Emily took great pleasure in observing his countenance, the quick life in his face. She examined it quite secretly, she felt: he was occupied and quite unaware.

They were seated in a private curtained booth to the back of the dining room. He asked the waiter how long the lamb had been hung and detailed questions about the sauce. He appeared in his element, ordering extravagantly, both precisely and vaguely, with great care. The other diners had all looked at them when they came in, and had remarked upon them quite openly, she felt. She had never before felt so prominent in a public place, and Emily was not sure how that made her feel. Yet at the same time, as ever with London, she was so marvellously secret, anonymous, away. She felt beautiful in his company.

They ate and drank lightly but well and were

185

very frivolous and very gay, egged on by Firle's extravagant mood. Emily caught it, the speed and precision of his thoughts, observations and discourse, responding to it with something of her own wildness and spirit. She felt free to exercise her curiosity.

'What do you like to do? What are your occupations?'

'I have already told you,' he replied. 'I have none. In this country, gentlemen have pursuits—it's far safer.'

She laughed. 'Pursuits?' she repeated, feeling very daring.

'Hunting, fishing, shooting—the eternal round. We are very partial to our pleasures in Europe,' he said, with his usual lightness, but a greater concentration in his gaze.

'Lord Firle, I don't think we should—'

'Of course we should not. You are quite right.' He turned away from her, raising his hand. 'Waiter, my account.' He looked stern, displeased, and just for a fraction of a second reminded her of her uncle. Then he smiled. 'I must take you home.'

They took a cab. It was cold and she held herself away from him, only allowing herself to observe him out of the corner of her eye. He did not try to speak to her—all the ease and hilarity of the evening seemed to have disappeared.

'I think I have behaved like a fool,' she said at last, quietly but quite distinctly.

'You did not consider that a minute ago,' he replied coolly.

When he handed her out into the cold night she felt his disappointment in her and an utter misery at their parting that was quite absurd. The horse stamped and snorted and the driver stared straight ahead.

'Have you ever been kissed?' he said at last, quite gentle.

She shook her head, feeling sudden tears. 'No.'

'Would you like to be?'

She could not answer, only looking at his eyes that had lost their colour in the darkness. He made a move as if to leave her and she reached out for his sleeve. When he kissed her it was all there was.

Miss Emily Hudson   Grosvenor Square, SW
—— Square
Mayfair, SW

5th June, 1862

My dear Miss Emily,

I am taking the liberty of writing to you at the earliest opportunity to enquire whether you would do me the honour of calling on me this morning.

I am not formally 'At Home' until this afternoon, so we shall be quite undisturbed.

Yours truly,

Caroline Trelawney

             *   *   *

The grandeur of Caroline's house in Grosvenor Square far exceeded even her uncle's establishment at Boston, but Emily did not think about that as she was ushered up the stairs. It was only the wild tired joy of the evening that filled her head and heart. She was exhausted with happiness and dry-eyed from a strange hunger and lack of sleep.

'So good of you to come,' said Caroline, moving forward among the ochres and greens of the splendid room. Emily blushed. 'Will you take some tea with me?'

'You are very kind.'

Miss Trelawney rang for it to be served and then led her into a small withdrawing room at the back of the house filled with bowls of flowers. 'I have them sent up from Richmond,' she said, when Emily remarked upon them. 'I miss my gardens so when I am in town.'

Emily looked for the rosebuds she had admired with Lord Firle, but of course they were not there, her exhausted gaze took in only a blur of almost moving colour to suggest each petal. 'They are lovely.'

Miss Trelawney motioned for Emily to sit down and she found herself perching uncomfortably opposite her, in a velvet upholstered chair: not close enough for intimacy, Emily felt, but with an awkward distance between them.

'My dear girl, I have spent the night reproaching myself terribly.'

So full of her impressions of the last few hours, Emily could only ask, 'Whatever for?', concentrating with difficulty on the meaning behind the words as if at the background of a painting she had come to copy.

'Making your acquaintance and then neglecting you so shamefully until last evening. As a foreigner your cousin is not the correct person—he cannot be relied upon to introduce you to society. He does not have the experience of the way things should be done. I knew it, and there has really been no excuse for it.'

'Please. Miss Trelawney, there is no need whatever—'

'Caroline.'

'Caroline. I did not expect—'

'You are friendless in this city and—'

Emily smiled a tight smile, trembling. 'It is easy to behave foolishly, I know.'

Caroline narrowed her eyes. 'What would your cousin say if he were to hear of your conduct last night?'

'He has far greater forbearance than I once credited him with. He can be capable of great kindness.'

Her companion continued as if she had not spoken. 'Do you have any notion of what this means?'

It was unavoidable; she was to be warned, admonished, scolded and, unlike with her uncle, from a deep affection she did not deserve. Sensible of this, she could not prevent herself from responding sharply and feeling almost cruel towards her friend. The curious thing was that she could not feel ashamed. Her longing to see Lord Firle, and everything that concerned him, must be protected; she must close her mind to all other distractions.

'I do apologise, my dear.' Caroline's voice was kind. 'I do not mean to infer that you are not capable of thinking for yourself. May I speak plainly?'

'Please. Please do.'

Emily reminded herself that Caroline took only the liberty that Augusta might, in similar circumstances, and so she had no especial right to be offended, but she felt peculiarly numb.

'My dear—' When Caroline took a breath, struggling for words, Emily felt no mercy towards her. 'I will try to explain. It seems to me that you are in a very delicate situation indeed, and I am fully conscious of my own responsibility for putting you there. I feel that you are quite able to see that there are two paths open to you.' She paused while Emily remained contemplating her, quietly. 'One would be to allow me to take you under my wing: chaperone you, introduce you, behave to you as a sister and advise you in the ways of this world as a sister might. Or the other—'

'I could choose to go my own way and become a fallen woman to whom no decent person would ever speak, and who cannot marry. All this on the evidence of a shadow of one flirtation.' Emily did not know her own rapid speech and bitter voice. She could see that it shook her friend. 'It may surprise you to know that I intend never to marry.'

Caroline leaned closer. 'Do not speak so frivolously.' Before Emily could reply she hurried on. 'I do not speak of marriage. I speak merely of being accepted in this world. In London, young ladies are *never* escorted home alone from the theatre by gentlemen, unless they are close relations, regardless of whether these gentlemen are married or unmarried. They do not keep any sort of company with gentlemen at all unless in the presence of a respectable chaperone. As you know, Lord Firle is married. His reputation where ladies are concerned could hardly be worse. Do you have

190

any notion of what this means?'

'I—'

But Caroline continued as if Emily had not spoken. 'I do not know how I could have allowed you to make his acquaintance at Richmond—and to agree to his idea to go to the theatre, that was inadvisable; I will always reproach myself for it. It is just that he seemed to want it so.' She rubbed her forehead, looking at her flowers, quite distracted. 'I entertain him for my own amusement, and besides, he is immune to my charms.' She smiled.

Emily noticed how preoccupied Caroline looked, how weary, how concerned, as if afraid her new acquaintance were falling prey to some disease, and she felt the first stirrings of responsibility. And she did not want to think of ladies and Lord Firle. On a sudden the elation left her and only the exhaustion remained.

'I have never had such a delightful time as last evening in my life,' she simply said, beginning to lower her head.

Caroline pulled her chair closer and took Emily's hand. 'He is splendid company. But respectable people can be amusing, too, you know. My dear, you are very young.'

'I know it. I know.' This was not a fact she could ever deny, ignore, or conceal.

Caroline left a pause, as if to give her words more weight. 'I am equally sensible that you are of an independent mind, and I admire you for that. But you must decide upon your choice before it is too late, what it is you truly desire for yourself— because if you are ruined, it will be for ever.'

Emily looked at the bowls of flowers so

thoughtfully and unimaginatively placed around the room, at the pale countenance and brown hair of her friend, and could say nothing. Every object she observed conspired to defeat her.

'This evening I will be holding a small reception in these rooms. We gather to hear poetry read, and afterwards there will be a light supper. Tonight we shall listen to the poems from a collection by Mr Browning. Might you attend if I send my carriage?'

'Of course,' said Emily, feeling the light dim. 'Of course.'

*　　*　　*

Bitter tears stung her eyes as she quitted the house—hot wells of tears. 'But not of shame, not of shame,' she muttered to herself with no attempt to wipe them away. She wished she believed in God; then she would pray for deliverance. She felt as a child, but that did not defeat the feeling: of all the people in the world now breathing, Lord Firle was the one whose company she desired, craved, and he had been forbidden to her. She walked for some long time through the London streets: cool spring squares, the arching trees, shops full of beautiful things she could not afford to own. She would not go to the school today. It was impossible.

Crossing Park Lane she ventured into the wide expanse of the park, her eyes searching for a horizon as infinite and uncrowded as her hopes. On a sudden she longed for the ocean. Sitting down upon a bench she sat and cried, and thought of her mother, and the spirit of her family. She thought of the evenings by the stove and the music and the books and the laughter. And she cried all the more. When she had finished crying she dried her eyes and walked across the park to school.

Miss Emily Hudson   Lowndes Place, SW
—— Square
Mayfair, SW

5th June, 1862

My dear Girl,

Last evening you gave me great happiness. I can think of nothing but you. Send to me when you are at liberty to do so.

Arthur Firle

Miss Augusta Dean   Mayfair
Hotel d'Angleterre, Rome

June 5th, 1862

Sweetest Augusta,

This evening I attended a supper party given by my new acquaintances, the Trelawneys, at Grosvenor Square. That sounds very gay and it was not, but to call it a poetry reading makes it sound altogether too sober, which again it was in no danger of being. It was altogether pleasant and agreeable. I find that wealth makes many things pleasant and agreeable. Such an observation must make me sound ungrateful—and I must admit my spirits are not buoyant. I dare say they will mend by and by.

Caroline sent her carriage for me so I was safely conveyed to her establishment. Everything was arranged with the utmost elegance, and the company refined and intelligent. One of Miss Trelawney's closest acquaintances, a Miss Wentworth, is to be married shortly, and there was much chatter in happy anticipation of that event. This class marries itself and all these fine young ladies will vanish from London and become mistresses of large estates before I learn to remember their names. (William says unkindly that they will all turn into horses.) They were very cordial to me. I was a novelty. But I felt a dark little thing tonight—certainly not the girl William used to be convinced that absolutely everyone would be dazzled by.

We listened to readings from that great poet, Mr Browning, given with a theatrical aplomb that was almost comic. I did not know the works in question, they were taken from a volume of his called *Men and Women*. I am sure my cousin is intimately acquainted with them, and I intend to procure my own copy today, but I scribbled down a line from one poem. It is a question: 'What of soul was left, I wonder, when the kissing had to stop?' Dear friend, I do not know the answer, but is it necessary that a kiss should diminish the soul? Does it not enlarge it? Must bodies and souls be enemies—should they be forced to war with one another so cruelly? You—in Italy—the

breeding ground for all passion, it seems—
have you become degenerate? I think not! Is
feeling passionately for another human being
so terrible a thing? I long to know. I ask in all
innocence—what do you know of the sensual
life? Forgive me this outburst. I am perturbed
at present by a matter I will communicate to
you by and by.

I am working very hard at the school on a
study of a mother and child; a difficult task
with a clothed model and a painted doll for an
infant. All the girls giggle. But I progress.

Do you realise we have now been separated
for more than a year?

I do not want to end this letter—it is so
unsatisfying. I feel I am striving and
floundering with enemies old and new, and you
are further away than ever. I am losing sight of
your ambitions, feelings, plans—and of my
own, sometimes, I fear. I cannot even picture
this Mr Harper who has taken his place among
the saints of your life. And where would you
settle in your wedded bliss?!—if I dare make so
bold.

Forgive me for sounding so angry.

With deep affection—

Emily

*　　　*　　　*

William was waiting for her outside the Art School
and Emily experienced that momentary jolt that
occurs when a familiar face appears in an
unexpected setting. He had a copy of a periodical

195

under his arm that Emily guessed contained his most recent story.

'Tell me I have not made a mistake? This is not our day to dine?'

'At this hour?' he replied. 'Indeed not. I thought I might take you to tea.'

He took her to an establishment on Piccadilly, close to the Burlington Arcade. It was exactly the kind of place he would choose: luxurious, dark as a lair.

'Shall we sit at the back? I must rest my eyes—it is far too bright today.'

'But it has been very pleasant, William, has it not?'

'You are very quick with the correct phrase, these days, my dear.' He looked into her face, uncharacteristically direct. 'How is it with you, Cousin?'

Emily found she could not answer right away. 'It goes well. My work absorbs me. Miss Norton is a hard taskmaster.'

He looked at her sharply. 'Not too hard, I hope. I fear I have been ignoring your studies. I have not so much as glanced at your portfolio.'

'I have been working on the human form. The tenderness between mothers and their children—it all stems from minute observation, not merely of feeling, but of form. I am drawing from life but there is an objectionable amount of clothing to contend with at our sittings.'

He rubbed his eyes. 'That must indeed be hard. And your lodgings? They are comfortable?'

'Of course.'

'And does Mrs Denham make herself agreeable?'

'I have only seen her rarely, but she has not

scolded me yet.'

'An acquaintance of mine saw you at the theatre with the Trelawneys. He said you were beautiful, if quaintly dressed.'

Emily laughed. 'My allowance does not stretch to the latest fashion, Cousin.'

'Do you require more?'

'That is not what I said—or meant to say. It is kind of you to ask.'

'I was surprised you accepted the invitation when I heard that this fellow, Firle, was in the box. I imagine you did not know he would be of the party.' He had come to the object of their encounter at last.

Emily felt a rare impulse to touch her cousin's hand, lying upon the table-top like a thing discarded. Looking directly into his cloudy eyes she said, 'I knew he would be. It was he who invited me.'

William's lips tightened and an expression of disdain—and something keener, harder for Emily to understand—came into his eyes. 'My dear, I do not know what it is you have been allowing yourself to believe, but I expected greater things from you.'

Her heart beat with a feeling of sickness. But she could not be angry, hesitating uncharacteristically before she could speak. She did not dare tell him about the supper. 'You always scold me, William,' she said at last. 'But the truth is, so did I.'

Miss Augusta Dean   Mayfair, SW
Hotel d'Angleterre, Rome

June 15th, 1862

My dearest Friend,

Thank you for your sweet letter. It is true
that I was very troubled when I last wrote to
you. I remain troubled by the question I put to
you, and I must admit to feeling that your
claim to know nothing of the sensual life
because you are unmarried a little—how can I
put it?—fantastical, or at the least, difficult to
understand. I hope you do not take that amiss,
for I know you have always been wholly
forthcoming with me.
So perhaps it is simply that we are very
different: you are content at present to be
admired, and that is enough. If that is the case,
I envy you. I own to conducting a battle with
myself and I hope you will not laugh or think ill
of me when I say I cannot tell you more about
it at this moment. Perhaps I should be content
with my ignorance, call it innocence and have
done with it. But your soothing words were a
great comfort and I promise not to forget
them.
With love,

Emily

Miss Caroline Trelawney   ——, Mayfair
Grosvenor Square, SW

June 15th, 1862

Dear Miss Trelawney,

I wonder if you might do me the honour of
acting in a delicate personal matter on my
behalf. I enclose a letter sent to me by a
mutual acquaintance. I opened it ignorant of
its sender.

If you could be so kind as to beg of Mr
Trelawney the favour of returning the letter to
its rightful owner, I would be more than
grateful.

I trust that if Mr Trelawney were to explain
that I am naturally unwilling and unable to
enter into an improper correspondence with
any gentleman that might compromise me in
any respect, the matter could be concluded
with all speed.

With grateful appreciation of your discretion
in this matter,

Yours truly,

Emily Hudson

[Enclosed: Lord Firle's letter to Miss Emily]

Miss Emily Hudson   Carlton Club, SW
Mayfair, SW

June 17th, 1862

My dear Cousin,

I have opened an account for you at the
dressmakers ———— in Albemarle Street. I
believe she will attend to matters of dress and
appearance satisfactorily and that you will
proceed without extravagance, but with an eye
to the proper presentation of yourself to the
world.
    Until next we meet, I remain,
    Yours etc.,

    William Cornford

              *   *   *

'Your dress is very pretty.' William spoke with a
lively return of interest and affection, and Emily
was relieved.
    They were walking side by side in the Green
Park observing the sheep; he with his stick, she
with her portfolio. The day was warm and full of
the future.
    'It is for the summer season. Caroline helped me
to pick out the correct style,' she said, with some
pride.
    'And embellishment. I could grow fond of that
bonnet.'
    'Oh really, William.' Emily laughed. 'I should
have thought you far too serious to become fond

200

of a bonnet.'

'Then I am glad I can still surprise you,' he said, his face agreeable, if a little embarrassed. 'When does your term come to an end?'

'I forget. July at some time.'

'I am to take a house by the sea for the summer—I have decided. We shall go there: you and I, the Trelawneys, perhaps one or two other sympathetic souls. Some sort of chaperone. I will write and you will sketch. We shall walk the beach. It will be like that pure Newport time.'

She turned and smiled in the dancing sunlight. 'When all I desired was escape.'

'Not only that, Cousin—you gloried in each moment, as I recall. And allow yourself to reflect. You desired travel, you have achieved it; you desired the time to explore your talent, you have been given it; you desired not to be forced to marry and that ambition too you have attained.'

'It is strange how in this English light the wishes and the answers do not appear the same.'

'They never do, Cousin,' he said. 'More and more they never do, I find.' They walked on in silence for a while. Emily noticed that there were lovers ahead of them in the grass. 'Look at me and tell me I still occupy that place in your heart where your Newport dreams began.'

For once he did not avoid her searching glance. 'What a strange question. You have surprised me again.'

'You have not answered me.'

'You will always be in my heart. As my first true teacher and someone in whom I have absolute trust.'

He smiled at her and made as if to touch her

cheek, but when she inclined her head towards him, he allowed his hand to drop.

Miss Augusta Dean   Mayfair, SW
Hotel d'Angleterre, Rome

June 30th, 1862

Darling Augusta,

Allow me to offer you my very deepest and most sincere congratulations! Mr Harper has secured his prize, and my sweet friend the promise of her wedded bliss. You say the ceremony may be as early as autumn—I am so happy on your behalf!

Darling girl, visions of you in white with orange blossom—or perhaps mistletoe—are singing through my soul. If you were to come into France and the wedding was to take place in Paris, perhaps William might accompany me to the ceremony. I would have to wait for the right opportunity to ask, but I can think of nothing I would like more.

My dearest friend, I hope your beloved endeavours every day to deserve you. And I am so delighted that his love of Europe equals yours, and you will not be forced to return to New England until you are so inclined. After so long away one tends to forget that there would be little joy in setting up housekeeping with the country at war with itself and tearing up the soil.

You will have so much freedom now,

Augusta—you could come to me in London if you so desired, travel and live where you will, see whom you please, read as you like and when—provided he is as indulgent as you say he is.

But here I am, becoming so caught up in the golden ideal of your union that I am in danger of running away with myself. Do not feel, my sweet friend, that you are in any way obliged to write to me only of happiness. If you have doubts or thoughts—I will not go so far as to call them misgivings—you may find it easier to share them with your old friend—and I promise to cheer you on from the stands as if it were Saratoga.

Love to you always and my respectful good wishes to Mr Harper.

Emily xxx

Miss Emily Hudson   Lowndes Place, SW
Mayfair, SW

1st July, 1862

Dear Miss Emily,

I have received an indication in no uncertain terms from Thomas Trelawney that you would prefer not to correspond with me.

I must take this opportunity to explain that your making my letter available to the Trelawneys places me in an awkward position for which, as a foreigner and untutored girl, I try not to reproach you.

Despite this embarrassment—despite myself—I long for us to meet again.

Firle

[Letter destroyed unread]

Lord Firle   Mayfair, SW
Lowndes Place, SW

July 5th, 1862

Dear Lord Firle,

I shall shortly be quitting London for an extended stay at the South Coast, and when I return there will be no resumption of the season and so I do not expect to find you in town.

I write to say goodbye. In truth I do not know why I write as I have forbidden myself all further correspondence with you, or even a glimpse of your last letter.

But this afternoon, as I was arriving at Christie's with my cousin, I was convinced that for a fleeting moment I saw you ahead of me at the top of the first flight of stairs. Your back was turned entirely to me, and by the time I had gained the main landing, with its painful branching choice of direction, you were gone. I could hardly have begun pursuing you—if it was indeed you whom I saw—through the rooms like a mad thing, but the truth is, I wanted to—very much.

I was beguiled to discover on leaving that there is another street door on that first floor that you could have taken; or you could even have been present all the while within the rooms, concealed from my sight.

If that is the case I do not think you saw me.

Emily

[Letter unsent]

*   *   *

'Caroline?'

'Yes, my dear.'

They were picnicking on the lawn leading to the banks of the Thames at the Trelawneys' house at Richmond. Emily had never known a picnic quite like it, with china and a silver teapot on its stand. It was a light summer day, a little undecided, with flashes of colour that turned the grass emerald when the sun pierced the clouds.

'I thought it always rained in summer.'

Caroline smiled. 'I am beginning to know you, Emily, and that is not what you were intending to say.'

'Oh, do look at William peering at us from his window! I am certain he is only pretending to write up there. No one could stay inside and work on a day such as this.' From the house behind them, a shadowy form was visible at a high window.

'It is pretty, but not as altogether warm as I would like,' said Caroline, untroubled by the prospect of William, shading her eyes in an attempt to see Emily better.

'The perfect summer day,' said Emily. 'Each of us longs for it, but I fear in a lifetime there are very few.'

'You are very philosophical today.'

'I am not entirely thoughtless, you know,' she replied lightly, glancing at her friend.

'That is not what I meant,' said Caroline, patiently. 'What were you about to ask me?'

'I was going to ask your permission to paddle.'

'What? In that filthy river? Amongst the ducks! I absolutely forbid you to. You will die of the cholera.'

Emily laughed. 'Oh really, Caroline!'

'I am quite serious. We must take every precaution until they find out the proper cause of the disease.'

'Indeed. I forget. They discover new things about diseases every day, it seems.' She looked away, towards the water. 'But I do not care to pursue the subject.'

'I could take you to the stream in the little wood. You could paddle there. But it would be very cold.'

Emily remembered the freezing woodland streams of her schooldays.

'No, thank you. I am far too contented with my strawberries and my contemplation of the river. I shall paddle when we go to the sea.'

'I think we should go into the house. I don't at all like the look of the sky.'

It was true, the cloud was increasing and it was noticeably cooler. They rose to go into the house, Emily following Caroline reluctantly. As Caroline went to the kitchen to order more tea, Emily started up the stairs to fetch her shawl. Her eyes were not accustomed to the light; she did not immediately make out William standing still on the landing. The door to his study beyond was ajar.

'You made a delightful picture on the lawn,' he said. 'Quite perfect.'

'Will you come down and join us now?' She felt awkward, the staircase above her shadowy and high.

'I will be down presently. To renew my study of you.'

Emily coloured, embarrassed. 'I hate it when you discuss me as if I were a character.'

'But you are one of my characters, dear heart. You are my experiment in life—essential for the experiments on the page to progress as they should. But forgive me, I am keeping you from some errand.'

Emily paused. 'I hope you are teasing me, Cousin,' she said at last, irritated and confused, unwilling to pass him. Seeming to sense this he retreated, going back to his study and closing the door, without a reply.

CHAPTER THIRTEEN

Miss Augusta Dean   Marsh House
Hotel d'Angleterre, Rome

July, 1862

My dear Augusta,

It seems I am on the brink of another adventure—and this one so beautiful I hardly know how to describe it. Marsh House is a long, low-ish structure, redbrick in the tradition of a farm or cottage, but built recently enough to encompass the long windows so beloved of the Georgians, and so it is all lit up inside. And the country! I did not know England could contain anything like it—but then I have been so starved of natural landscape in my time in the city that I had begun to forget there was any countryside whatever, and how essential it is to the soul.

We are at Old Romney—which is where two marshes converge—and there is a vast soft flatness around us with the distant downs behind and the sea ahead, just out of sight. Everywhere there are sheep and birdsong and no other sound but the occasional rattle of wheels, no other interruption of the sky but a church spire—in this ancient country it seems they are very devout! I shall indulge my passion for walking as far as I please across the fields— and William promises he shall accompany me because the land is so flat he has no excuse for straining his back.

It does not make me think of Rhode Island at all here because for all the sky above it is so defiantly small—there is a church almost next door to us, we are on a bend in the lane, we have a front garden with a straight garden path, a warm enclosed garden behind and a little meadow to the right as you face the house through a gate. Much of the land about belongs to the property so William says there need be no fear of trespass—but he has also explained that when he has come to this country before no stranger has ever been suspicious or proprietary regarding his explorations. How could it create envy, such a place as this?

As you can see I am enraptured. My window faces front on to an apple tree, vigorous and newly planted, and the warm salt air comes off the sea and even the clouds are gentle.

We have come here in advance of the Trelawneys so as to open up the house. It has been let to us by a widower who, since his loss, has not the heart to continue to live near the seat of his happiness, and I think has gone to sojourn with his relations in the North of the country. I do not know how recent the bereavement is and I do not think William cares to discuss it for fear it might make me morbid. I hope there were no little ones to be left motherless, but the house speaks to me of youth, so I should not wonder.

It feels a little how I imagine being a newly-wed might feel. William treats me with kindness and great affection and is in very high spirits; higher, in fact, than I have ever seen, and we find ourselves in perfect accord, sitting with our books by the summer fire in the evening.

There is a housekeeper who comes every day. I find her quite alarming and cannot understand all that she says, but William has made it clear that Mrs Phelps—Caroline's aunt, who will accompany them when they arrive next week—shall supervise household matters and so I must not trouble my head. I cannot imagine it would be any good if I were to try!

The country is renowned for fresh fish and the sweetness of its lamb—I cannot wait for the apples to ripen!

All my love,

Emily

PS. On another more pressing matter, I think Mr Harper is quite right to be concerned about the possibility of unrest reaching Rome with the trouble that has come into that country. We are living in strange times when countries cannot leave themselves alone and must eat themselves up in the name of nationhood. There are so many enemies of life for one reason or another who would deny it to others, and when it is gone there is no way of wresting it back. If you should quit Rome in advance of your wedding I would be more at ease. The preciousness of your own life is close to the hearts of too many people for you to endanger it.

Miss Mary Cornford   Marsh House
Cornford House   Old Romney
Boston, Mass

——, 1862

Dear Mary,

It seems an age ago that we agreed to correspond—forgive me for having taken so long to begin writing.

I understand from William that he has

already told you that we have taken a house close to the sea—not as close as at Newport but you would appreciate its charm, I think. So there is no need for me to tell you more at present but that I am wildly happy, in a very ferment of delight, in fact. Your brother concerns himself (unnecessarily) with my every comfort, and we pass our days deep in conversation as we used to at Newport Beach, in the midst of what he calls 'The English Pastoral Idyll'—but not on the grand scale, you understand!

I must confess to feeling more at ease here than in London, which, though stimulating, tires me frequently.

I have set up a small painting corner for myself in the sitting room, and I wish I could say I was more industrious than I am, but William insists that this is an opportunity for rest rather than work. I think of you often as I sit doggedly at my sketchbook—despite his advice—hoping to achieve something of merit. You and I share a devotion to our work, I believe; I remember how you used to shut yourself up in your room to write and think.

I hope your health is proving strong enough to allow you to venture out, and that you are occupied in studying without allowing it to exhaust you, because you know your father would wrest that pen out of your hands at the earliest opportunity were he to see you weaken! Forgive me if my attempt to joke is clumsy.

Let me know how you do.

I remain yours, affectionately,

Emily

*   *   *

'But my dear, this could not be more perfect!' said Caroline.

The Trelawneys and their relation Mrs Phelps had alighted from the cart and the entire party was standing in the front garden of the house, admiring its modern proportions and delightfully picturesque air.

'And we have had bright sunshine every day.' Emily said it as if she were personally responsible.

She had never seen Caroline look so enchanted. 'It can be very wet in this low country,' her friend said. 'Especially in spring, which has passed, thankfully, but we have come prepared for every event with all sorts of outdoor apparel.'

'We shall play at having our own establishment with everything as we please,' said Emily.

'There shall be no playing about it,' said Mr Trelawney. 'I shall press wildflowers and categorise birds until you beg me to leave well alone.'

'Do not forget that we are your hosts,' said William, taking his cousin's elbow in a proprietary manner.

'And William shall write every morning and I shall paint and draw and walk to my heart's content,' said Emily, with a smile.

'I fear idleness,' said Caroline. 'I am not used to it. But I have the dogs. They shall help me find occupation.'

'Do not allow them to chase the sheep,' said William.

'But this is a time expressly for your recreation, my dear,' said Mrs Phelps to Caroline, in her widow's weeds and cap and kindly plumpness fulfilling exactly Emily's wishes for a chaperone. 'You do not have two houses to run, and the world to entertain, so you shall read and improve your mind and go walking and have picnics on the beach. But not too much air, my dear, remember what Mr Cornford said about the damp.'

'We shall visit Rye,' said William. 'I have an especial desire to see it.'

'That you can do alone, Cousin. I do not wish to see another building for a long time,' said Emily.

'Fresh cream from the farm,' said Mrs Phelps. 'I shall explore the kitchen and larder directly.' And she was gone.

'There is something I have been wanting to ask you, Caroline,' said Emily, drawing her aside beneath the shade of the tree. 'Do you consider, do you think we might—just while we are here—dispense with our corsets? So we can walk freely, and be unfettered?'

Caroline laughed, looking Emily firmly in the face. 'But of course we cannot, my love,' she said. 'Whatever gave you that idea?'

Miss Augusta Dean   Marsh House
Hotel d'Angleterre, Rome
July ——, 1862

My dearest Augusta,

I cannot describe to you my feeling of relief

that you are settled on removing from Rome, although I understand that in your opinion there is no real danger. I feel entirely unqualified to advise you on where you choose to remain for the time being, but I understand that Paris in the summer months is not to be recommended. If it has anything approaching the airlessness of London at this time of year I can fully appreciate the difficulty. I have heard that Switzerland and Vienna can be delightful, and I glory in imagining you in a slightly fresher climate.

In my already beloved Marsh House the good weather continues unabated. I must admit I had not expected it to hold. I write this before dinner in a beautiful extended twilight that seems so delicate and especially English. Moths are beginning to flutter close to the lamp that I have just lit, so I will be brief.

Today we journeyed to Camber Sands with our picnic basket. There at last was a shore to compare with Newport! We had to beg a ride from the farmer in his cart but he did not begrudge us our pleasure, agreeing to deposit us at noon and return for us at four o'clock. We were quite stranded. Mrs Phelps begged to be allowed to remain at home with her needlework, even though there was no breeze that could have disturbed her and the glare was not harsh.

I became almost entirely out of breath scrambling along the dunes, but would not give up—the higher you climb the more of that extraordinary yellow shore you can see, and then sliding down is almost like tobogganing on warm sand! I scratched my hands on the marsh grass though; it is quite fierce.

Caroline has become quite placid, she stayed on the rug beneath her parasol watching her dogs, and the gentlemen walked along the shore. I ran down to join them. I had forgotten how hard the sand is with the ribbed pattern of the waves when the tide runs out, and as I came closer the waves breaking was like a gentle rushing sound, so like a stream or a waterfall you forget it is the ocean—or the sea, as they call it here. (The word 'ocean' seems to provoke hilarity in the English, as do so many American words and habits of speech.)

William has become quite absorbed in his many talks with Thomas Trelawney and his watchfulness of him makes me consider that he is using him for some character or other. His look is almost hungry, sometimes, when he considers him; it is strange, very like, I must admit, the way he frequently looks at me. It is peculiar because when we are all three of us together I see him hesitate occasionally as if questioning whom to favour. I only walked with the gentlemen for a short time, they were so occupied with one another: one so clean and English and upright, the other so stooped and tall and peculiar.

Dear William has brought down the manuscript of part one of his first full-length novel for me to read, which is a tremendous honour—partly, I think, because he knows I will praise it as I praise all his stories, and with justification, of course. His writing has a delicacy and a menace that can be unnerving and feels altogether unique. If I could produce a painting with his eye for detail and his exquisite variation of light and shade and, above all, mood, I would truly have achieved something considerable.

As I walked away from them back to Caroline I thought of Captain Lindsay with a stab at the heart that was quite acute. I have not forgotten him. That I have not mentioned him in my letters does not mean I do not think of him often. But it is part of my attempt to see him as a friend and in memory only that I do not write of him. Yet I found it impossible today to walk along close to the water without him coming into my mind. I wonder how it is with him. I have written to Mary but did not enquire after him for fear of bad news—but I cannot go on. Even when I am so happy—as now—a fierce sorrow for the past is still with me.

We ate strawberries and cream on the rug— the best I have ever tasted. After lunch I took off my shoes and stockings and paddled and made the gentlemen paddle too, though Caroline refused. It was properly warm. I am determined that next time we shall play together in the waves, and she will see—she will see how simple joy is.

Later, before bed

The moon is full. We have the most delightful times at table here. Sometimes I sip some wine. It is very informal—we serve ourselves. Mrs Phelps often retires early, leaving us to talk into the night if we wish and I can become as excitable as I please. If the evenings continue warm I hope to persuade her to allow us to carry the kitchen table outside so we can enjoy our dinner under the stars.

Acquaint me at the earliest opportunity of where you have decided upon settling next.

Affectionately, as ever,

Emily

*   *   *

'Who shall accompany me to Rye today?' said William, looking only at Emily. 'I would like to climb that famous bell tower and see the world spread out before me.'

'Merely England, my dear fellow,' said Thomas. 'And a small part of it at that, not the world.'

'I could not stir from this place on such a lovely day,' said Emily, and when Caroline also demurred, Thomas said he would gladly go. Mrs Phelps was pressed to accompany them. Emily sensed her cousin was displeased at her flat refusal, but she had no mind for sightseeing.

'Will you not reconsider, my dear?' said William, when they were left alone amid the bustle of preparation.

'I have no desire for it. You would not insist, surely? You must go and confide your impressions to me on your return.'

He gave her a somewhat bitter smile before saying quite gently, 'Very well.'

'How shall we amuse ourselves for the day now that we are quite alone?' said Caroline. Arrangements to borrow a neighbour's conveyance had already been made and the party were gone by ten o'clock. The day was bright. The women waved together from the door.

'Will you walk with me?' asked Emily.

'I went earlier with the dogs. I think I will stay inside and read a little.'

'Would you mind if I were to sketch you? I have so little opportunity to work from life.'

Caroline smiled. 'Not at all.'

Emily fetched her sketchbook and pencils, busying herself with setting up her equipment just as she liked it, beginning to experience the clarity of her working mind as she let the real world recede.

'Emily—forgive me for asking—do you have any notion of how long you will remain in this country?' It was as if her friend could not ask her while she had her whole attention.

Emily was a little taken aback. 'Why? Do you wish me gone?'

'Of course not. It is merely that I cannot imagine a life of so limited a horizon as yours.'

Emily looked up sharply, although by now she felt she should be accustomed to her friend's frankness. 'You mean unlimited,' she corrected, regarding Caroline with all seriousness.

'Believe me, I do not.'

'I can do as I please. I am without responsibilities.'

'Are you quite sure that is the truth, my dear?'

Emily found she could not answer. 'I am going to arrange you in profile now, looking out of the window. You must try not to speak.'

'You are unusually evasive,' pursued her friend.

'I am concentrating. There is a difference.' Caroline wore a simple brownish sprigged dress with a white collar. Her hair was drawn back from her face. 'You could be my Madonna,' said Emily.

'Except that I am not beautiful and I have no child.'

'Wait a little—I will furnish you with a baby,' said Emily, and quickly deposited a small tapestry cushion in her lap. 'Lower your head a little as if to look into its face.'

'Emily, there is no face.'

'Try.' Caroline adopted the age-old posture of bending neck and lowered eyes, as if it were ordained. 'Good.'

Emily worked for some time, and Caroline was an obedient model, still and quiet. The heat mounted in the room, for they had not opened the windows and it was past noon.

'Your aunt has left a little bread and cheese for us. Shall we eat it, and perhaps, if you are willing, continue in the afternoon?'

Caroline turned to her and, nodding, appeared moved. 'Would you like to show me what you are doing?'

Emily took her sketchbook to her friend's side. 'These are the preliminary sketches from the model at school. Her features are far coarser than yours.'

'But she is pretty.'

'Yes. Very fair. She reminds me of my dearest friend, Augusta—I have not seen her for more

219

than a year.'

'How many sketches must there be before you can start the portrait?'

'It is not a portrait exactly—too much must be imagined. I want her to hold the child against her breast, loosen the dress to show that, but I have no model.'

'I see.'

They went into the kitchen that was cool and dark and helped themselves to cheese and bread and cold water. Then they went out into the garden at the back of the house, smelling grass and contemplating sheep and butterflies. A sweet lethargy was stealing on the afternoon.

'I find I am rather tired after staying so very still and dreaming,' Caroline said. 'I think I shall go and rest. We shall have tea by and by.'

When Emily did not reply she continued, 'I wonder how the gentlemen are finding Rye. I hope they are not wearing out Aunt Phelps with walking. Excuse me.' And she was gone, taking her formality with her.

Emily lay down and fell asleep in the grass.

*   *   *

When she woke it was to the sound of a clattering of china in the kitchen. The grass was soft and itchy. Rising to her feet, Emily went into the kitchen where Caroline was boiling a kettle and collecting crockery for the tray.

'Shall we take it in the front garden?' she said. 'Look at you, Emily!' and she reached out and touched Emily's hair. 'All grass stains and tangles.'

'I slept well. Did you?'

220

'Happily. Emily, if you wish, I will sit a while longer for you. And if you were to assist me it would be easy to unhook my dress.'

They looked at one another in the dark room, Caroline's eyes serious and full of feeling and trust and Emily felt thankful. They finished their tea in the kitchen and returned to the drawing room, taking the places they had relinquished.

'The light has changed.'

'It is lower. No matter.' Emily stood behind her friend to unhook her collar and loosen her dress. They took her arms out of her sleeves and bared her breast so that only corset and light undergarments remained. 'You can preserve your modesty, friend,' she said.

Caroline laughed. 'Hardly.'

The rosy translucent quality of Caroline's skin, the way her hair fell against a bare neck— loosened, yet still pinned up as it was, the ineffable generosity of unclothed arms encircling the cushion, provided a transcendent beauty that had been absent before. The pose imbued warmth and depth of feeling to the scene that otherwise could not have existed.

'I am for ever in your debt,' said Emily. 'But I shall have to try to remember the colour of your skin.'

'If you would like to fetch your paints I could be patient a little while longer.'

Emily laughed, but a low, satisfied laugh, not one of merriment or wild delight, and as they looked at one another the sound of carriage wheels came upon them and then the sight of the conveyance coming around the corner and stopping at the gate.

Emily saw Thomas jump down and help Mrs Phelps while William almost ran ahead, glancing at them through the long windows but unaware of what he saw.

'Emily!' he called. 'Emily, I must—' She did not think she had ever heard him sound so excited. In an instant he was in the room and Caroline, having got to her feet, was fumbling with her dress, blushing deeply, Emily attempting to help her.

'Please, ladies. Forgive me,' he said, and immediately withdrew.

In silence Emily helped Caroline dress as she heard her cousin say, 'Let us go into the parlour. The ladies are absorbed in their work in the drawing room.'

Caroline gave Emily a look of pure shame and terror, then she passed her by, leaving her alone and running up the stairs.

In another instant William returned, remaining in the doorway as if too close a proximity to his cousin might endanger him. 'What in Heaven's name did I just witness?'

His anger was so intense that there was no opportunity for her own. Emily tried to summon her courage but the tears were in her eyes.

'Caroline was modelling for me—for my study of the—'

'Please, do not go on. Madonnas, of course, have to be in a state of dishabille.'

'The Renaissance Masters often showed—'

'You are a little American girl. You are a poor, sick orphan! Who are you to stand in the house that I have provided for you in your skimpy grass-stained dress and talk to me of Renaissance Masters? Perhaps my father was right. You are a bad apple. Poor Miss Caroline—how will she look at me now without knowing I have seen her in so shameless a state of undress—'

'She was beautiful.'

Emily thought he might lose control of himself with rage. 'I think you had better go to your room,' he said.

*   *   *

Upstairs it was like her uncle's house at Newport once more: the confinement. Nothing was changed, she thought, in the strangled sensation in her throat and the pain in her eyes that presaged a waterfall of tears. How arrogant she had been, how pitifully arrogant, to believe that her appetite for feeling, truth and beauty could influence William's outlook, his character and— But she could not think. He was as cruel as his father, as his mother, as them all. She could hear their voices downstairs: William, Thomas and Mrs Phelps taking their tea in the parlour and exchanging commonplace observations about the events of the day.

She could hear Caroline weeping quietly in her room through the wall, and for the first time she hated William, purely, cleanly and simply, as if she were watching a bird flying upwards in the sky. The interior voice, the undercurrent of shame, her habitual fear of ungratefulness was extinguished in this passion, or rather united into one cry. She sat still on her bed looking at the garden in the evening, the red and green of the apples on the tree, and felt a great anguish and heat. Going to the window and opening it there came not a breath of air. The golden day had become something altogether different, almost sinister in its stillness. She must get to the sea.

Without so much as changing her shoes or finding a bonnet she stole down the staircase, but without fear: she knew no person would emerge from any room to block her. She left by the front door—she had only the garden path to cross and a few paces to the bend in the lane and she was concealed from view. The church bells chimed six. The light around her seemed almost lurid—a warmth bathed her, held her almost buoyant as if she were in water, and she glanced at the sky. There were no usual white fluffy clouds that often resembled skeins of white silk, but a general darkening as if a watercolour blue had been smudged with charcoal—contaminated by a dirty hand. There was still no air.

She walked at her fastest pace. She had never gone to the sea on foot before, but she knew the way. She would follow the lane until it met the coast road: she could either follow that until she found a track to the ocean's edge, or strike off by instinct across the country towards the water. She felt very light, almost as if she had no body at all— the road made no impression on her feet in their kid slippers, the airless air nonetheless giving her the oxygen she required. She did not know how long she could continue at that pace—it was sufficiently unreal, her speed, for her to know it would not last. But she did not think they would follow her. Even if they noticed she was gone, there was no means of transportation at their disposal. And after all, it was only an evening walk. They would not understand she had to reach the sea.

No vehicle passed her on the open road and she experienced the strange sensation of seeing herself as others might see her—a lone girl, respectably if untidily dressed, exposed and vulnerable to any passing stranger. But she was not afraid: this was not London where beggars might accost her in the twilight, hawkers and sellers and thieves of every description play their game. Here there was no one. If somebody passed by with a cart of straw she would be an oddity. But what about in darkness, what about in cold? The thousands of nameless destitute wanderers she had seen in the city, on the high roads, began to press themselves into her mind and she did not know if it were pity or fear she felt. It was only speed that mattered.

She had a pain in her side and an ache in her chest and her vision began to blur with the tears she let fall unchecked. She must get to the sea. It was Camber Sands she wanted—that glorious expanse—but it was too far. She felt a little sick, but not faint, never faint, never that. Ladies who faint are merely domestic animals, she thought: she did not know why. The sky was darkening, the high road brighter. A storm was coming and she had known and she was glad.

Turning off the road she began to hurry across the fields. Sheep lifted their heads in brief enquiry, the bumps in her path made her stumble for she could not discipline herself to pick up her feet. It was difficult to find the gate. The next field had a ditch between her and the one after; she waded it without thinking, clambering up the bank on her hands and knees. And then she saw the sea— pewter-coloured close to her, with gleams of sunshine on it near to the horizon. Out to sea the sky was blue and the storm had already passed. The air was thickening and she clambered on, over marsh grass that grew through the sweet grass and then replaced it until she was on the dunes and below her lay the beach. She sat down until she had finished crying, then lowered herself into a hollow in the sand to wait out the storm.

It was not long until the rain began in almost stately slow and heavy drops that became more rapid and urgent. There was little wind. At first the rain eased and cooled her, then it insisted itself through her pretty blue dress, streaking and darkening it, penetrating her hair, splashing her neck and hands and face and she could see very little. Then the wind began. She was protected from its worst by the curve of where she sat. It did not hurt her when it blew but made her cold. This is what you wanted, she thought.

When the rain stopped the sky was only briefly sullen, a sullen evening sky. She stood up and, taking off her shoes and petticoats, rolled them into a bundle on the sand. Walking down to the beach was laborious, the sand was so heavy and wet. She walked into the water without hesitating. It was surprisingly warm after the rain. She had never let the water reach more than her knees before, but this time she waded to her waist. Her skirts billowing about her made progress hard. A wave could knock her off her feet. She could not swim. But the sea was lazy. The sky ahead looked secret and ungiving and she was crying again, but no longer with rage, with longing. She looked at the sky for a long time; then she turned her back on the sea, wading to the shore, stumbling across the great beach in her heavy choking clothes, climbing the first bank she came upon. She was very tired and entirely wet—the cold stung. Falling to her knees, she curled up like a cat and fell asleep.

*   *   *

A face was leaning over her and a dog sniffing at her neck. 'I do not want to be found,' she said. But he did not appear to hear her. He was old, a countryman, weathered, stupid, kind. She closed her eyes. He was shaking her. 'Miss. Where are your friends? What is your name?' Then he lifted her and she was drowsy and she slept. She dreamed she was in her bed at home with her mother bending over her, turning down the light.

*   *   *

The doctor had a cold stethoscope and a cold eye but she was very hot. 'Young lady, you have a fever. I am, however, more concerned for your chest. Does it hurt?' It hurt. It rattled when she breathed. It did not want her to breathe—thick as if bandages were inside her lungs. He held her hands. 'Will you not speak to me? There is only myself here. Your cousin and your friends are deeply concerned for you. We all are.'

She began to cry but without sobs. 'Mother,' she said.

*   *   *

'Why did you walk into the sea?' It was William's voice. The room was dark and she could not see him. 'Why did you want to leave us?'

She did not want him there. She tried to sit up and breathe but she was coughing again. She shook with it and the soreness in her lungs. He lit the lamp and placed it beside her. He looked ghostly. She could not stop coughing and he pressed a handkerchief into her hand that she held over her lips. And then it came and she knew there was blood on her handkerchief before she could even look. It was dark and bright. All the colour in the room. He saw it too and he said, 'Is this the first time?'

'Yes.' She shook, recognising it, crushing the handkerchief into a warm ball in her fingers.

'You are so beautiful,' he said. Taking the handkerchief into his own hand he tenderly wiped her mouth. They looked at one another; in his eyes was pity and a kind of triumph. 'Lie back on your pillows, Cousin. There.'

She struggled to breathe, cold with terror, and he waited.

'I have things to tell you. I am going to go away for a little while—Thomas will accompany me. Mrs Phelps and Caroline—so long as they wish— will remain with you here until you are stronger. Then we shall see what is to be done.'

She could not speak to him, looking at the handkerchief clutched in his fingers.

Presently she said, 'Open the window?'

'I do not think that would be wise, my dear.' And he was gone.

*   *   *

It had come to her at last: Emily saw with her

228

whole self that she had merely been waiting for it to happen. She shuddered, her body heaved, her muscles cold and without strength. How much more of life would it give her? Weeks? Months? A year? She did not want to die. She was not ready to die. She was afraid to die. She wished that William had not left her alone and yet partly she was relieved to be free of the scrutiny. She could not help it, imagining the moment of her death—then nothing. She could not contemplate a life beyond. She must not think of it, the vision of her coffin going into the aching empty ground. Where would she be buried? Now that she had sent Captain Lindsay away, who would truly mourn her? Why had she lived at all? And yet she would not bring him back to her now. She would not force him to be the one who had promised to keep her, always keep hold of her hand.

'Mother, help me to be less afraid,' she prayed.

*   *   *

The doctor sat by her bed. It was evening. She could tell from the light outside her window that made the curtains glow. When she was hot she put her wrists against the cold brass of the bedhead as if running them under a tap.

'And this was your first haemorrhage?'

'Yes.'

'And when did it take place?'

'I do not know—yesterday, before my cousin went away. Miss Trelawney will tell you.'

'Have you had another, since?'

'Yes, in the night.' It had been very dark and she had had to light the candle to see it and try to clean it up.

'And what happened after it passed?'

'After it passed I slept.'

'Good.' He sat up very straight next to her. 'May I listen to your chest again? From beneath your shoulder blades?'

'Of course.' She was more prepared this time and shut her eyes. He was merely carrying out his vocation, like playing the piano or ploughing a field.

He paused a long time when he had finished listening. 'Miss Hudson, I think it is only one lung that is affected. But I am not a specialist. I would strongly advise Mr Cornford to find one and I shall write to him to that effect.'

'Is there medicine?' She knew the answer to that question and wondered why she should exert herself to ask it.

'There is none. Only rest. I can give laudanum for the pain—if it is acute.'

'No, thank you. I would rather not.' Thoughts of her mother beginning her last illness came over her. 'I do not need the drug.'

He began to pack his case.

'What shall I do?'

'My dear young lady, these lungs will not heal themselves. You must do nothing. They need rest and fresh air, preferably warm, dry air, but in moderation. No exerting yourself on walks. I am surprised that a young lady with your disposition and constitution should have counted walking and sitting on damp ground among her pursuits, let alone wandering out of doors in a storm.'

She could have said, I must be outside for my work, for my sketching and drawing. I must be by

230

the sea for my soul. I must sit upon the grass because I am young and alive. But she did not. 'I am not fond of parlours and still lives.'

'You are an obstinate girl. This is a serious condition.'

A flash of anger. 'Do you think I am not sensible of that?'

His eyes remained cold. 'I scarcely know you at all, Miss Hudson.' And there were her tears rising again. 'If you are to recover it is with plenty of rest—no excitement—and I shall see that your cousin calls in a specialist. Good day.'

'Good day, Sir.'

*   *   *

After then she cried: weak and useless feminine tears. It seemed she was at fault, at fault for her own condition as well as her desires.

There was a knock at the door. 'Emily? It is Caroline.'

'Come in.' Before she even had sight of her friend, Emily said, 'I am so sorry, Caroline—please forgive me for the embarrassment I caused you—'

Caroline sat on the bed and held her hands. 'You are very pale.'

'I am sorry, I—'

'I do not want to talk about the storm. You were distressed.'

'I don't mean that, I mean putting you in such a position—because of my work—'

'I do not care about that. I care only for my friend. In any case, it was my idea, I share the blame. We must get you better, with plenty of warm milk and bread and honey. Plenty of soothing, clean, pure food. Don't cry, my dearest.'

'It is because you are so kind.'

'Thomas has gone. He has taken the dogs so we will have quiet. Now that this is just a house of women we shall be gentle with one another and get along nicely. We shall mend you.'

Caroline's hand was still closed over Emily's.

'When it comes, it is—'

'Try not to be frightened. Call me and we shall manage it together. The basin and jug are just a few steps to the other side of the room. There will always be clean towels.'

'Yes.'

'I shall come to you by and by and see if you will take a little gruel.'

Caroline kissed her on the forehead. Emily watched her straighten up in the dim light. There were so many images she must commit to memory because she did not have the means to sketch them now.

CHAPTER FOURTEEN

| Emily Hudson | The Pheasant Inn |
| Marsh House, Kent | York |

—— August, 1862

My dearest Cousin,

I send this by the hand of a highly respected physician. He knows everything in modern medicine about your condition, having even visited the first sanatorium in ——— that has been operating for three years past.

You must tell him everything and hold nothing back if he is to help you.

You are in my thoughts.

Thomas and I are occupying ourselves with looking at horses; he has a mind to buy another hunter for the season and a riding horse for his sister. There are many journeys and sojourns in uncomfortable inns but I console myself with the notion that I am gaining insight into the life of the English gentleman: it is so dominated by such pursuits I cannot be ignorant of them. Considering I have no interest whatever in chronicling the lives of the poor—I will leave that to the vulgar taste and Mr Dickens—I must take every opportunity to observe the friends I have in this adopted country of mine. More and more I lack the desire to return to our New World.

I have always found August a difficult month, however, as one is not expected to work and I do so loathe any form of idleness. I must admit that I am missing more literary society and the conversation at my club not a little, but London is deserted and my acquaintance are all abroad or shooting.

You must be brave.

You are brave; I do not presume to instruct you on that.

My dear girl, write to me soonest.

Your unquenchable spirit will always be an example to me.

Affectionately,

William

It was as if she were already dead.

*   *   *

The doctor who brought the letter was bearded but much younger than she had expected. She wondered what he might look like beneath his beard. She did not think his chin was weak—he had a very determined and decisive air but a quiet one too, as if at ease with himself, as if he did not require the good opinion of the world.

She was strong enough to receive him in the parlour, but with all the energy it had required to dress and descend the stairs she almost regretted it, and reading William's words under his watchful eye was disconcerting.

Caroline had brought him into the room. He smelled of the summer outdoors.

'Dr Cooper?'

'Miss Hudson.' He took her hand lightly and let it go, sitting at a respectable distance while Mrs Phelps brought in the tea. Then she stood beside Caroline and they were like two sentries on duty. 'May I request an interview alone?'

In her strained smile, Emily detected all Caroline's fears. 'I promise to tell the whole truth,' she said, looking at each of them, and they, in turn, withdrew. She was concentrating so much on the doctor she did not hear their murmured excuses, if any were made at all.

He poured the tea for her and put the cup on the table beside her chair.

'It is very good of you to come such a long way, Dr Cooper. My cousin should not have put you to the trouble.'

234

He smiled. 'I enjoy the countryside. Although it is a little warm today.'

'By all means open the window. I shan't complain.'

He did so, allowing in a few inches of air.

'The daisies on the grass are very pretty, aren't they?' she said. 'I like touching the warm stone wall out there too.'

He turned towards her. 'It is a terrifying condition.'

'Yes.' She had not expected this directness, this warmth and this calm. She looked at his watch chain. A solid gold watch.

'You are studying to be an artist?'

'Yes. Did my cousin tell you?'

'He has written me a long letter all about you. He is very fond of you.'

This was not the doctor's business or his concern but she did not mind. She did not say to him: he has many feelings about me—too many, but the curious thing was that she should want to.

'Yes. He took this house for me—for the summer—for us all. He wanted to give me happiness.'

'I am sure it has been delightful for him too.'

'I regret to say I cannot call it that. At first we were very happy here.'

He did not press her to continue, but she found that she did. 'Then we quarrelled. I am very wilful, you see.' She rubbed her eyes, pressing her knuckles into the sockets.

'I do not want to tire you, Miss Hudson. If you could tell me a little about your attacks.'

'Attacks. Yes. That is what they are. My cousin must have told you I was out in a storm. I think it is about a fortnight since. I collapsed. I had a fever and then fits of coughing—and then the first one came.'

'Have you had fits of coughing before?'

'Yes, last winter in Boston. But I recovered. I have been perfectly well.'

'And had there ever been—blood, in Boston?'

'No.' She remembered the blue dining room on New Year's Eve and Captain Lindsay's face; the smell of the Christmas tree and the candles in the ballroom. 'No. Nothing of that kind.'

'Have you ever been unwell before last winter?'

'I was indisposed at Newport, in the summer.'

'With what?'

'A cough. It passed after a day or two.'

'How indisposed?'

'I was confined to my bed.'

'Was a doctor called on either of these occasions, allowing for your family history?'

'No. And I would not have wanted it.'

'Of course not,' he said mildly, as if this made perfect sense. 'May I examine you now?'

She nodded. He listened to her chest, and then gently motioned her forward to listen at her back. He listened for a long time. 'What colour is the blood?'

'Bright.' She shuddered and began to cry. He put away his stethoscope while she wiped her eyes.

'Do you ever take sugar with your tea?' he asked.

She lifted her head and laughed. 'No.'

'I think you should. You will find it quite the thing, very reviving.' He poured a new cup, added a spoonful of sugar, and passed it to her, taking care to avoid touching her hand. Then he withdrew to the sofa as she sipped.

There was more silence. It was as if they were on a picnic rug listening to the sea: there was no imperative, no question of life or death.

'Doctor ———, who saw you first, was quite correct. It has only affected one lung. And it is in its early stages.'

She found she could say nothing.

'But it wants to take hold. I say this not to frighten you, but to make you understand. If you have more than three haemorrhages a day I must be called. In the meantime, you must eat. You must rest. You must take plenty of nourishment.'

'I shall die of boredom!'

'Why not ask them to make up a bed for you down here, by the garden windows? It is so warm and you can watch the sky and fields, see if anyone passes on the road, perhaps sketch a little or read. Would you like to return to school in the autumn?'

'Very much.'

'Good. Take a little air, but not if it is damp. You may go outside as long as you are closely wrapped, but not for another two weeks.'

'You have a schedule for me, Sir?' She pronounced it in the American way.

'Without a "schedule"'—he echoed her pronunciation—'we are in confusion. That will not do.' He smiled again as if he could see the future.

She shook her head in agreement with him, once more unable to speak.

'Next time I come, may I look at your drawings?'

'Of course, I would be delighted.'

'One more thing. Do not excite yourself. Try not to disagree with anyone. Or let anyone disagree with you.' There was humour in his words and a kindness held back. He gave a slight bow, a dignified, almost comical inclination of the head and said, 'Good day, Miss Hudson. I am privileged to have made your acquaintance.'

'Good day, Doctor.'

Emily felt at ease in her rest after that, falling asleep there and then on the pretty sofa he had sat upon. Caroline came with an eiderdown to keep her warm.

William Cornford, Esq   Marsh House
c/o Carlton Club, SW

August ——, 1862

My dear Cousin,

Thank you for your kind letter and for the doctor who was equally kind. I am pleased that you are occupied, if not with the seashore at least with your friend, and I am reassured that there is to be no quarrel between us. I strive to be of good heart and spirits.

Please convey my warmest regards to Mr Trelawney.

With love,

Emily

Miss Emily Hudson   Dr G A Cooper
Marsh House   Harley Street, W1

Dear Miss Hudson,

Please accept this volume of verse in lieu of a prescription.

Read at least one day.
I am, etc., yours respectfully,

Dr G A Cooper

The book was Elizabeth Browning's *Sonnets from the Portuguese*. Emily put it aside in her drawer.

* * *

It was a slow process, recovery, and sometimes Emily lacked the ability to distinguish between illness and convalescence. But a part of her knew that if she were to mend her lungs she must believe it could be done. To her many follies she dreaded adding the false hope of the invalid, but there were such an avalanche of fears in her path she must choose her way carefully for there to be any progress at all. Haemorrhage continued—a nightly battle, though she believed there was less blood. She found it very hard to sleep. She knew the restless energy of the consumptive was a danger but she did not want to take any form of draught. To succumb to that put her in mind too much of oblivion.

* * *

The weather continued warm and there were no storms. Dr Cooper visited once a week.

It was three o'clock on a Thursday afternoon. 'You could set your watch by him,' Caroline said.

Emily looked forward to his visits in a way she could not admit, even to herself. If the night before had been feverish and the blood had been bad, she felt less afraid simply because she knew he would be present for her to confide in the following day. He regarded her illness as a significant and serious thing, but in his eyes it was in every way separate from her, her true being and essence. She was enduring it, and she was taking all possible steps to combat it, but it was not her: just as Emily's mother's illness had not been what made her uniquely herself. The elopement and manner of her death would be for ever connected in the eyes of the world, whereas to Emily, to her father and dear family, they had always been entirely distinct.

To Dr Cooper's tolerance and complete understanding was added, to Emily's mind, a complete lack of pity. Or if he felt pity he concealed it. Equally, she did not feel ashamed—ever—in his presence. He did not exaggerate her hopes of recovery, nor did he pander to her fear of death. He tried to teach her patience, she supposed: it was no use wishing her circumstances were not what they were, or that her illness would miraculously disappear, but there was always quiet and profound hope.

After a month Emily's haemorrhages ceased. It was like the incessant clamour of a fire bell and its accompanying thundering hooves suddenly being wiped away, leaving only silence and birdsong and the colours of the sky.

They would not let her sit upon the ground, but put a daybed in the garden for her, protected by a parasol and an awning that the ladies constructed from a tablecloth attached to two easels. 'My pagoda,' she called it. She tried to be gay, always.

240

'A mournful invalid is not to be countenanced,' she said.

Sometimes she closed her eyes in the open air and allowed herself to drowse and remember the ocean and her first walk with Captain Lindsay, the quarrel that led to their first understanding of one another; how happy and whole that had made her feel, almost as carefree as a child. She relived their walk, their handshake, the dancing waves; she remembered the sound of the carriage wheels when they had taken their only ride together, the feeling of laughter and how easy it was to laugh. What had happened to him? Was he suffering, and she not there to help? She thought of the comfort she might have given him as his wife in doing his duty for his country and her refusal of him seemed suddenly trivial and unnecessary, perverse as the whim of a child. Then she remembered that in doing so she had protected him from seeing her wasted like this, weak and recovering from fever, but waiting, always waiting to be pulled down under the water again. Their innocence would never have survived. But it was very hard, and she would be forced to turn from the thoughts and memories, squirming, shift her body away from the source of the pain so that she no longer lay upon the wound.

Miss Emily Hudson   Ludlow
Marsh House
September 7th

My dear Cousin,

Doctor Cooper writes that you have been untroubled by haemorrhage now for above a week. Thomas asks me to tell you he has said a prayer of thankfulness.

We are returning shortly to town and then I will come and visit for the day.

Affectionately,

William

Mrs R W Harper   Marsh House
Hotel Splendide, Vienna

September, 1862

My darling Augusta,

I am delighted to hear that you have chosen Vienna. It sounds the perfect place for your wedding trip. I am only sorry to have missed your wedding, but from your description it was so perfect and private an affair that I was not needed.

Forgive me for being so very feeble a correspondent this summer.

I fear I have become lazy what with the beauty of this place and the unending brilliance of the light and coolness of the shade. They have quite overwhelmed my senses and I have been overtaken by a certain lethargy, contentment, call it what you will, that has even forced me to neglect my work.

Besides, it is possible, I have discovered, to have little news!

William has gone into Yorkshire in pursuit of horses (most unlike him, I know!) and this is a house of women, peaceful and quiet.

Write to me of Vienna—I am told its opulence is quite austere.

Love always,

Emily

Miss Emily Hudson   Cornford House
Marsh House   Boston, Mass

September 15th, 1862

My dear Cousin,

I have heard from William that you have been most seriously ill these last weeks and I am heartily sorry for it. He also says that you are beginning to be stronger. I look forward to hearing how you do by your own hand, but please do not tire yourself to reply until you can do so without taxing yourself.

Thank you for your letter. I have passed a pleasant enough summer at Newport Beach and I have been in sufficient health and spirits to venture into society with my mother a number of times. I have taken to writing a daily journal of these events and I must admit I find it very rewarding: a life catalogued is more definite and worthwhile than one conducted in perfect solitude. My father has been very busy with his work and I trust that in Boston this Fall I shall continue to make my forays into the world undisturbed, for I find that I take pleasure in observing it—it affords me no little satisfaction.

It seems hardly possible that more than a year has passed since you spent the summer with us there. This cruel war has so far spared my beloved brothers. I pray for them every day.

Please keep me abreast of your condition and try to remain hopeful.

Yours affectionately,

Mary

Miss Mary Cornford   Marsh House
Cornford House
Boston, Mass

September 25th, 1862

Dear Mary,

Just a few lines to thank you for your kind letter. It is true that I am improving. But it is very important to me that my condition is not generally known. I have not admitted it even to my dearest friend. It is a kind of pride, I suppose, and a feeling of being at a disadvantage in the world. I have no hesitation in believing in your discretion, having never had cause to doubt it. Your brother has always been similarly discreet.

I struggle every day to be of good heart.

I shall write again presently, but allow me first to tell you how gratified I am to hear of your improved health and spirits and the increased activity of your daily life.

Affectionately,

Emily

*   *   *

Emily was standing when William came into the room. It had become so familiar to her, that drawing room: every line and shadow, every simple piece of furniture, and as he came in she could not help but remember the last time he had surprised her there. He was awkward. His face bore the marks of exposure to the sun and open air, but had not benefited from them. If anything he was thinner.

'William, you look so different!' she burst out.

'As indeed do you, I am glad to say.'

'Thank you for your letters, and the doctor.' She felt embarrassed. It had not been so long ago, after all, that they had fought bitterly. And now she was thanking him once more.

'It was nothing.'

He was waiting for her to apologise. Breathing and swallowing, she plunged in, entreating him with her eyes not to punish her, hating herself for doing so.

'I am sorry we quarrelled. I am sorry I have been so ill and caused you so much worry and trouble.' She knew as she spoke them that these were not the words he wanted, but she had no others.

'It is not so much the illness but the recklessness that caused it. Admit that you are sorry for that, too. And tell me you are free of it, Cousin. That this has taught you to be?'

She felt a great weakness in her legs and on a sudden found she must sit down. 'I have always thought that you admired my unique spirit.' She tried to sound close to merry, arch and light-hearted, but knew that she did not, that it was the old painful struggle resurfacing.

He bit his lip and an opaque look came into his eyes, the flush that presaged emotion came to his cheek. He moved to the window and looked out. 'This is indeed a beautiful view. I am soothed to think you had occasion to draw strength from it.' He did not appear soothed in the least.

'The house has been a peaceful one, William.' But for the night terrors, she longed to say, and the blood, and the housekeeper pounding the linen to remove it.

'You have been safe and warm here,' he said. 'Untroubled?'

'Indeed.'

He turned towards her. 'Might you consider staying here for the winter? You need not be lonely. You could have visitors.'

'I had not thought of it.'

'If you return to town you will be alone again with the weather, the mire in the streets. Winter is filthy here, you know. There is not the blue of Boston.'

246

'You talk as if you have already thought of an alternative.'

He seemed resolved to speak dispassionately. 'There are warmer climates. Italy—perhaps Rome. Augusta—'

'Augusta has, I understand, removed from there and is at Vienna. And she is on her wedding trip, which I could not disturb.' He was still staring out of the window. She did not like it.

'Understand that I cannot undertake to accompany you abroad, should you desire it. I have submitted my novel and am embarking on a series of stories that will keep me hard-pressed all winter. It is unlikely I shall emerge from my study at all.'

She found she could not gauge his wishes. Did he indeed want to be rid of her? 'I have heard of women at the school who sometimes travel alone,' she said.

He took a step towards her. 'Chaperoning one another?'

'Not always, I am informed. Sometimes they are quite alone.'

'That is out of the question. If you were in company it would be another thing, not a very respectable thing, but I am tired of lecturing you about that.'

'I do not consider it practical to think of travel now, when I have so lately been ill.' She tried to sound measured and calm. 'And England has become my home. I would like to continue with my studies here.' She was not going to say that even she would be afraid to go abroad unaccompanied.

The expression in his eye was that of someone wounded, but she could not imagine why. 'So I

247

shall not be keeping this house on? You are determined to return?'

'Yes.'

'Very well. You shall remain in London then. Although, as I have explained, I can neither recommend the climate nor determine the society.'

'All I ever asked of you was to take me to London,' she broke out.

'And I have done it,' he said bitterly. 'On my own head be it.'

She knew better than to deny him this speech, this summation of his disapproval. But they could not embrace after these words, or comfort one another or talk of the future. There was no hope of that now.

*　　　*　　　*

'My dear girl, he has distressed you.'

Caroline found Emily in the garden on the stile looking into the field, her face all wet with tears.

'He is not proud of me.'

'Dear, dear girl.' Caroline clasped Emily in her arms. 'You are still as thin as a bird!' she laughed, releasing her.

Emily shook her head. 'No. I shall be a fat London pigeon by and by.'

'Will you not stay with me at Grosvenor Square when you return to town?'

'No. I could not. You have been kind enough. It is time for us to resume our daily lives. I have my pursuits, you have yours.' She straightened up and smiled.

'But we shall see plenty of your sweet face?'

'I do hope so.'

Miss Emily Hudson   The Carlton Club
—— Mayfair, SW

September 25th, 1862

My dear Emily,

I write because I fear our last interview was unsatisfactory to us both.

It would please me greatly if you would understand that my desire for you either to continue your sojourn at the South Coast, or to journey to a warmer climate, springs purely from my disinterested feeling for you. You are an orphan in a country far from that of your birth; I have undertaken a responsibility for you, which I owe it to myself, and to you, to fulfil to the best of my ability. By this I mean consulting the best doctors, and attempting to provide you with the best surroundings for your condition.

Your denial of my attempts to come to your aid when we last met left me not a little exercised. I regret that I spoke to you in anger.

It is important that you should be aware that I am at present extremely taken up with my work and its pressing obligations, and therefore may not be at liberty to call on you as frequently as I might wish now that we are both re-established in the city. Nor can I undertake that I will always be able to keep to our weekly appointment to dine.

I ask you, therefore, in all earnestness, please to apply to me if you feel your health may be weakening in any particular. I cannot impress on you more strongly how severe the English winter can be; not in the extremes of temperature you may recall from New England, but in the acuteness of the all-pervasive damp.

Dearest Emily, please understand that you yourself are responsible for your position, but that a word from you to myself could change your circumstances immediately, and—in my opinion—for the better.

I am aware that you cannot bear to be serious, to feel bound in any way, or to be crossed in your wishes. But please heed my warning.

With sincere affection as ever,

William

Dr G A Cooper   Mayfair, SW
Harley Street

September 30th, 1862

Dear Dr Cooper,

Thank you for your kind letter enquiring after my health.

I find I am not in need of your assistance at present, but I am extremely grateful that you are willing to be of help to me should I so desire it, and also to hear that you will be in London for the winter, should I have need of you again.

Much as I have enjoyed making your acquaintance, I am sure you can understand my reluctance to say that I hope it will shortly be renewed!

Please do, however, allow me to take the opportunity to thank you for the kind visits you paid me. Your faithful attendance played no inconsiderable part in my recovery and my friends and I are deeply grateful. But I must stop, lest I become too emotional for both our sakes.

Yours truly,

Emily Hudson

Miss Emily Hudson   Grosvenor Square, SW
—— Mayfair, SW

October 1st, 1862

My dearest Emily,

No sooner have I unpacked my trunk than I find I must go away again.

My widowed aunt, who lives in the West of the country, is extremely unwell and without a nurse or close family of any description. I must go to her at once and have left instructions for Thomas not to fall quite into the worst habits while I am away.

I wish you could accompany me—I do not like leaving you—but I know you will not, so I shall not ask it of you.

Write every day—or as often as does not tire you.

Affectionately and in haste,

Caroline

PS. Please do not work too hard—your health is of far greater importance than your studies.

CHAPTER FIFTEEN

Autumn was coming upon the Park, the air cooling, sky hardening, leaves brightening, and there was mist and dew when she walked across it to school. Solitude made Emily light-headed. Even in class she could spend all morning without speaking, simply bent over her work, listening to her own shallow breath.

She had gone with a group of her fellow students to the National Gallery and Miss Norton herself had instructed them on one painting only. Emily's fear of the place really should be over and done, she thought, but she was nonetheless uneasy in its environs. They had studied Rubens' 'Samson and Delilah': so much tenderness entangled with so much dirt, she felt. Delilah's swollen breast and contemplation of the conquered Samson—his magnificence—these intimacies, these feelings she would never experience both animated and weakened her. The work of art was more alive to her than the play she had attended. When the class dispersed it was to different engagements and Emily was left alone looking at the painting, except for Miss Norton, who was busy gathering her belongings. She would lunch alone again, she thought wearily. She had found a reputable place where they would give her soup. She had promised

Dr Cooper and she ate there nearly every day.

'Miss Hudson, are you quite well?' Miss Norton's voice broke in upon her thoughts. 'You have been looking pale these past days.'

Emily flushed. 'Thank you, but I am perfectly well. A little tired sometimes perhaps.'

'This city is not kind to those without protection,' said Miss Norton. 'I should like to satisfy myself further about your health. Is your cousin in town?'

'Not at present,' said Emily. 'But he will return shortly.' It was the first time she had ever told a lie out loud. The truth was she had seen William but once, for tea, since her return to London. It had been a strained occasion and they had foundered for words; he preoccupied, she unusually afraid.

'Be good enough to advise me upon his return.'

'I shall.'

'My dear young lady, there is no need to look so woebegone.' The lady smiled. Emily wanted to catch at her hand and beg her not to write to her cousin about her concerns, or communicate with him in any fashion, but she feared alerting Miss Norton to her duplicity. All she could do was remain still before the painting, waiting for her teacher to take her leave. At last, chiding herself for her lack of discipline, she quit the room.

Standing at the top of the flight of stairs to the crowded vestibule, not ten feet away—as if their meeting were pre-arranged—was Lord Firle. She saw him immediately. She had forgotten how tall he was. He had a sternness about him she did not remember. She was not surprised, for she thought of him so often, that he should appear, but after the clarity of the first look, it was all confusion. He looked entirely serious—no air of amusement when his eyes were on her, but his look seemed to allow her an importance she held for no one else. She had the presence of mind to allow him merely a brief nod of acknowledgement before continuing down the stairs. He followed her. She could tell this without turning. She knew his step, just as she knew his eye, his lip, his gleaming hair, and had imprinted them on her mind. She was shaking. She could see them both on the staircase as if from above.

'Will you not stop and say good day?' he called lightly. She would, she would, of course she would: it flooded her that there could be no alternative. After all the tedium and solitude of her illness she would not send him away. She turned to look at him with the sudden joyous anticipation of looking at the sea.

'Good day, Lord Firle.'

'Miss Hudson, I am enchanted to see you.' And he embraced her with his eyes.

'You are very kind.' They did not say anything further for a while because she should have been walking away.

'I trust you have passed a pleasant summer.'

The painful blood-soaked interim and the sweetness of the meadow at Marsh House all mingled in her consciousness as she looked at him. He could have no idea. She was a different girl.

'Indeed I have, Sir. And so—I trust—have you.' She should be making her excuses. She should be hurrying away. 'What brings you to the Gallery?' she asked.

'You must believe I have rooms here,' he said, and smiled. 'But I am giving them a picture, and

254

they are not contented but that we must talk about it constantly. I shall certainly never give them another.'

'It is good of you to bequeath something from your collection to the nation.' Her words were coming out quite independently of her thoughts.

'I suppose,' he said. 'I had never thought of it that way. But I am not dead, you know, young lady. It is only because they will look after it far better than I.'

'Is it a portrait you have given them?'

'No, a landscape. I keep the portraits at the Hall.'

'Of course.'

'Taking care of things is such a bore, you see.'

She looked at him firmly, as if making a decision. 'I agree. It gets in the way, rather, I find.'

He approached her, standing close by so that they could not be overheard. 'May I see you? May I see you this evening?' The eagerness and urgency in his tone was so unlike his accustomed drawl she would have laughed if she had not been trembling. 'I could wait for you wherever you wish in a cab— you would not be seen. I would take you somewhere private. It needn't be as you fear it.'

It was exactly as she had feared it. She could not disguise from herself that she understood everything his invitation implied. She felt alive and filled with an improbable overweening joy.

'I will be on the corner of Gower Street and —— at seven o'clock,' she said and, turning, walked rapidly away.

* * *

255

All that afternoon she sat at her window, her chin upon her hand, and thought. It would be easy not to keep their appointment; he would not have the indelicacy to call at her address even though he knew where she lived. She kept seeing his face, the change in him she perceived towards her, the urgency. She had remembered him as so dismissive, so superior, so amused. The contemplation of her desires only seemed to sharpen the clarity with which she saw her situation—aware that everything and nothing had changed since their last meeting. Before she had had no awareness that she may die within the year, although she had held a dread of the disease, held it tightly, like a charm. Now it had shown itself to her, had tried to drown her in blood and terror. The thought of Lord Firle and the darkness around him presented itself in many ways as a refuge, a deliverance.

Above all she was tired of fighting and struggling, struggling with her own nature—her own being. He, of all people, longed for her nearness with the same potency as she for his— and no other creature alive held such an interest for her, or charm.

All these thoughts and many others paraded themselves before Emily, sitting as still as a portrait, in the window of a house that was not her own.

*　　*　　*

He was waiting on the corner as he had described. She could see his face clearly even in the twilight. He pulled down the window and motioned for her to climb in, but she remained outside, looking at him calmly as if unaware of the danger of being seen. She thought he admired that, but could not be sure.

After a while he said, 'Did you know that the sight of a young girl—young lady—looking at a picture can be as much a work of art as the masterpiece itself?'

Emily smiled.

'I am in earnest. The expression in your eyes the first time I saw you—I shall never forget it.'

'I try to burn each picture I study into my brain—to remember.' She did not tell him she was doing so at that very moment, with his face.

'Is that why you had ceased to sketch that day and were simply gazing?'

'You ask a great many questions.'

'Have you none to ask of me?'

She could not tell him that her mind was blank, only her eyes were full and her blood thrumming.

'I have not ceased to think of you,' he said.

'Such remarks are unwelcome.' She smiled at the beauty of his face.

'Ah. But I do not believe you.' He continued to look at her. 'You were the picture of innocence that day. Always, you are the picture of innocence.'

'Lord Firle, you should not talk to me in this manner.' She said it happily, still smiling.

'Nonsense. These are the words that every female heart longs to hear. It is the purpose of your sex to be worshipped and adored.'

She wondered how many times he had said that and to how many women. She did not care.

'There are many purposes for which all of us are born.'

He laughed. 'That is a very sober New England speech. Come closer, I must kiss you.'

'In the street? Through a carriage window?'

'It was on the street last time.'

She hesitated but did not look around her.

'Climb in, just for one second.' He held the door open for her and gave her his hand. She took it and stepped in. He closed the door, pulling down the blind, and they kissed for a long time. It was a promise of a homecoming.

'You are not going to cry, are you?' he said.

'Why should I cry?' His face filled her eyes. 'I am happy.'

He removed his gloves and stroked her throat. 'You do not regret this?'

'Do you think I am so naïve as not to know what I am doing?' And she took his hand and in her turn stroked his throat, putting her own kiss on his lips. 'May I ask you a question?'

'Certainly.' But he drew back.

'What can you offer me?'

His eyes narrowed. 'I do not understand you.' He paused. 'My heart?'

'That I have no use for.'

'Now you are cruel.' His tone was flirtatious, but wary, worldly.

'I do not think so. Conditions—and temperaments—do not augur well for our alignment.' He took her ringless hand and played with it. 'I have a . . . tenderness for you,' she continued. He made as if to kiss her again, pressing both her captured hands. 'But I cannot see you again.'

He smiled. 'Methinks the lady—'

She shook her head slowly, looking directly at

him. 'No.'

'Why not?'

'Because it would be wrong.'

He smiled. 'Wrong because I am married?' He pronounced this as if it were a minor objection. 'I would still decorate your hair with diamonds,' he said, loosening her bonnet and touching the strands that escaped. 'I would still show you off to the world.'

She caught his hand. 'Wrong for my soul. And I do not care to be ruined. I am to be an artist. Not some ruined, dying girl.'

He let her hand out of his grasp. 'Dying, you say?'

'I am not a wholesome young lady for a— flirtation. This you should know.'

He sat back in the cab away from her and into the corner, averting his face. 'Which of us is wholesome?' he said; then presently, 'Did America give you this honesty?'

When she did not reply he took her hand again, more gently. She looked at their hands clasped together and thought the image beautiful.

'My dear Sir, I am fond of you in spite of myself. I desire your company against my own judgement. But I have made up my mind. This is to be the last time.'

'I should feel myself aggrieved that you are playing with me so carelessly,' he said. 'But I do not.'

They did not look at each other but he kept hold of her hand. 'I could give you such pleasure,' he said. It was too dark for him to see how she blushed when he said that.

There was a silence between them and then it

started to rain. She could hear it drumming on the roof. 'Are you sad?' he said.

'Not at present. Because I am still with you. When you are gone I shall feel the lack of you.'

'Let me ask of you one thing, Emily.' His voice was low and not without emotion. 'If you are ever in trouble—the winters here are quiet, and filthy and cold—will you call on me? Send to my address. I shall endeavour to treat any request with the respectability it deserves. There would be no need for us to meet if you did not desire it.'

Her breath caught in her throat, answering him. 'You are very—kind.'

After a while with only the sound of their breathing, he climbed out of the cab.

'I shall direct the driver to take you through the Park and then back to your lodgings,' he said as he left her.

She felt rather than saw him go. When he brushed her hand as he passed her heart was too full to allow her a reply.

When she returned to her rooms she cried for a long time. If he had given her a love token, now would have been the time to return or destroy it— but he had given her nothing.

Mrs R W Harper   London
Hotel Splendide
Vienna

October 14th, 1862

My dearest Augusta,

Autumn is settling in here with such a storm
of rain and tattered leaves the streets are filthy
with it, and I worry for the comfort of the cab
horses and the people whose living is taken
from the streets.

My dear friend Caroline continues absent
and since I have completed my portrait of
mother and child I find I am not concentrating
on my studies as I would wish. I long to work
outside the studio again but of course
conditions do not permit—indeed the studio
itself is so cold that the girls complain of
chilblains.

Cousin Mary has written to me sending me a
knitted shawl and gloves with no fingers—they
are ugly but a comfort. Her last letter was very
brief. The war goes on in painful
circumstances—my uncle continues to ignore
it. He quite refuses to allow his own concerns
to be eclipsed by this appalling slaughter, most
recently at Corinth. How can the war continue
with such casualties? And all for what they call
strategic victories! Thankfully my cousins
continue to be spared. Mary has been well
enough to write consistently in her diary: she
may not have William's power to act in the
world but she has his inclinations. I am glad of

261

it. No word of Captain Lindsay. The thought of him continues to disturb me. I do not dare to imagine his fate—but that is a lie, I imagine it constantly and curse my own imaginings. I pray the omission of him from her letters augurs well and not badly.

There is very little to distract me from my thoughts, which I own are not always of the most cheerful. Unlike in Boston, there is no autumn season to speak of here. Houses are shut up and unoccupied and what society there is remains closed to me without Caroline. My cousin dines with me now only very occasionally, and our conversation has become considerably strained since our sojourn by the sea this summer. I believe I have disappointed him so very deeply that there are no amends to be made.

I cannot but admit that I am wounded by it and wonder if I should make some appeal to him and our longstanding friendship, the bond of trust between us. But I am proud and he is more so, I think.

I continue to expand my knowledge, not only of the History of Art but of the contemporary style. Painters such as Barbizon and Corot are concentrating on scenes actually set upon a beach, so the ideas I have been brooding over, of bringing the outdoors in all its colour and movement into a painting, may be not be as far-fetched as all that. If I were to begin to work in this way, however, I would need a more favourable climate for it!

I long for news of Vienna—although I understand that a girl on her wedding trip has other things on her mind than writing letters.

Do not worry for me, it is solitary but it is what I have chosen.

Affectionately, as ever,

Emily

Mrs R W Harper   Mayfair, London
Hotel Splendide, Vienna

November 11th, 1862

My dearest Girl,

Forgive my confusion, but I realise I can no longer call you that for you are a married lady now—unless I can count it as a sign of our continued intimacy, which I hope I can, can I not?

I was delighted to hear from you this morning. It has felt like such a very long time since I last saw you with my eyes instead of my memory or fancy, especially in these last days. I am so happy that your married state suits you so very well. He does indeed sound 'a capital fellow', as they would say here. Is your existence now utterly devoted to enjoying his devotion of you, or are you continuing with the pretence of educating yourself in Europe? I am teasing you, and you must take it in good heart.

It has rained all day today. I must admit that until I came into this country I had no notion of what it is to pass a rainy day! I have lost count of the number of times I have been

263

soaked to the skin and it is so difficult to feel wholly warm and dry after a drenching, however short. My feet and stockings are quite soaked and as for the hem of my pretty new dress and coat you would think they had been dragged through the woods that used to surround our old school so long ago. Despite the fire and the warm, if indifferent, dinner, I am still shivering. All except my face, which for one reason or another seems to be burning hot. It must be from sitting so very close to the grate.

I do not want to leave it for my cold bed. I am convinced the very sheets are damp. I must remember to ask for a hot brick another night.

I walked a great deal today for I did not want to go to school. I wanted to be outside. I could not cough in the studio where they are all working, in any event. It would not be fair to the other girls and Miss Norton would disapprove.

I long to hear your voice. Sometimes I imagine I almost do.

Have you seen the white horses in Vienna yet?

Are you crammed with cake, whipped cream and opulence?

Do you love the music or are you tired of the waltz?

I must lie down but I do not want to go to bed.

Goodnight, my dear sweet friend.

Emily

[Letter unsent]

*   *   *

When Emily woke in the night with the blood
rising in her throat and in her mouth she felt very
calm, as if it were all inevitable, she had known it
and had only been marking time before its return.
Her first thoughts were of Mrs Denham's sheets.
She must not dirty Mrs Denham's sheets. Her
existence could not continue if blood were to be
found on the sheets. She coughed into the folds of
the shawl that Mary had sent her and that she had
worn to bed, lifting it from her shoulders and
pressing it to her mouth. When the fit had passed
she did not know what to do with it. It was warm
and thick with new blood. It would be impossible
to wash it out in the basin, there was not sufficient
water, and she risked it being seen as it hung to
dry. So she folded it as neatly and tightly as she
could and hid it quickly in the back of the
wardrobe, only to rummage for it frantically
almost immediately and bring it back to bed with
her in case she should have need of it again.

Dr G A Cooper   —— Square
Harley Street, SW   Mayfair, SW

November 12th, 1862

Dear Dr Cooper,

    I write to you in complete confidence.
    I fear I have had a recurrence. Indeed I know
that I have. This disease is no respecter of

265

situations but I believe is more afraid of you than of me. Could you come to me at my London address—above—and intimidate it for me once again?

I will wait for a word from you.

Yours truly,

Emily Hudson

PS. Not a word to my cousin, if you please.

Miss Emily Hudson   Carlton Club, SW
Mayfair, SW

November 15th, 1862

My dear Cousin,

I fear I have neglected you of late. As Thanksgiving approaches I find I think of you, and as my closest living relative on this continent feel I should bestow a little of the Old World style on your hardworking nature.

Might you accompany me to a supper party on Thursday next? It is by no means a grand occasion but a few sympathetic souls will be present. I would appreciate your looking your best so as to honour the company not purely with your opinions but also your person.

Yours affectionately,

William

*   *   *

William's letter came so soon after the terror of the illness had begun again that she found herself grasping at its information as if this one occasion could salve all her woes. He was offering her another chance at society: she must take it firmly; make him proud. Then perhaps there would be peace between them and her path could be straightened out. She would order a new dress; she had had no evening clothes since the spring and must obey the fashion and the season. Although Emily did not consider herself frivolous or vain it gave her joy to choose the stuff, order the trim, decide on the pattern. She even visited a selection of drapers' shops for the lace. For this occasion she was determined to make herself the subject of her art.

At the fittings she could see how thin she had become in the mirror, but the dressmaker's talents transformed this paucity into elegance: the corsetry and the undergarments gave her a silhouette as sharp and clear as a cameo, even if she felt all blurred inside. It was comforting to be tended to even by virtual strangers. It was a solace merely to converse with them after another day of wandering and not having the heart to go to school. They gave her water when she coughed and tried to press more refreshments on her but she did not want to put them to the trouble. Besides, she had no appetite. They tended to her as if she were a fly caught in a web, these benign spider-women who were neither friends nor strangers, but who had one function only, to present her to the world.

Sensible of what an honour the occasion was for her in William's eyes, she resolved not to argue with any soul; she would not speak, she would be peaceful and silent and sympathetic and as pleasing to the eye and ear as she could make herself; and all the clever gentlemen could pronounce on her, on themselves and on the world and she would say nothing. She would take care to have her reticule with her always in case the worst should befall her.

Dr G A Cooper   Mayfair, SW
Harley Street

November 20th, 1862

Dear Dr Cooper,

If you have been absent from town I hope you are now returned. Forgive my bluntness and brevity, but please send to me as to when I might receive your visit or come to you.
Yours truly,

Emily Hudson

Miss E Hudson   Harley Street, SW
——— Square
Mayfair, SW

November 22nd, 1862

Dear Miss Hudson,
Please accept my apologies for the delay in writing to you. I have taken the liberty of

forwarding your letters to Dr Cooper, who is at present in Switzerland at the behest of an esteemed colleague.

He shall either reply to you directly, or instruct me further at the earliest opportunity.

In the meantime, should I be able to be of any further assistance please do not hesitate to contact me.

Yours faithfully,

Nathaniel Mayhew
Secretary to Dr Cooper

*   *   *

It took a long long while to make herself ready for the supper party, for she was feeling not a little weak. Mrs Denham kindly lent Emily her own maid for the dressing of her hair. Lizzie, she was called. Together they achieved a muted splendour. She had been going to wear her mother's necklace but could not bring herself to take it out of its box. It reminded her too much of Captain Lindsay. After Lizzie had gone she sat close to the window waiting, gazing into the square.

William came up to her rooms when he called for her, and Emily realised with a shock that this was the first time he had set foot in them since depositing her here that long ago day in April.

'You look beautiful,' he said. 'I am happy to see you again.' He spoke the words without reservation, the way he used to talk to her at Newport, when there were no clouds in the sky; as if he appreciated her, the way he had used to when he turned her head with the notion of her rareness

269

of spirit and beauty, when he did not believe her damaged and selfish and spoiled. His look was the look she remembered, and felt ashamed to have craved. She was relieved to find him so real, so flesh and blood and solid, and in so benign a mood—indeed, she could feel herself almost overwhelmed.

'Oh, William—I am glad to see you.'

'You sound a little emotional, Emily, are you quite well? Would you like a moment to compose yourself?'

'I am perfectly composed,' she said, swallowing the nerves, imagining swallowing the blood. He must not know. 'I don't believe I have ever thanked you sufficiently for all these beautiful clothes.'

'My dear girl, it would be most uncomfortable if you were to spend your time constantly thanking me. We have an agreement, we honour it, that is all.'

She nodded. 'Shall we go?'

He guided her out of the room in that proprietary way he adopted when an occasion was to be public. She did not like it while finding it comforting. She wondered vaguely if the world would always be this confusing.

'We are going to my friends the Pettifers. Thomas will be there, I believe.'

In the hansom she listened to the horse's hooves. Strange it was how alike they all sounded. She wondered if she had ever travelled by the same horse without knowing it. She wondered about this one's name. It was raining again as they descended on to the pavement. William opened his umbrella elaborately and held it over her head as they went up the steps, the railings glistening in the lights from the house. She was very nervous. She remembered she did not like parties. There would be strangers and she carried the well-known enemy within.

The sound of laughter from above could be heard as they trod the crimson-carpeted stairs. Their hostess, a handsome woman, no longer young, greeted them with all courtesy in the haughty English way, and the company was lively enough, fortunately, and of sufficient numbers for Emily to feel inconspicuous. She stayed close to her cousin. The large room felt dim even with all the candles blazing.

Mr Trelawney quickly found them. 'My dear Emily, it has been an age. You are looking exquisite.' But his eyes held little confirmation of these words, and a very slight coolness. She had caused him trouble, after all. No gentleman liked that.

'How do you do?' she said, 'I am so glad to see you,' urged to affection by the memory of him on the beach at Camber in earnest confabulation with her cousin.

William adopted the same proprietary air towards his friend as towards Emily, and they talked of Caroline's continued absence, of horses and of mutual acquaintance. Emily thought, this will be perfectly all right.

At dinner—it was definitely a very formal dinner and not the supper William had described—Emily remained quiet, affecting only small talk with the gentlemen and observing the ladies' dress, jewellery, the way the light fell upon their hair. It was a strange dream-like sensation to be so detached. She remembered Boston and Captain Lindsay down the table and wondered again what had become of him. Mostly she did not want to know if he were dead or alive: it was safer preserving him in the amber of the past, but tonight she longed—longed acutely—to know. Had it mattered so very much whether they married if they were both condemned to die?

The talk was of literary matters only briefly, before it turned to society, of which Emily was largely ignorant. It was not the occasion she had always imagined attending with William in London, where important artists and painters talked into the night with coffee, brandy and cigars, and the ladies would not have to withdraw; where there would be an informality between the ladies and gentlemen and not this feeling of constant watchfulness and assessment; where they would not be served countless courses at a long reflective table, but would move freely in small groups, or perhaps even be an intimate party, known to one another with affection—friends. Would she always view every occasion in her actual social experience as if from a great distance, while intimately observing every physical detail should she need it for her work? The way the candelabra flickered and burned down, the dull glow of the silver and the far greater brightness of the flowers, all these impressions of colour and light took her attention.

So absorbed was she in these thoughts she did not notice that the gentleman to her right was addressing her.

He had a full set of reddish-grey whiskers of which he was obviously very proud. 'So this country of yours is still intent on its civil war?' He pronounced 'country' with a sneer.

'I believe so.' Emily answered gently but her heart was already beating faster. Would this gentleman continue to mock at these struggles of life and death, or would he refrain?

'I wish that they would not,' she said, looking directly into his eyes and hoping her firmness might check him.

'Is that why you left your home and came away?' he asked.

His question felt overly intimate to Emily. 'Indeed, no. I simply wanted to take the opportunity to—to—' and she felt a horrible blush stain her as she fumbled for the words. Words were clearer in her head than in her mouth tonight. She stopped, swallowed, started again. 'I came into this country to study to be an artist.'

'How unusual,' he said, with complete lack of interest. 'But tell me, my dear—why are your countrymen a nation of such savages? First they subdue the Indians, and now they are at one another's throats.' He began to raise his voice and attract the attention of the table. 'These people behave with primitive barbarity, while continually going about making declarations—is that the word?—about rights and other such nonsense. At best they are fortune-seekers and would be better off acknowledging the fact.'

William looked at her. She must not disappoint him. 'Indeed,' she said mildly.

'You haven't got much to say for yourself, have you?' he expostulated. 'I thought American girls were meant to be so independent, cast quite in a different mould.'

'It doesn't do to generalise,' said Lady Pettifer easily, and seemed about to change the subject.

'But it is impossible not to in this case. If there were ever a people so intent on impressing their wrong-headed ideas upon the world—'

'I think you could accuse Napoleon of that, before the Colonials,' said Thomas Trelawney, with a smile and to general laughter.

'Yes, it is true that we are the only ones to have escaped these absurd revolutions,' her companion continued, triumphantly.

'Charles the First was executed,' said Emily, in a clear, carrying voice. 'We learned all about it at school. Men have been killing each other for no discernible reason since the dawn of time.'

'You are not comparing a brief and shameful episode in our domestic history to the continual lack of respect with which these other countries approach the future of the world? Everywhere, revolutions—the old order is being destroyed, and for what?' He was very exercised now, and his whiskers were trembling.

'It will be trains and factories that do the most damage to the future, I think,' said William quietly.

'It is all moving too fast. But these Yanks are a bad lot, posturing savages in tailcoats, nothing but criminals and fanatics, the lot of them, nothing but criminals and fanatics. We should never have let them go.'

'You could not control us,' said Emily, reddening again. 'We are not to be controlled.'

'Are you a patriot? If you care for the fate of your nation so deeply, what on God's earth are you doing sitting here with me?'

274

'I am no patriot, Sir,' said Emily. 'Merely a human being who cannot abide a stupid opinion.'

A silence fell upon the table as complete as a fall of snow. Emily, breathless, cheeks throbbing, got up from the table, murmured her excuses and stumbled from the room. There seemed no alternative. Her uncle would never have allowed her to stay.

*   *   *

The drawing room was empty, made ready for the return of the company. There were mirrors on the walls. She had not noticed before because there had been such a crowd when she arrived. In the mirrors she looked tiny and ridiculously dressed, like a doll with red-painted cheeks. *Une poupée.* It would be better in French. What must she do? She must leave the house—but she could not go without an apology to Lady Pettifer, without saying or writing something. What she had said had seemed inevitable just a moment ago, but it was not. She burned with shame, with pain, with longing, with loss, with the utter loneliness of her predicament, lit from within by the fire of her disease. She began to shiver.

Perhaps William would come. He did not. Neither did her hostess. Nobody came. It was so very English: they must be pretending, going on as if nothing had happened; no appalling ill-judged words had been spoken. She had been angry with this gentleman for engaging her, with his fat whiskered cheeks and his fat lands and doubtless his fat healthy family—but she could not defend her actions even to herself. She knew that her rage had been indefensible. She too must be an American savage, unable to disagree quietly with an overbearing gentleman at dinner, unable to keep her feelings to herself. It must be another accomplishment learned by English young ladies that she had not been taught.

She thought all this as she hurried down the stairs. In the hall, the butler approached her and she asked him to call her a cab. He sent a footman out while he helped her into her things with a blank, impenetrable expression that she felt it delighted him to adopt. It was not until she was safe in the darkness of the cab that she began to cough. It was just about to pull away from the kerb when she saw William come down the steps without his coat. He called to the driver to stop, approaching her with a horrible deliberation, white in the face. It seemed to take a long time for him to reach her and she could not stop coughing.

They looked at one another through the cab window without speaking, his eyes narrow with rage.

His voice, when it came, was full of disgust. 'I shall never take you anywhere again. You can be assured of it.'

She was coughing and thought she could not stop.

'I am tired of appealing to you. It is at an end.' She threw out the words. That was not what she had intended to say. She had not realised she was angry with him; she had thought it had only been shame.

With one of his abrupt changes of tone, he took a step towards her with an expression of concern. 'Are you ill again, Cousin?'

'Please—keep my secret,' she whispered. That was all she cared about now, her own privacy, the refuge of it.

'I have always kept it,' he said. And seeing her draw away from him, hissed, 'I have always kept *you*.'

'And what have *I* kept, William?' she burst out before the cough choked her again. 'What have *I* kept? For *me*?!'

'At this moment I never want to lay eyes on you again,' he said. He tapped the cab. 'Driver, drive on—take her where she wants to go,' and, turning his back on her, he remounted the stairs.

*   *   *

The blood was very bad that night.

Emily could not rise from her bed in the morning, she had not the strength for it after a sleepless and terrifying night. At nine o'clock Mrs Denham had tea brought in to her and stood at the foot of the bed looking elongated and frightening in her dark widow's colours. I must not be frightened of her, thought Emily, nor must I show my fear.

She must try to think what to do. It seemed a crisis—severe, inescapable—was impending in her illness and so in her life, and she must think what she must do. She knew she was feverish. She recognised the symptoms. It had been hot in the dining room but cold in the streets. Now it was both hot and cold. There was no further possibility of Dr Cooper. Even if she beseeched him he could not come to her.

Her only thought was flight. It was a foolish

desperate thought but it was all she wanted. She could not write and beg the help of Caroline. It would be immediately forthcoming, she knew, but Caroline had her own private family obligations and their bond, although warm, was based on only a few months' acquaintance.

Of her cousin she could not think without a shudder of the spirit. He had wronged her. They had wronged one another. He was ashamed of her. And this brought her to the worst of her predicament. It was his fortune that fed her, clothed her, kept her from destitution; to reject his protection was to take away her means of survival. And yet had he not intimated that he regretted extending it to her? As a gentleman who thought well of himself she did not think he would willingly withdraw it—but . . . Her head ached. She could not allow it to continue, this debt to him.

To call upon Firle was out of the question, although she believed he would make good his offer and wrap her in his wealth, should she ask it of him—even if the rapid change in her, her sickly feverish mien, repulsed him. But she did not want to accept his help and she had sufficient vanity, or pride, not to want him to see her without her beauty.

Perhaps she could pawn her necklace and secure enough for a safe passage, but she could not bear to leave it behind. And where would she fly to? What would she fly towards? It was perplexing. These feverish fervent wishes, this longing to be gone, to be free, was it death itself she wished for—the extinguishing of all her worldly trials? But no. It was not. She did not want to die. She wanted to live and live freely. It was difficult to puzzle out.

It made her cry.

*   *   *

She slept, waking to more haemorrhage. When it had passed she slept again, coming to consciousness at the sight of Mrs Denham in her room once more. This time she approached and sat upon the bed. That was very strange.

'Miss Hudson, I believe you are gravely ill.'

'Indeed.' Emily smiled. There were no grounds for denying it.

'I am sorry for it. But you must understand that I cannot undertake to nurse you here, in my house. You are making us quite frightened. I would like to send to your cousin.'

'You cannot. He left for the country early this morning.'

'Did he leave no address?'

'No. He will return tomorrow. I beg you to wait until tomorrow.'

'Perhaps I should call for a doctor then. You cannot merely be left in this condition.'

'Please, Mrs Denham, I have sent to my doctor. And I shall send again to him today—the letter is written. He will come tomorrow, and I have friends—I will remove from here with all speed. But please, do not send to Mr Cornford today.'

'Very well, my dear. I will respect your wishes. The ill so rarely have their wishes respected, I know that for a certainty. But if there is no doctor by noon tomorrow I will send for one, and to your cousin. I cannot bear the responsibility of this illness of yours alone. If you were my daughter, I—'

279

'Please. Before you go, could I have pen and paper? They are in my writing case, on the chest of drawers. Could someone take a message for me? Would it be too much trouble?'

'I shall send for Lizzie. She will attend to you and it will be despatched with all haste. First try to take a little gruel.' But Emily could not.

When Mrs Denham withdrew Emily cried: human kindness made her cry.

*   *   *

Lizzie brought the writing materials to her bedside and adjusted the pillows so that Emily could sit upright. She remained in the room while Emily wrote, turning tactfully away. Tact, thought Emily, another virtue I have never known. When she had finished, Lizzie promised to deliver the letter with all speed and wait for a reply.

After she had gone, Emily put on her clothes. It was the simplest of tasks, but it took a very long time because of her frequent bouts of dizziness and her trembling fingers. She rested before beginning to brush her hair. Then she sat in the window and waited until she saw Lizzie's bonnet appear amongst the heads of the passers-by at the corner of the square. The day was overcast but the sky had not yielded up its rain.

The contents of the note were satisfactory, and she prepared herself to leave the house, to make that desperate effort, because it had to be done.

'Is this wise, Miss?' said Lizzie. 'If Mrs Denham were here I am sure she would not be pleased to see you attempt any journey alone.'

'It is only a little errand. But I must perform it.'

The banking hall was as hushed and high as a church. Mr Sinclair greeted her promptly and ushered her into a private room. He was very deferential, and younger than she had imagined him, but he made her feel afraid. Anticipating what she was going to say sickened her and her head ached terribly.

'Miss Hudson, I am delighted to make your acquaintance. What can I do for you?'

They were both seated. Emily did not believe that any person from the other side of a desk had ever spoken to her in such a way before. If she had been in health and high spirits, what a terrific joke it would have made. She tried not to shiver but could feel her flesh begin to crawl.

'Mr Sinclair, I understand that my cousin has arranged with you that if I were ever in sudden need of funds beyond my weekly allowance that I should call on you. That time has now come.'

'I see. What sum would you like me to advance you, Miss Hudson?'

Emily told him.

He did not raise his eyebrows, he did not appear to take a breath, but simply said again, 'I see.' Now he would ask her for what purpose she needed the money and now she must say what she had prepared. But he did not.

'I shall arrange for the draft to be made out directly. Do you require any ready money?'

'I should like it all in cash, please.' Emily tried to appear sensible and cool.

He paled slightly, but did not argue with her. 'It

281

is fortunate that we have such a sum put aside for you by your cousin for such eventualities.'

'Will Mr Cornford have to be consulted before the funds can be released?'

'Indeed, no. Did he not explain to you that these arrangements were made solely in your name?'

'He did. It is just that I imagined such a sum . . . He is very generous.'

Mr Sinclair looked a little taken aback that he should be asked to comment on any personal characteristic of one of his clients. Perhaps he was used to extravagant young ladies. Perhaps he thought she had lost it at cards. He made a sort of brief sound of assent accompanied by an awkward nod, but avoided meeting her eye. Emily began to sweat, feeling clammy and cold.

'If you could care to wait here for a few moments, I shall make an arrangement with the cashier and return directly. Miss Hudson, might I ask if you have considered the wisdom of carrying so large a sum about your person?'

With trembling hands Emily opened her reticule and produced her mother's jewellery box with its lock and key. Opening it, she showed him wordlessly that the jewels and velvet had been removed, leaving what she hoped was sufficient space.

'The lock is sturdy?'

'I have no reason to doubt it.' She felt an acute discomfort. She hated questions unless it was she who was asking them.

'Please excuse me.' He left the room quite silently. She wondered if this were a pre-requisite for his position at the bank.

It felt as if she were waiting for a very long time.

She had to try with all her might not to cough for fear she would not be able to stop. When he came back into the room she half expected him to be accompanied by an outraged, white-faced William. But he was alone, apart from a brown paper packet. Sitting down carefully, he cleared his throat and adjusted his chair before opening the envelope and deliberately counting out the money with his practised fingers.

Emily had never seen so much paper money in her life. There had been her allowance, handed to her by William in an ostentatiously unostentatious manner at the end of the weekly dinner they had together; everything else in her existence was charged to him. Seeing that crisp heavy paper so beautifully embossed, she wondered how it must make William feel to have so much of it—how it must make any gentleman feel. That he had been prepared to give it to her 'in case of emergency' seemed a most curious fact. William had never given her anything freely—and now she was taking. She was robbing him. Any minute she expected the police to storm into the room.

But the transaction was reaching its conclusion. 'If I could just ask you to sign for the amount, Miss Hudson. Here.' He indicated a generous space on an official-looking document, which she was too blinded by panic to read. Her signature surprised her by remaining steady and when she had finished she passed him the paper and his pen and looked him full in the eye.

'You will be careful, Miss Hudson?' he said. 'If any thief or vagabond on this city's streets should have any intimation you were carrying such a sum—'

'I do understand.' Her heart was hammering. She stood up and he stood also, because she was a lady.

He accompanied her into the murky throbbing street and she felt London's vastness and her own insignificance very keenly.

'Might I secure you a cab?' he asked. He does not want his bank's money to be jostled, thought Emily, with one of her gleams of understanding of the comedy of it all.

'Thank you, Sir, but no. I would prefer to walk.' She did not want him to know where she was going.

He bid her goodbye on the pavement, aware, she felt, of the gravity of the situation but not of its true nature; that she fervently hoped.

Emily might walk in either direction to reach her destination: up Lower Regent Street to Piccadilly and along to the corner of the Hyde Park, or along the Mall. She felt a little confused about the clearest, quickest way, sick and trembling in the winter daylight. Not caring for the sight of Buckingham Palace, an unprepossessing building at the best of times, she turned up Lower Regent Street, clutching her reticule and attempting to breathe as deeply as she could. If there were a world of some description where she could walk without being encumbered by lacing and undergarments, she longed for it.

Looking into the windows of the saddler's and the apothecary's, and the splendour of Fortnum & Mason, she began to feel a peculiar gliding sensation. She was in the city but not of the city. It was truly nothing to do with her. She had loved its majestic splendid buildings, its generous thoroughfares, the grandeur and newness of its plan, its history and its beauty. But she shrank from its chaos, its filth, its poverty kissing riches, its greed.

She thought of the pictures in the galleries she had loved—at the memory of lifting her head to gaze into St Paul's cathedral that glad day in April and her feelings of awe and rejoicing and wonder—and how in so short a time she had reached the end of the road. Was she so tainted that everything she touched turned to dust and ashes, or was the world so encrusted with cruelty and sadness and lies that it had diminished her without so much as a pause for breath?

Pause for breath. That is what she must do. She had been wandering and thinking of the past, when she must think of her destination—that was what mattered, she must reach it if she were to accomplish everything she had planned. It would not do to weaken now.

It began to rain, the streets immediately beginning to ooze with filth, the pavements becoming slippery with dirt. Passers-by began to hurry for shelter because the downpour was considerable. She was now nearly on the edge of the Park and could clearly see the Winged Victory ahead. She had passed all the coffee houses and shops in which she could have taken refuge and now it was just her and the traffic, the blinkered horses and shouting drivers, the bicycles and carriages and carts.

She could make out a woman coming towards her, a respectable working woman, holding a child by each hand. She could see her coming closer and closer, intent on the way ahead as she was, the safety of her children. Emily must speak to her and ask her to help her find a cab, for she had no strength to essay the confusion of Hyde Park Corner by herself. Was she not ill? Did she not have the consumption? She should not be wandering abroad quite by herself. William would not approve.

Reaching out her hand to speak to the woman she became aware of a terrible sound of rushing in her ears and pains in her chest. Then it all went black.

*　　　*　　　*

The hardness of the fall brought her back to consciousness quickly; she was on the pavement and faces were gazing down.

'I am perfectly well,' she heard herself say, in a gasping voice that sounded foreign and distant. The woman and her two little children: golden-haired girls with solemn expressions, were still discernible, and it was she and an errand boy who helped her to her feet. The boy stopped a cab for her within a few moments while the woman remained sturdily by her side, the rain falling on them both.

'Your dress is spoiled, Miss,' she observed.

As she climbed into the conveyance Emily tried to thank her but she seemed to have gone.

*　　　*　　　*

'You realise you are in no fit state to travel, even if I were to write to my acquaintance about receiving you.'

286

Emily sat with Miss Norton by the fire in her office, a blanket around her shoulders. Her clothes had been taken away to be dried.

'Please—I am sorry for the imposition. But I must go. I have no choice, there is no one else to turn to.'

'What an absurd thing to say.' Miss Norton appeared unaccountably angry. 'You are surrounded by friends, well-wishers. Your cousin—'

'Must not know where I have gone. I will write to him once I am settled.' Emily began to cry. She hated herself for her weakness, for playing on another's feelings.

'So you have quarrelled with him. I cannot be party to such a deception and you should not ask it of me. I make it a rule never to interfere in the private lives of my pupils.' Emily did not remind her that it had been she who had first enquired as to her health in the Gallery in October.

'Please, Miss Norton. I fear prevention.'

Miss Norton frowned sharply. 'Why should you fear it?'

'He would prefer me to stay, I think. I have no independent means. I am not my own mistress. I can no longer stay here. It is impossible.'

Emily watched Miss Norton rise to her feet and go to her window. Outside the rain was still falling in sheets. 'You are not at liberty to divulge the reasons why you are afraid?'

'No.'

'Do you fear he will harm you? Hurt you in any way?'

'Only in my spirit.'

Miss Norton turned and looked at Emily with a very different expression in her eyes. She sighed

287

and neither spoke for a long full minute. She put her hand to her forehead in an unconscious careworn gesture before continuing.

'Yours is a dilemma not unfamiliar to me. I do not like to be reminded of it. I shall write for you. But I shall not conceal anything should Mr Cornford enquire after you. I detest surreptitious behaviour, unless it is absolutely necessary.'

'It is absolutely necessary,' repeated Emily.

'Then I will make the appropriate arrangements. And do not distress yourself, I shall do so with all speed.'

PART THREE

CHAPTER SIXTEEN

Emily would always remember that long journey through a haze: the cold of the boat train, starting so early in the London fog, the damp on her chest like a real thing, the pain in her lungs, the coughing. She remembered ignoring the coughing, it could not matter to her now, it could not claim her attention. Wet fields and wet cows and gungrey sky, the boat with its wheeling gulls and slurries of water on the deck and great waves beyond. She could not keep warm. And after, the change of trains at Paris with the distinctive burnt smell of the Gard du Nord, and after so much time and confusion, to reach the train she longed for, the one with the word roma emblazoned on its front like a banner, made her feel warmer, as if it could be done.

She slept deeply on the train, listening to its clanking, with French darkness around her, and woke only once in the night at the border with what looked at first like shadowy painted mountains looming out in the dim light, while the officials checked her papers with the brightness of their lanterns reflecting on the snow.

Her mind was calm. As the landscape changed before her eyes; rivers and streams and rocks to hills and pines to olives and cypresses and all those beloved unknown longed-for names—Pisa, Napoli, Firenze—flooded past, she felt she might be coming home.

It was morning again when she arrived, the last station, Roma, Italia: the goal of myriad pilgrimages, this last being her own. She thought of Augusta and the idea that this had been her city for so long, had held her golden vitality and given her so much happiness, made her spirits rise. In spite of her weakness, her clamminess and the faintness in her head, the taste in her mouth was sweet.

It was raining outside the station and she wanted to laugh at her own dreams: in her imagination the Roman sky was for ever like the Titian in the National Gallery when she had first seen Firle, and the ground a carpet of flowers. But this was November. It was winter here, too.

She had no time to gain any impression but of rain and red rooftops and a seemingly vast piazza before being approached by a small plump figure, dressed plainly and wearing spectacles.

'Miss Hudson?' The lady looked up at her, like a respectable maiden aunt, but brusque in her manner, with untidy hair and an air of self-importance that was not without charm. She wore stout boots and carried an umbrella. 'It is Miss Hudson, is it not?'

'Yes. Yes, indeed. How do you do?'

'I am Miss Drake. Miss Catherine Constance Drake.' She pronounced her name with amusement as if it did not belong to her.

'I am Emily.'

'I know. Miss Norton told me that in her letter.' Emily wondered how—with an introduction so awkward—the rest of their discourse would proceed.

'I can hardly believe I am arrived at last. It is good of you to come and meet me.'

Miss Drake did not reply to this, glancing around

her as if looking for something. 'I shall arrange for your trunk to be sent on, and we shall walk. Where is it?'

'I did not pack a trunk. I have left most of my clothes in London. They did not really belong to me.'

'You have come with nothing?'

'Only a small suitcase. And my portfolio, of course.' She indicated them at her feet.

'They shall carry those, then. We can hardly be expected to. Have you an umbrella?'

'No.'

'Then you shall share mine.'

Her companion pronounced Emily so pale that she insisted they stop for breakfast in the square. In the darkened interior, among the leather booths, Emily had her first taste of Italian coffee and brioche with sugar on top.

'This is so delicious!' she exclaimed, with her mouth full, like a child.

'Everything is delicious here. It is the way they are,' said Miss Drake. She put her head on one side. 'Are you well enough to walk? Miss Norton wrote that you have been suffering from a cough.' Her look was intrusive, but not unkind.

Emily could have opened her mouth and said, I am suffering from the consumption; so little is known about it that I might recover, die within months, or I might give it to you. (She would have added, of course, that she always took great care not to breathe too closely upon any companion for fear of such contagion.) But she could not do it. She could not arrive an invalid in Rome.

'I have been suffering from quite a severe chill. I must admit I have had a fever and am rather weak

293

with a cough. It may take a few days to recover fully.'

'You require sunlight. My studio has plenty of that. Shall we go?'

Miss Drake rattled her cup and tapped her spoon and wiped her mouth in a way that Emily had been told never to do. She quite liked it.

They walked together in close proximity under the umbrella, which Emily carried as she was the taller, and that is how Emily was first introduced to the wonder of Rome: walking as if waking out of her dream and into another so extraordinary she had no words in her head to describe it.

'How do you live every day with such beauty, such grandeur, such history?'

'Very happily,' said Miss Drake. 'Very happily indeed.'

William Cornford, Esq   c/o Poste Restante, Rome
Carlton Club, SW

December 1st, 1862

Dear Cousin,

I hardly know how to begin this letter. Firstly, I must apologise for quitting London in such a hurry and without bidding you goodbye. I was afraid you might not have let me go, nor afforded me the means, and now I see that in your eyes it may very well be for the best that I have gone. I am sorry that I appropriated your funds in what can only be described as an underhand manner. My judgement, I fear, was

294

clouded by excessive emotion, as I am sure you will say is the case always where I am concerned.

I can only say again that I am sorry we quarrelled so violently. I try not to brood over it and hope you will do the same.

Again I am sorry that I took money for the purposes of my journey without your knowledge. I shall find a means of employment and repay you, to the last farthing.

I am at Rome, staying in the apartments of a respectable connection of Miss Norton. I am safe. I am tolerably well. I cannot imagine that you should need or desire to know my address, but at present I feel I must withhold it. If you care to write to me, please do so at the *Poste Restante*.

I am convinced that I must somehow attempt to forge my own way and that this is the place where I shall either succeed or fail.

With love, as ever,

Emily

*   *   *

'Why are you crying over a letter?'

Miss Drake stood in Emily's doorway. Her rooms were on the first floor of a crumbling pink palazzo in the foothills overlooking the city. She had given Emily a small spare room for her bedchamber, but it had a beautiful window and a door opened on to the loggia, where Emily knew that in the warmer weather she would sit and gaze and be peaceful. She had a little iron bedstead and a washstand.

'We must find somewhere for you to hang what remain of your clothes,' Miss Drake had said.

The main room, also opening on to the loggia via three sets of French windows, was used as a studio: Miss Drake slept in a curtained-off recess in the corner. It was piled with canvases and paper and art materials of every description, neatly organised and stacked. The floor was of red tile. Miss Drake was frequently barefoot even in cold weather, and the colour came off on her feet. She wore no corset and her clothing was loose-fitting and what Caroline would describe as frumpy. She often covered her whole dowdy ensemble with a large apron to protect it from the paint. Emily had never seen any female person like her before.

'It is to my cousin. I left without saying goodbye. It is the first time I have deceived anyone in my life.'

'In my opinion one is usually driven to it,' said Miss Drake.

Mrs R W Harper   Rome
Hotel Splendide, Vienna

December 7th

Sweetest Augusta,

It may come as a surprise to you that I am all of a sudden arrived at Rome, having decided that a change of air and society would be very beneficial after the many inconveniences of London. So many journeys—we are both wandering souls it seems! And yes, before you

296

shake your head, it is true that I am being evasive, but it is also true that I am under the protection of a thoroughly respectable if unmarried lady. She is proof that even a lone female can become respectable quite easily, providing she is no longer young and no gentleman is interested in making love to her.

Miss Drake is originally from Pennsylvania, but has lived at Rome these ten years. On reflection, you may have heard of her, although sadly she has not heard so much as a whisper of you. (Unsurprising, considering the very different circles in which you must have moved.) She is an artist. Occasionally she travels to Venice for the light, and to Florence purely for Florence. She is far more disciplined than I make out; I fear my thoughts are fluttering and I am unable to put her into words satisfactorily. I am still most terribly tired after the journey.

She runs a studio here that caters principally to young Americans, although all nationalities frequent it: young people embarking on their grand tour, overwhelmed by their own ignorance and the city's beauty, longing for structure and tasks to which to apply themselves—individuals not so different to myself, in other words. She teaches class in drawing and painting, gives lectures, arranges tours of the antiquities. I declare she is an authority on every subject connected to Rome. I have yet to see her caught out on a single point. And this living museum, or city of memorials to the dead, somehow feels contained when she constructs her thoughts around it.

Indeed I must admit to a certain relief that we are in the hills and not among the throng of moving and disturbing beauty—I think it would overwhelm me quite, and as I said, I am very tired. What I have seen of the city has been from a carriage where I have been wrapped up, and Miss Drake instructs the driver about the correct route in perfect Italian.

In addition to this very busy life, Miss Drake is also dedicated to producing work of her own; what I have seen of it is very fine, and an inspiration. Her technique is excellent, her style her own. At present she is painting me on a *chaise longue* with drapery. It is a source of great amusement, but she says it is necessary to keep me still and I must remain still for the time being, so I obey. She is easy to obey.

Miss Drake's servant, Anna, completes the household; she has a fine little boy of ten, Paulo, and together they cook in the evenings and we light a fire. It is extremely convivial, the supper so simple and delicious, the hot pasta and the pungent sauce and the home-baked bread.

I am determined to seek a means of employment, but Miss Drake assures me that time is measured quite differently here and that I must not exert myself prematurely. She has a habit of scrutinising me that I find disconcerting but not uncomfortable. I am sure she thinks I am suffering from a broken heart. When that is mended (in her opinion) she can unloose me upon the world! Then I can begin to explore Rome as I would wish.

As for you, married lady, is it to be Christmas among the Viennese?

I send you so much love,

Emily

Miss Caroline Trelawney   Rome
Grosvenor Square, SW

December 10th

My dear Caroline,

I admit to feeling extremely embarrassed to be writing to you and wonder if perhaps you might not invite the correspondence, having no doubt learned the sudden circumstances of my departure from my cousin, a departure that became expedient for reasons I feel I cannot wholly confide to you on paper.

If I have caused you pain or embarrassment I apologise unreservedly. I am so grateful to you for your friendship—more than that, your nursing—and time spent in your company, even the most difficult, always holds a glow in my mind. But my life in London—as I am sure you had eyes to see—simply became untenable. I long for an afternoon of conversation with you to explain, and at the same time I do not, partly because of your English reserve and partly because I sense you already know more than you might say.

Here at Rome I am resting after a long journey in the care of a thoroughly decent connection of the principal at my school. She is very well established in the city, and although at present I am somewhat dependent on her hospitality I am looking forward to the day when I can make some real contribution to her *ménage*.

Please write to me of your aunt's health, of your brother's, and more importantly, of your own—and, of course, your spirits.

I miss you and keenly hope you are not regretting our friendship.

Affectionately,

Emily

Miss Mary Cornford   c/o Poste Restante
Cornford House   Rome
——— Square
Boston, Mass

December 11th

My dear Mary,

I do not know how much your brother would have made known to you about my whereabouts, but I feel I must tell you that I have removed to Rome where I find myself quite safe and well looked after.

Relations between William and myself had, I am afraid to say, deteriorated to such a degree that I felt I had no choice but to take this step. As I do not wish to be the cause of any quarrel or misunderstanding between you and your brother, that is all I shall say; and may I add that in addition I hope that you and I will continue to correspond freely.

I was so very touched by—and grateful for—the shawl and mittens you sent me: they comforted me in the coldest part of the English winter. I do not even recall if I have thanked you as I should.

I shall write more anon; in the meantime, tell me how you do.

Affectionately,

Emily

*   *   *

'When you set out upon a picture, what are you hoping to achieve?'

Emily and Miss Drake sat close to the fire in the huge draughty studio, black night around them and city lights in the distance.

'A glimpse of life,' said Emily, drawing up her knees and hugging them with her arms.

'Life as it is? Should be? Never was?'

Emily smiled as if at a memory. 'The beauty of it.'

'The beauty of what, my dear young lady?'

'The way the light falls upon a woman's face, or a flower—or even a crumb upon the tablecloth.'

'Only a glimpse, you say?'

'A glimpse of perfection. I do not think it is possible ever to gain more.'

'Indeed.' Miss Drake's wry tone was nonetheless encouraging and she studied Emily openly.

'And at the risk of sounding morbid, in the world

301

there is so much pain and confusion, I long to show that there is always beauty to be contemplated, grasped, if only for an instant—'

'Always beauty? Is it to be found everywhere?'

'No. You are right to correct me. Indeed it is not. But is not the purpose of Art to uplift the soul, through the senses?'

Miss Drake laughed, a gruff, snorting sound. 'Thousands before you have held to that truth. I dare say it is what we all believe or we would not strive at it so.'

'Art is the only permanent thing to hold on to, is it not? The only illumination? The only record that we have lived?'

'Quite so, young lady. Now it is late and time for you to go to bed. You look pale and wan and it is absolutely my fault for keeping you up. I have left an extra blanket on your chair, should you require it.'

*   *   *

Emily's lungs were sore and she had bled since coming to Rome. There were no miracles to crown her pilgrimage. But she hoped the haemorrhages were sufficiently small for her to be able to conceal them from Anna and Miss Drake. She washed out her stained linen herself at her washstand, and if it were too besmirched, disposed of it discreetly when no one was looking. She began to nurture a sustaining hope of improvement, if not recovery. In a little under a fortnight she had come to fear her condition less.

Miss Emily Hudson   Carlton Club, SW
c/o Poste Restante, Rome

December 15th, 1862

Dear Cousin,

I write to acknowledge my receipt of your
recent letter.

I find I must ask you to return the money by
which you have funded this latest rash journey.
I cannot be seen to endorse financially or
otherwise your stay in a house and with a
person unknown to me.

Regarding your (somewhat petty novelette-
ish) concern about maintaining the secrecy of
your address, you may rest assured that as you
have seen fit to act entirely without my
guidance, advice or friendship, I seek no
renewal of our intimacy, correspondence, or
any other form of intercourse.

I remain, yours truly etc.,

William Cornford

*   *   *

'What—more tears over a letter?' said Miss Drake,
coming upon Emily huddled in a draughty corner
of the studio among the unfinished canvases.

'It is my cousin. He is very angry. And he places
me in a difficult position—financially.'

'Allow me to read it.'

Taking the letter from her hand without waiting
for an agreement, Miss Drake perused it quickly;

when she had finished folding it and saying coolly, 'He is fond of words, if only to disguise his own feeling. It is quite clear what must be done. I shall lend you the money and you shall work for me. You certainly seem strong enough after a month here—almost healthy in fact.'

'But what shall I do?'

'Aid me in supervising my classes. The young ladies in especial do tend to giggle so. Model for my students and for me—if it does not offend you. Put your brain to work on my books. In addition, there is always research to be done. Employ yourself. A person must work. It is the greatest discipline, the cure for all ills, bar the most acute, of course.'

They sat side by side and Emily was grateful not to be forced to look into her companion's eyes at the mention of illness.

'But Miss Drake—'

'And in return, you shall have board and lodging. You need no longer be a guest. That should please you.' The lady paused, allowing herself a tiny, beady glance at her new friend, 'And perhaps a small allowance will be included.'

Emily saw clearly that she was exchanging one dependency for another, but this was a fairer, more honest pact than any she had made with her cousin.

'I gratefully accept!' she burst out, somewhere between a laugh and a cry.

William Cornford Esq   Rome
Carlton Club, SW

December 21st, 1862

Dear William,

    I write, as you can see, enclosing a banker's draft for the full amount I had occasion to borrow from you.
    While I continue to hope you understand that I did not intend to injure you, nonetheless I remain well aware that I did not behave honestly—and for that again, I am sorry.
    I shall not seek a renewal of our intercourse unless I hear from you to the contrary.
    Should you have occasion to visit Rome I would of course be pleased to receive you.
    Yours truly,

    Emily Hudson

Emily was forced to cross out the last line, because she could not convince herself that it was at all true.

Mrs R W Harper   Palazzo
Hotel Splendide, Vienna   Rome

January 1st, 1863

Dear Augusta,

    The turn of the year and life moves on apace. I am delighted that your first married

Christmas has been so delightful in Vienna. It seems you cannot tire of amusement, and that is how it should be for newly-weds in my opinion. I am at pains to imagine, however, that any Viennese cake could rival an Italian concoction!

Regarding your letter's many questions concerning my abrupt departure from London, I am sorry to say that I cannot at present be more specific even to dearest you, not until we meet again. Forgive me. Try to understand that I had no cause I can explain in writing and do not worry for me. That is all I can say. (For your part I sense a hankering in your letter for a return to your adopted city. I can only encourage this in you, as my longing to see you is as strong as ever.)

I have had occasion to visit many of the sights of Rome in the company of Miss Drake and her students. Whether observed in solitude or in a small or large group, the eternal city never ceases to amaze. Miss Drake says that the weather gives it an austerity it will shake off in the spring and summer, but I find that hard to imagine: a piece such as the Ecstasy of St Teresa or the grandeur and wild joy of the fountains in the Piazza Navona appear entirely undimmed by rain, wind or dull skies. The idea that light could make them more exuberant even than they are at present is hard to conceive.

I simply love it here. Every day I wake up in my peculiar little iron bed, in my barely furnished room, and I understand what made you so ardently happy. It is not a contentment I feel, but a deep joy.

Neither am I short of convivial company. The young ladies and gentlemen who come to the studio share my awe about Rome, and if they do not appear to notice it and are vulgar or brash, I find that amusing, although—I hasten to add—not (I think) in a cruel way. After all, they are young and feel the joys and pain of youth as I do, and so we are connected—although I must admit that I feel a great deal older than they.

When we have our expeditions through the city and pass a crumbling column by the side of the road, abandoned-seeming, unattended, and so beautiful and so old, it always makes me want either to laugh or cry.

And when I see the French troops (here for our protection as I am sure you remember), all I can think of is how favoured they have been to be quartered in this place. This European war does not seem half so real to me as the one at home—partly, I think, because I am still young and frivolous enough to feel the detachment of a foreigner, and one who has not a single loved one connected to it, and partly because of the feeling of utter impregnability this ancient city has to the trivial quarrels of our time. That is what gives Europeans their arrogance, I think, the mere fact of their centuries of survival—an arrogance so different from our own, which concerns itself with proving that we have a right to exist at all. The sight of the soldiers, however, cannot but remind me of the barbaric war we have left behind.

I wish you had had occasion to meet Captain Lindsay. I find I cannot wholly forget him, and hope passionately that he has been spared without daring to discover it for certain. I have tried to put the ocean of distance and time between my past self and his—but even so, he will rise up to meet me at the most unforeseen moments and there is no advantage to be had from the memory, therefore even if I cannot excise it quite, I must endeavour to try. It is simply that there seems so much left unsaid, and only this blankness remaining.

Back in this time and place, there are so many impressions. The poverty I witness—the women begging at the gates of churches with their ragged children—is both horrifying and pitiable: that you must also remember. The crowds of *beau monde* I occasionally see or hear from a passing carriage seem blissfully far removed from anything that concerns me.

I have started working again. That fact makes me feel clean and whole and as if my struggles have not been entirely in vain. It is only a little study of Anna and her son Paulo, but I am drawing them in the kitchen preparing our lunch. When it is warmer I shall put them on the loggia and attempt to convey the light and colour around and through them, and so I am impatient for the summer to come.

You would not recognise me. I have put aside my corset (it is much easier to breathe) and I own only one or two work dresses and one for best, just like Miss Drake. I still put up my hair, of course, but it is far lower on my neck, easier to pin for myself. It is such a relief no longer having to care how I present myself to the world. I do not trouble myself very much with a looking glass.

My dear Girl, forgive this endless, trivial letter. I fear it is inconsequential. Perhaps all calm and near-content sounds essentially frivolous, I do not know.

Do give me news of your adventures.

How do you do?

Affectionately as ever,

Emily

Miss Emily Hudson   Trelawney House
c/o Poste Restante, Rome   Richmond, Surrey

January 5th, 1863

My dear Emily,

So here we have all been, your English friends, beside ourselves with worry for your safety and state of mind, when on a sudden you write to me of this Nirvana you have come upon. I own I do not think it sounds comfortable in the least, but you are a romantic—this I know—and you have found the right spot for it in Europe.

All I ask of you is that should the city appear threatened in the least by this so called unification that you will quit it; and secondly, and perhaps more importantly, that you will try not to quarrel with your new-found saviour. That would be most unfortunate. Needless to

say you are finding my tone scolding—and I
admit it is partly because I have been so sick
with fright on your account and William would
tell me nothing but that you had 'Gone to
Rome for your health.' He looked so
thunderous at this announcement that I did
not dare ask him anything further. I must say
he can be very intimidating for one so young,
and for a person who gives an impression of
such outward fragility.

I have an idea that I will see less of him now
that you are gone. Thomas continues to
mention him, for they meet at the Club and
share a bond that is quite independent.

My life here, so long taken up with nursing,
then with funeral arrangements, and more
recently with the usual confusion about the
estate, is beginning to settle back to its familiar
pattern.

I have removed to Richmond and am
resolved to remain here for the time being:
London is quiet and rather dreary at this time
of year. Everyone of consequence is still away.

I wonder when I shall see you again.

Now that you have affronted your destiny
with such daring my advice about conduct will,
I am sure, go unheeded. But please, do not
neglect your health or squander your virtue.

Affectionately as ever,

Caroline

Miss Caroline Trelawney　　　　Palazzo
Trelawney House, Richmon　　　　Rome

January 15th, 1863

Dear Caroline,

   Your last letter sounded not a little
melancholy and I detect bitterness in your
tone. I hope your disapproval, though well
deserved, is waning.
   I am sorry. Your advice is sound.
   Visit me. I can think of nothing better.
   Only the best hotel for you—of course.
   With love as ever,

   Emily

Miss Emily Hudson　　　　Trelawney House,
Palazzo —————, Roma　　Richmond, Surrey

January 31st, 1863

My dear Emily,

   You are incorrigible. My scolding inspires
only silliness and levity in you! But the tone of
your letter made me laugh, once I had
recovered from the irritation.
   I am disinclined to make any journey
whatever—especially in February!
   I shall visit you, when the time is right.

In the meantime keep me apprised of your doings and your health. Do not neglect it. To ignore the dangers we have both witnessed, dearest friend, would be folly of the surest kind.

Affectionately,

Caroline

Miss Emily Hudson   Boston
c/o Poste Restante, Rome
January 13th, 1863

Dear Cousin Emily,

Rest assured that I am relieved to hear that you are at Rome, where I understand the climate is more favourable to your condition than the famous damp English weather.

Your adventure sounds extremely romantic, but I would be deceitful if I were to say that I did not concern myself as to your well-being.

Even though my brothers were both amongst us, Christmas in Boston was quiet and sad—this war, you see.

Affectionately,

Mary

Miss Mary Cornford   c/o Poste Restante,
                        Rome

Cornford House,
Boston, Mass

February 8th, 1863

My dear Mary,

Thank you for your kind letter. You express yourself with a delicacy I fear I cannot match.

I remember that this time last year we occupied the same house in Boston and indeed had experience of many of the same vicissitudes. Here I am, once again among virtual strangers, but I am fortunate enough to be being received with all kindness.

You do not mention it but I trust you are in tolerable health and spirits? Please write further when you have the opportunity. I am quite quiet at present and have a peculiar sensation of waiting, as if something—at present unidentifiable—is about to happen.

With love,

Emily

CHAPTER SEVENTEEN

It was May and with the coming of spring, the wildflowers and the warm weather, Miss Drake and Emily made an expedition into the Campagna. A pony and trap were procured, driven by Anna's brother, and a rocky meadow close to a pile of picturesque ruins with a view of the city was found with little difficulty.

'This is my favourite pursuit at this time of year. I have refined my approach to an art,' said Miss Drake. 'In the early years I would bring too much, in the middle years too little, but now I have just the right amount of luggage to supply our needs for the day.'

'You have a reassuringly practical mind.'

'Let us sit upon the ground, it is by far the most pleasurable way to enjoy the countryside.'

Emily could not help but think of William, and his loathing of sitting on the sand dunes at Newport. In their loose clothing, with their parasols propped among rough stones and their rug spread out with perfect smoothness beneath them on the dry earth (Miss Drake could not abide wrinkles), they sketched in companionable silence for the morning, breaking off only to find a stream in which to cool their hands and throats.

'I love the wildflowers. The haze of them,' said Emily.

'It will turn to yellow very quickly.'

'It has a golden quality even now.'

'Yes. And the reds, and the speedwell blues.'

'I must bring my easel and paint in the open air,' said Emily, narrowing her eyes at the distant sky, blue and promising the heat of the summer to come.

'The light would change. You would not be able to control it.'

'No matter, I would try to remember it. Work it out later at the studio.'

'It could certainly be done. Cumbersome, but

possible.'

'If I chose a place nearer the palazzo, I could walk to it every day.'

'You are too impatient. Concentrate on what you are doing now.'

It was strange that Emily did not object to Miss Drake telling her what to do—because she understood.

They ate their lunch of bread and meats and cheese, the first tomatoes and cherries, and they drank the lemonade that Anna had made them that morning. Miss Drake had a keen appetite and Emily loved eating with her because they could be greedy and not speak.

'It is strange to think I have done this alone these past ten years,' said Miss Drake. 'And now it seems quite comfortable to be lunching and working with you.' Miss Drake did not usually speak about herself, but on this occasion did not appear embarrassed, even though she did not look at Emily.

Emily glanced at her friend's profile, so solid and determined. 'Will you stay always here at Rome?'

'It is my home. One cannot turn back and leave aside all that one has come to know, exchange it for—'

'For what?'

'That kind of new darkness they mistake for bright dawn, our countrymen and women.'

Emily tore off a piece of grass and began to examine it, listening.

'Not that one is treated with any great understanding here. The Italians think I am eccentric—everyone does. But at least I can live and work unmolested according to my own lights.'

'What of your family?'

'I am an only child and, like yours, my parents are dead. When it became clear that I would never marry I became—restless, and I began to think of what I could do. I have a little money. I had always travelled. When I reached Rome it came to me that I could not be anywhere else.'

Emily smiled. 'Do you not tire of being brought to think of God and passionate human love, death and sacrifice so continually?'

Miss Drake turned to face Emily and look at her full in the eyes. 'It is better than to be turned to stone. When I have longings of the heart, or am brought low, I work, that is what I do.'

Emily fought tears that surprised her by coming into her eyes, dropping her head so that they could not be seen. She could hear the sound of the tethered horse snatching at the grass beneath the trees, of children playing in the distance—they must have come out of school—and the tinkle of harness when the horse's back shivered away a fly.

'I was indisposed for quite a long time one winter,' Miss Drake continued, 'and I discovered the habit of learning a poem every day. It was a great discipline. I had to keep to my bed and was frustrated. But at the end of every day when I could no longer point to a sketch that I had made, or a paper I had written for my students—for I was obliged to close my studio—I at least knew that I had learned a poem.'

'A—friend gave me a book of poetry when I was ill once.'

'Indeed?'

'I have not opened it.'

Miss Drake laughed, sharply. 'You are in a

316

position to choose not to accept gifts?'

'I did not think of it.'

'The young are very peculiar,' observed her friend. 'What was the book?'

'It was Mrs Browning's *Sonnets from the Portuguese*.'

'Ah.'

Emily laughed. 'What does that signify?'

'You will discover it. You could read one each day even if you did not learn them. It would be good for you.'

'The gentleman advised me of the same thing.'

'Wise counsel. One must increase one's stock of images, every day, in language as well as through the eyes. Neither should one be afraid to listen to advice.'

'They settled at Rome, did they not?'

'Mr and Mrs Browning? Yes, they did. I had occasion to meet them once.'

'It was my cousin who first encouraged me to read—truly to read and think,' said Emily, with a sudden stab of wistfulness at the memory.

'He is not entirely without merit then.'

Emily began to rip her little piece of grass into infinitesimal shreds.

'Do you think you will remain at Rome?' Miss Drake asked.

She shivered. 'I do not know.' The cloudless day, the warm meadow, seemed infinitely more precious at the mere idea of their precariousness. 'I shall work, I shall see, and I shall discover.'

'In time you will desire your own establishment. But understand that you are always welcome to share mine.'

Emily looked at Miss Drake: her thick eye-

browed, close-featured face, her air of
determination and resolve, the restraint of her
feeling, and was moved. 'I believe I am fortunate
in you.'

'Yes, my dear; I think you are.'

*   *   *

In her narrow bed that night Emily began to read
the first Sonnet from Mrs Browning's book.

I Thought Once How Theocritus Had Sung

I thought once how Theocritus had sung
Of the sweet years, the dear and wished-for
  years,
Who each one in a gracious hand appears
To bear a gift for mortals, old or young:
And, as I mused it in his antique tongue,
I saw, in gradual vision through my tears,
The sweet, sad years, the melancholy years,
Those of my own life, who by turns had flung
A shadow across me. Straightway I was 'ware,
So weeping, how a mystic Shape did move
Behind me, and drew me backward by the hair;
And a voice said in mastery, while I strove, —
'Guess now who holds thee?'— 'Death,' I said.
  But there,
The silver answer rang, 'Not Death, but Love.'

*   *   *

The days continued warmer, and in her brooding
heart Emily began to ponder over the past and her
treatment of her cousin. Had she been cruel and

318

unthinking, unheeding of his feeling of her? Might the outcome between them have been different if she had deprived herself of her selfishness? Had he not loved her sufficiently tenderly (she could think of no other word now that he was no longer present to shrink from it) to devote himself to her keeping, deliver her from his father, from the bonds that had chafed her so terribly? Did he not pay for her to live, to go to school, to pursue her every ambition? Had he not introduced her to Caroline, the chaperone in every sense most suited to lead her into English society? Had he not found a house for her for the summer, sensible of her love for the sea? And she had thwarted him with her conduct and behaviour, embarrassed him with her dalliance with Lord Firle: would she not behave differently now that she was a little older and far wiser? At first she had considered herself innocent and injured. It came over her that perhaps she had been deeply at fault. She felt it keenly.

And at night-time with her candle and poetry book, the passionate love that Elizabeth Browning felt for her soul's equal, her profound gratitude, this moved her, and she berated herself for never having counted gratitude among her blessings.

When she thought of Firle it was of the intoxication that his presence had always given to her—the dizzy sense of freedom at the brazenness of his intentions and invitations; but where before she had flattered herself that it was her charm that had inspired these attentions, now she wondered if it were merely her defencelessness. When she thought of Captain Lindsay it was with the old tenderness and pain, if she could bear to think of him at all; her mind and heart shied away from it. Beyond that she had a sense almost of shame. What would have become of his faith in her if he had seen how she had conducted herself with Lord Firle? The liberties she had allowed him to take?

In her moments of reflection in the studio or on the loggia, observing the sparrows in the eaves or making patterns in the sky; the vault of Rome's heavens, the roofs and spires and domes beneath, she questioned each action, each feeling, from her arrival at Newport to her flight to Rome, and could draw no other conclusion than that many of her actions, thoughts, feelings, had been the height of selfishness and folly.

At the memory of her dear mother and father she would still flinch with instinctive hard inner pain, and when that passed she could see her mother's goodness, not as the angel of their house as Mr Dickens would have her be, but as solid flesh and blood; her devotion, what she had taught about duty and work and love and truth to one's heart, and she thought that these teachings were not entirely unlike the way Miss Drake spoke and acted. She did not intrude upon Emily with questions. Every day she was kind: to Emily, to her students, to the flowers of the field, and she gave herself up to the life she had chosen with such discipline, such single-minded American zeal that Emily was put in mind of the pilgrims her friend so affected to despise. It was a tangle. It was a coil. She could not puzzle it out.

*　　　*　　　*

They were breakfasting on the loggia and it was

already warm. The bright morning sunlight defined the shadows. Emily liked feeling warm in her bones. It was as if she were being held by a divine hand.

'I notice that you no longer appear consumptive,' said Miss Drake.

Emily nearly dropped her coffee cup. They looked at one another.

'I am glad of it. I dare say you are too,' she continued, tartly. 'Do you know, I have never seen you speechless before.' She broke a brioche and covered it with thick black jam.

'I thought you had no idea! I thought I had concealed it.'

'In the first instance you are entirely transparent. In the second, consumption has a very distinctive face. In the third, it is impossible to conceal anything from me. How long since you last coughed blood? A month?'

'Six weeks.'

'You have more flesh on your bones. And you sleep better at night. I do not hear you move about as I used to.'

Emily shook her head and began to laugh, pressing the backs of her hands to her eyes to quell the water, as she always did at the first starting of tears to her eyes. 'I think it has left me. For the time being.'

'Well, let us make sure it does not come back, shall we?' smiled her friend, taking a saucer of milk to the corner of the loggia and calling for Anna's cat.

William Cornford, Esq   Palazzo ————,
Carlton Club, SW   Rome

May 30th, 1863

Dear William,

  Forgive me for writing when I had assured
you in my last letter that I would have no
occasion to.
  It is a simple thing I have to say: *mea culpa*. I
am truly sorry. Perhaps it is being surrounded
by the many candle-lit penances of Rome (I
apologise for my jest—the city has not robbed
me of an inability to be serious), but I have
come to understand that I have acted selfishly
and thoughtlessly throughout our friendship
and that I have injured you.
  You are the person to whom I owe my very
existence beyond America and I have used you
ill in return for your generosity.
  I do not expect a reply, nor ask for one, but
merely desire you to have the comfort—should
you require it—of knowing how very sorry I
am.
  With love as ever,

  Emily

Miss Caroline Trelawney   Palazzo
Grosvenor Square, SW   ——————, Rome

June 1st, 1863

My dear Caroline,

Thank you so very much for your last letter: I am delighted to hear that you are enjoying the start of the season and beginning to initiate a whole gaggle of new young ladies into the pleasures of poetry readings and suppers. Your *soirées* must be a welcome respite—for most, I would imagine—from their mammas parading them through the Park and to every party and ball imaginable in search of a husband. Or should I correct myself—it seems that in your country young ladies marry houses rather than gentlemen. Forgive the bitterness behind my observation. (Doubtless if I had had a dowry and been courted I would have been contented enough; I fear I am like those who are not blessed with beauty becoming acid-tongued about the joys of love.)

But I did not mean all this in the least—there is so much more to tell you, and I have not even begun it yet.

But before I do, let me tell you how happy I was to hear about your new puppies. It must be difficult for you to tear yourself away from them at Richmond, but presumably when they are older you shall be able to bring one or two to London to run with their parents in the Park beside your carriage. I can picture it now. And I am so touched that you should name one after me. Let us hope it proves more sweet-tempered and biddable than I!

The days are beautifully warm here and we are fortunate that the palazzo is in the hills so we do not suffer from the heat and are quite the perfect temperature.

I am feeling very well—extremely healthy, in fact. In the mornings I go for long walks and rambles in the hills before settling to work and that seems only to increase my energies.

Miss Drake and I have been working diligently on preparing an exhibition of our and our students' work. There are many difficulties: we lack sufficient hanging space in our studio, and the palazzo is quite out of the way, but that has not deterred my friend. We are striving to make the occasion a celebration of our students and all their endeavours.

The truth of the matter is that the whole occasion comes very close to being a party, or reception, what you will, because there will be invitations, refreshments, perhaps even music. (You should taste what they eat and drink here—you would die of pleasure after just one grape!) We have been so quiet these past months that I have nothing at all suitable to wear and fear I must venture into a shop or dressmaker's or disgrace myself for ever in my work clothes.

Dear friend, I am really quite excited and must take my high spirits away from the paper for fear of stabbing it too hard!

With much love,

Emily

Miss Emily Hudson   Carlton Club, SW
Palazzo ————, Rome

June 10th, 1863

Dear Emily,

   For some days I have been at a loss as to how
to reply to your letter.
   On the one hand your habit of bounding
from one feeling or attitude to another appears
to have remained intact; on the other, if I
could believe in a true change of heart in this
case, I might come to hold once more to the
idea that my faith in you was, after all, justified.
   I hope you can appreciate that my
ambivalence is well-founded.
   If you should care to continue in a
correspondence, delicately, I should not object.
   Yours truly,

   William Cornford

            *   *   *

Emily received this letter on the morning of the
exhibition when there was such a commotion of
preparation that they had hardly had time to take
breakfast. Miss Drake had risen especially early
and was already beginning the hanging in the
studio with the help of a selection of her most
favoured students. The sight of her surrounded by
this group of tall young men and women had
caused Emily great amusement over recent days.

One glance at the familiar handwriting caused a sensation of nervousness Emily had not enjoyed for some months and rather than read it on the loggia, she carried it down the small outside flight of stairs to the quiet balcony garden where plentiful pots of geraniums, a honeysuckle and an entire wall of dusty roses and plumbago competed in their beauty to give her strength. It had rained in the night, refreshing the plants, washing the view of Rome, and now the sun fell on the back of her neck and hands with reassuring warmth.

She read it quickly, and then crossing to the balustrade leaned on it, looking ahead of her with blurred eyes. Of course he would not forgive her wholeheartedly—how could she have hoped for it, let alone expected it? The barb in his words, the familiar sensation of being put in the wrong, all chafed at her. But as she thought of it, she felt that, after all, he was entitled to look at her in that way. Without thinking any further she went to her room and wrote quickly:

William Cornford, Esq   Rome
Carlton Club, SW

June 15th, 1863

Dear William,

I have only just this moment received your letter.

My apology remains, as does my affection for you, and I can understand from your words why you doubt me. All I can add is that should we ever have occasion to meet again you would not deny the sincerity of my words.

Yours truly,

Emily

Then she hurried to put away the letter and join her friend.

Miss Caroline Trelawney   Rome
Grosvenor Square, SW

June 15th, 1863

My dear Caroline,

Today quite an extraordinary thing happened.

Anxious to escape from the continual preparation Miss Drake was making for the evening's exhibition, and fairly shooed out of the way as I was, I went to the Villa Borghese, having not yet had the opportunity to view the collection there.

Having been not a little shocked when I first came to Rome by the extravagant and overwhelming abandon of the Ecstasy of St Teresa, I found quite a different thing in Bernini's sculpture of Daphne and Apollo. It is almost the first sight to assail the senses when one arrives.

I am sure that as a well-educated and travelled young lady you have heard of it, but allow me to indulge myself with a rhapsodic— but quite inadequate—description.

Apollo pursues Daphne—she is cold white

327

marble, yet living, Daphne—and to escape him she is changing into a tree. The fierceness of his desire, the lightness of her escape and the sense of longing and flight—you could not but imagine the beauty of it—the living tree bringing a living death to that exquisite creature!

I have seen so much in Rome, so much that has filled my eyes and senses, but nothing that has moved me so absolutely as this. She would not have him. But indeed to what does she succumb in his stead? The tendrils of the tree, the leaves, the solid imprisonment of herself?

I walked around it for a long time, quite alone. Every detail is very delicate, and poised, you see.

Rome is fond of sacrifice and sometimes I am weary of it. I had to turn away.

And here is the extraordinary thing—I bumped straight into Dr Cooper! Can you believe it? Lovely, kind Dr Cooper. I had not even heard his footsteps, I had been so absorbed. I could not have been more surprised. It seems he has been in Switzerland plotting some new sanatorium with a friend of his and now he has come to see the sights at this most unseasonable time of year. Yet I suppose a doctor must travel only in summer when nobody dares to be ill! (Come to think of it, he travels in winter too, for he also went to Switzerland then, and I did not have the opportunity to bid him farewell before quitting London.)

He was so kind, as genuinely pleased to see me as I him, I think. He remarked that I had left no address. He has been away frequently over the last months in conference with this same colleague (who obviously has far too great a call upon his time!), and he enquired after my health in a manner that was genuinely concerned without being in any way untoward. I always liked that so much about him.

He remarked that I looked in excellent health, which was a little confusing, for I did not know whether or not to confide in him, what was the appropriate course in so public a place.

He too looked extremely well, younger in a peculiar way.

I invited him to attend our exhibition tonight—goodness knows why.

Tell me how you do. The London season has so many diversions I am sure you can think of some to describe for me. How are dresses being worn this year?

I still have not heard from you.
Affectionately,

Emily

*   *   *

At first Emily was afraid no one would come. The refreshments were laid out and the musicians were ready, the students trembling next to their work. Emily had never seen Miss Drake so nervous. She snapped at her and did not appear to listen to what was being said to her. But then little by little the tiled floor began to echo with footsteps and voices, and dear friends began to arrive. Hands were

329

clasped and jokes were made. The work was admired. Musicians began to play. Evening light streamed through the long windows, and candelabra inside the studio lit the pictures in soft and moving ways, giving them a mystery and depth that daylight could not bestow. Anna and Paulo fussed and fretted over the antipasti in the kitchen and the bowl of punch that Miss Drake had insisted upon as a reminder of home. There were little dishes of strawberry granita packed in ice in the small pantry off the kitchen. Anna's brother had been drafted in to help serve.

Emily took care to stand as far away from her own work as possible because it embarrassed her so deeply; in fact she wondered why she had agreed to show any of it at all.

Dr Cooper arrived with admirable punctuality, taking Emily's hand and introducing himself to Miss Drake with all his well-remembered formality, while a feeling of his loving-kindness towards her emanated from him. It was peculiar because while she had been his patient at Marsh House Emily had barely troubled herself to imagine his life outside his care of her, and at that moment there seemed very much more to discover. She could not help but think of the volume of verse he had sent to her, now so familiar to her she could not begin to recall it or she would blush.

'Have you a painting here?' he said. 'Might you show me?'

'I have several. But they are not—'

'Good enough?' He smiled. 'Of course not. Show them to me anyway.'

Emily laughed.

'Please, take me and show me.'

She showed him the study she had made of Caroline Trelawney at Marsh House the summer before. Its colours and its tenderness moved her still, even though she was sensitive to every fault, every line she could have made better.

'That is beautiful,' he said. 'I recognise Miss Trelawney in your English Madonna.'

'Indeed, you are quite correct. But I had to invent the baby. Here in Rome it is much easier to find models—children will come with their mothers—I feel much less like a criminal simply for pursuing my work. People understand how important it is.'

'You have made your home here?'

'I suppose I have. Among the antiquities.' She gave him a slightly wry smile and wondered why on earth she had done so.

'If you should ever become restless again, the place for any artist is Paris. I was fortunate enough to spend a few days there on my way to Switzerland. So much is happening in that city, there are so many new beginnings—'

'I fear you take me much too seriously, Sir. Indeed, it would be impossible. I know no one there,' she said in some rising panic and confusion, as if she were someone who did not know how to hold a conversation. It was most peculiar.

'Of course. I had not thought.' He spoke with sympathy.

She felt clumsy to have stalled all talk of Paris, when in truth she longed to hear everything about the city: its scandals and its glamour and its austerities, the salons and the cafés and, above all, the work.

'Well, if you will excuse me, I must attend to my guests,' she said, and blundered away into the kitchen where she stood, surveying the refreshments with unseeing eyes, distracting Anna and standing in the way. She had behaved foolishly in the light of his obvious interest and admiration and could not explain it to herself.

The crowd increased and with it the roar of conversation and the heat of the room. All the pleasure she had expected to feel in the evening was thrust out of the way with the worry that the doctor would not come near her again and she would not have the opportunity to enquire after his sojourn in Rome, even if it was too public a place for her to confide anything in him about her health or how grateful she had always been to him. There were a good many things she wanted to know about him. He must think she thought only of herself. And it was not true, she was curious concerning him, and longed to question him now that he had gone away.

Within an hour he came to her again, this time accompanied by a very tall gentleman with a patrician nose and receding hair.

'Allow me to introduce you to my friend, Robert Harrington.'

'How do you do?' said the stranger. 'I understand you are an acquaintance of Dr Cooper from England?'

'Yes.' Emily was grateful for Dr Cooper's discretion about the circumstances of what could only be described as their intimacy.

Mr Harrington raised his eyebrows. 'I understand from George that you had entirely disappeared from that country, leaving no trace whatsoever.' He spoke in the English way, as if mocking his own words. George must be Dr Cooper's Christian name, she thought stupidly.

Once again, Emily found she could say nothing at all.

'We must go and dine. The crowd here is dreadful,' said Mr Harrington.

There was a very long pause and then Dr Cooper said, 'Might I have occasion to call on you before I leave the city, Miss Hudson?'

'Of course, Doctor. You will usually find me here.'

He pressed her hand, inclined his head in that charming, awkward, formal way she remembered and was gone.

CHAPTER EIGHTEEN

A week of waiting and Emily was sure Dr Cooper had gone from Rome. She was troubled by how urgently on a sudden she longed to see him, but equally sustained and exhilarated by it. She did not know why she desired it so powerfully, but was dimly aware that in thinking about him she could no longer concern herself about William—his opinion of her; how matters stood between them. There was a great deal that she wanted to ask him and tell him both, without being confident that there would ever be sufficient time, and to be ignorant of a specific, appointed meeting was jarring to her heart. She began to remember three o'clock on Thursday afternoons the summer before at Marsh House with more affection than she could have imagined possible.

Sunday morning and Anna came out on to the loggia while she and Miss Drake were finishing breakfast. 'A young gentleman is here to see you, Miss Emily,' she said.

He had come at last, and she was a little perturbed at her own unexpected dismay.

'An odd day to choose to pay a call,' said Miss Drake, slowly. 'Where would you like to receive the gentleman?'

'Outside, if it is convenient.' Emily swallowed with difficulty in an attempt to hide her nervousness.

'Perfectly. I have a little business to attend to in the studio.'

As the women stood up in the bright morning light, a figure approached, coming towards them from the shadows: for an infinitesimal second sufficiently indistinct for Emily's heart to pound uncomfortably, when she realised with a jolting shock that it was William. He was immaculately attired as ever, and she observed how his eyes took her in: the smudged blue dress, the untidy loosened hair, the colour she had allowed the sun to bring to her face, and she could feel him storing the impressions in his mind as she knew he stored every instant that he experienced.

'My dear cousin,' he said, standing still, leaning on his stick. He extended a hand but did not smile. The vision of him almost jumped before her eyes.

Emily felt a deep blush, not only of surprise but at how unwelcome the sight of him was to her, sensible that her two passionate written entreaties had come as close to summoning him as any request.

'William. I am amazed. What brings you to Rome?'

'I am fond of travel, you may recall, my dear,' he said with an air of humour and veiled meaning, before glancing at her companion.

'Allow me to present my dear friend and employer, Miss Catherine Drake.'

'How do you do?' he said, with an air of perfect mastery of the situation that Emily longed to equal, forgetting he had the advantage of surprise.

Miss Drake scrutinised William in turn in a fashion that showed she did not care whether or not she appeared indelicate. Then she said, 'I will leave you to your conversation. You must have more than sufficient to say in private. May I offer you some refreshment, Sir?'

'A glass of water would be gratefully received,' he said, without so much as a glance in the lady's direction.

As soon as she was out of earshot he continued, taking a step towards Emily, 'You have no notion of how my eyes have suffered from the lack of you.' It was the most passionate and lover-like Emily had ever heard him sound, and yet there was no youth or ardour in him. Even so, she felt that if she had moved to embrace him he would have welcomed it. But she could not. She could not move at all.

'You look as if you are enjoying perfect health and spirits,' he said, studying her, musing, wondering, his eyes still firmly fixed on her own.

'It is true, I am.' She tried to smile. 'How goes it with you, Cousin?' Her heart was beating and she had to fight an animal desire to turn and run.

He opened his mouth and began to speak, exactly as he always had; he had always been able to give a fluent account of himself, had relished the opportunity. 'My first novel is published. It is a *succès d'estime*—I think that is the chosen expression. The world at large does not clamour for copies, but the people for whom I have respect have looked upon it very favourably. I have started to receive invitations to grander houses, as a man of letters. I am certain it is because I am so kind about the English aristocracy in my book, they believe they can trust me a little.' He smiled slightly.

Emily did not feel equal to a conventional remark about how she regretted not having read the early manuscript at Marsh House due to her indisposition, fearful of evoking their quarrel and her own despair.

'You have always been entirely trustworthy, Cousin,' she observed, feeling herself shrink at the truth of this.

They sat down together at the table and William took off his gloves and leant his stick against the palazzo's stone and stucco wall: it looked incongruous there against the pink and grey. Anna brought the water; William thanked her but did not look at her. Emily smiled, swallowed, turned to William, trembling.

'Do you still make your home at your club?'

'Indeed. How otherwise would I have received your letters?'

'Of course.' She had forgotten how stupid he could invariably make her feel, with what speed he could reduce her to confusion.

'And what of the Trelawneys? How do they do?

Caroline writes but . . .' She was aware she was questioning him rapidly to avoid any confidences: she knew he knew it also and was in command.

'Your Miss Trelawney has at last decided she is an old maid and a bluestocking. It is as well. She was only ever in love with Firle, and that did nothing but cause her pain. Now she fulfils her part in society usefully and remains excellently connected.'

Emily wondered feverishly how she could ever have been so blind to this feeling in her friend but determined to say nothing. Yet she recalled Caroline's blushes whenever Firle's name was mentioned, and the awkwardness of the interview they had shared when she had been so painfully chastised for associating with him. She was convinced William offered her the information about her friend not merely as a distraction, but purely as an invitation to reveal herself. She would not take it.

'How is dear Thomas?'

'He remains a gentleman who dabbles in the literary scene. A trifle lazy. But no more than befits his talent.'

A coolness came over their silence.

'And what of London?'

'It is as stimulating as ever. But never more so than when you were there, my dear.'

She looked at his narrow face and fine eyebrows, the immaculate preparation of his fingernails, steeling herself at the memory of all their time together, and a passionate desire to escape it. She wanted him to go away. Any notion of reconciliation seemed to belong to a long-ago phantasma.

'Thank you for your letters, Emily,' he said. His eyes were veiled but his voice betrayed unusual feeling.

'My apologies were sincerely meant,' she ventured, heart beating, uselessly afraid. Never had she sounded so false and conventional, she felt, and it was ironic to her that it should be in his presence.

'And they are gratefully accepted.'

She looked away, frightened still. The power of his indistinct glance had only increased since their last meeting.

'Would you care to examine our view of Rome?' she asked, desperate to stand up, to move away. 'It is very fine.'

'Gladly.' He got to his feet slowly and followed her to the front of the loggia, Emily grasping the broad stone wall with both her hands, William allowing his to rest upon its surface with a very slight pressure.

Her throat was constricted. 'This prospect is particularly fine in the early morning sun, and on Sundays, there are so many bells—'

'Yes, that is the flaw of these Catholic countries: so bad for the nerves.'

'I find the sound of praise beautiful—if occasionally melancholy.'

'You have become religious?' he enquired, turning his head. She was unsure whether he was amused.

'Indeed, no. It is only that I cannot but be touched by others' faith.'

'How extraordinary,' he said. 'I have always feared it.'

Recalling his father, Emily wished she had not

338

spoken.

He glanced towards the open door of the studio where Miss Drake could be heard moving about within. 'How is your work? Do you have any canvases to show me?'

'No,' she said swiftly, 'nothing is finished.' Turning from her contemplation of the city to look up into his face, she saw a flicker of expression in his eyes that revealed he had not forgotten any of the circumstances of their intimacy.

'I am sorry for the pain our nearness brought,' she said quickly, more honestly and simply than before. 'Such a waste of affection—and hope.'

'Aah. Hope, too,' he said.

She observed wholly how pale he was and in the morning sun how much older and iller he seemed.

'So you would not consider a return?' he said. 'I have kept your rooms as you left them.'

She imagined her beautiful dresses still hanging in the wardrobe. 'A return?' She groped to understand.

'To the old life—yours and mine.' He paused, as if deciding whether to continue. 'I shall not marry and imagine neither shall you. We could have our own small household, travel together, work. Maintain our . . . privacy, of course.'

Instinctively she took his hand and pressed it, full of sympathetic feeling, and he looked at her with an expression of such nakedness and yearning, such childlike devotion, that she realised he understood the gesture to mean assent.

'But William, I couldn't—you must understand.' She denied his look instantly: to prolong his nakedness would have been a sin, if she believed in sin, which she did not.

He withdrew his hand and tilted his head so she could not see his face. He cleared his throat. 'It was just an idea that I had . . . entertained,' he said in a muffled voice.

'I did not know that that was how you felt.'

He looked back at her. 'My dear girl, it is not a question of feeling but of convenience,' he replied. 'You cannot stay in a single room in a draughty palazzo with a spinster for the rest of your days.'

They looked at one another with complete clarity.

'Such decisions are for myself, alone,' she replied, quite without the old passion or defiance, deprived of the anger, in perfect command of herself.

'You have not changed at all,' he said, as if remarking on the colour of the sky, but then, dropping his voice, looking away, he added in a voice almost of wonder, 'except that you are even more beautiful.'

Had he seen her then, as truly herself, for the first time? Had he ever truly seen her? Or was this reverence at one with her final denial of him? Her eyes burned with tears.

After that she felt some part of herself struggle to fulfil the social obligation of the following minutes, the retrieval of William's stick and gloves, the saying of farewells, while in her spirit she felt a grief and an understanding so great that it almost rose up to choke her. Together they crossed the studio and came out into the hall, standing beside one another beneath the portico at the great door.

She watched him climb into his carriage and be driven away, raising her hand to him, as if in salute.

Emily turned back towards the studio like a blind person groping her way through her tears; her body was overcome by sickness and grief. Miss Drake was there to meet her; her hand caught hers.

She cried, wildly, 'Oh, I have been such a fool!'

'Do not try to speak, my dear. You shall sit down with me and you shall have some brandy.' They sat side by side on the *chaise longue* where Miss Drake had first painted her, and her friend called to Anna for the brandy.

'I feel so ashamed of myself.'

'Because your cousin has tried to take you back?'

'For my vanity in ever having been swayed by him. His attention—'

'Was almost too much for a girl of your tender youth and health. But you freed yourself—you came away.'

'Merely to summon him back again. It is only that I have never known what to believe of him. He once did me a great kindness.'

'And now—'

'Now, I am sure. There is something in him that would devour me.' Emily stopped crying and remained quite still, gripping Miss Drake's hand.

'It is not your fault. I will not have you blame yourself.'

Emily shuddered, recalling Newport, the lamplit hours, their bending heads.

'In truth, there was never very much peace between us. So much of it was what I wanted to be true—not what really was—'

'Sip this brandy. Do not try to speak. Remember you are not so weak. You have always had a mind to strive for a better, wider life; he did not furnish you with it. Your friends do not require your cousin to acquaint us with your qualities, they are quite apparent to us all. To know you is sufficient.'

Miss Drake closed her other hand over Emily's. 'You must forget him. You must forget them all.'

*   *   *

In the carriage William felt not grief, but rage, a pure white rage he believed he had never experienced before. He, William Cornford, had allowed himself to be refused, abased, by this insignificant creature, so obscure until he had raised her up, so insubstantial and abandoned. What a folly it had been of his to try to make a heroine of her. He felt her careless untidy beauty, standing on that ancient loggia, as an affront to his dignity; her very existence an insult to his own.

*   *   *

Miss Emily Hudson   Berne
Palazzo —————, Rome

July, 1863

Dear Miss Hudson,

Once again I fear our meeting has been delayed by the sudden demands of my work. The colleague I spoke to you of has had occasion to call me once more to Switzerland. I

342

shall not tire you with explanations.

I intend to return to Rome before the end of the summer and look forward to calling upon you then.

In the meantime perhaps you might consider writing to me.

May I venture to say that it was a great delight to see you once again.

Yours etc.,

Dr G A Cooper

*   *   *

The warm July days had soothed Emily's spirits and Miss Drake's kind companionship distracted her from her thoughts of William. 'You must push them away, these memories, my dear. Absorb yourself only in the present,' she said.

In the spirit of their intimacy she took the letter and showed it to her friend.

'This doctor has a very quaint way of expressing himself,' she observed. 'Quite old-fashioned, as if he had learned it.' Then she paused, pursing her lips. 'I dare say it is because he is not a gentleman and is fearful of making an error that might embarrass him or harm his practice.'

'If you had spoken properly to him you would have seen he is very sincere.'

'I do not doubt it: he is a sincere and scrupulous doctor. You say he did not have occasion to keep an appointment with you before you left London? He would like that opportunity now, I should imagine—in all probability his professionalism demands it.'

343

Emily longed to say, I think his feeling for me might be distinct from that—indeed I hope that it might be—before realising she had not the slightest foundation for this thought and wondering if William had indeed been right: she merely flitted from feeling to feeling, loyalty to loyalty, and had no anchor of any kind.

'Would it be indecorous to reply?'

'My dear Emily, are you looking so soon for another deliverer?' Miss Drake looked as strict as if she were dealing with a wayward pupil.

Emily felt so frustrated she was nearly in tears and longed for Augusta. Her companion's expression softened.

'What is in your heart, my dear? Forgive me for asking.'

'I am no nearer to understanding the world than when I was a child!'

Miss Drake said nothing while Emily composed herself. 'But what of this doctor? Are you sure of his wishes? Of yours?'

'*No!*' Emily burst out again. 'I am sure of nothing.'

'Then you must do nothing, my dear. Wait for the answer to come.'

Mrs R W Harper   Rome
Hotel Splendide, Vienna

August, 1863

Sweetest Augusta,

I write on immediate receipt of your letter. Never have there been such glad tidings!! That you are with child is the most delightful, glorious, bright thing to happen in so very very long! I can hardly write but must splutter on to the page!

I understand fully now why you have been quiet for some little time, because of course one must not announce these things before they seem a certainty. I am so gratified to hear that you have had but little sickness and that your appetite is returning. You are perfectly placed, with an excellent doctor, and a thoroughly sensible husband who can tell you not to fuss, to rest every day, etc. On second thoughts I imagine Mr Harper will be more likely to fuss than you will. In my experience, women in your condition are apt to be remarkably calm.

Oh, my darling girl—I long and long to see you, how could you doubt it? But are you certain that it is wise to attempt the journey from Vienna in the heat of the summer and in your condition? Of course if the doctor and your husband should allow it, I can only add that they must have good reason, and if this is the optimum time, I understand that too. I utterly sympathise with your yearning to spend your confinement in Rome; after all, it is where you met your esteemed husband and were so very happy for so long. But do give the move careful consideration, dearest friend.

I hope you will not take it amiss that I am being so terribly interfering, when really it is not at all my place. You are a grand married lady now—no longer my best friend at school—and I must admit to a feeling of sudden nervousness at the prospect of seeing you again. After all it has been over two years. What should befall us if—despite our happy memories of one another—we find that we have simply outgrown our intimacy, or even interest to each other? I know I should not say this, but no doubt you remember I have always had the unfortunate habit of saying or writing whatever comes into my head at any given moment.

I am so glad—also for your sake—that Mr Harper is the kind of fellow who writes treatises and publishes articles and so can afford to indulge you and take you to any city that you care to settle in without fear of abandoning his work. It is delightful to have that freedom and independence.

Oh, my dearest friend. I recall you in your girlish beauty as if it were yesterday that I held you in my eyes and arms. I long to see you blooming and matronly before another season has passed.

I will, with all speed, make enquiries about lodgings for you.

Please give my regards to your Mr Harper and all my love to your dear self.

Emily

Miss Drake pursed her lips when Emily said that Augusta was shortly to be returning to the city, and with child. 'How disruptive,' was all she said.

Miss Emily Hudson   Switzerland
Palazzo ————, Rome

July 23rd, 1863

Dear Miss Hudson,

I hope you have had occasion to receive my last letter. Time hangs heavy here in the evenings, and so I trust you will not object to my writing you another.

I thought I would tell you a little about my work. A dear friend and colleague has recently established a sanatorium for consumption here in the mountains, believing that the purity of the air can have a very beneficial effect on the condition. I was fortunate enough to advise him on its beginnings and am usefully employed in monitoring its progress with a view to beginning on plans for another. Indeed I have had occasion to refer one or two of my London patients here already.

I must tell you that the speed of progress has been remarkably good. The prevailing belief in the medicinal qualities of mountain air has been borne out by some remarkable improvements—even in a few cases, cures— and there is nothing more rewarding for a doctor than to see his patients thrive, particularly when they are subject to a condition so frequently difficult to defeat.

My colleague would like me to spend several weeks here every summer in order to continue to conduct my tests and observation, and I own to being tempted—especially if my visit can be combined with other, perhaps more stimulating, destinations.

But I bore you, I fear.

The trouble with my life's work is that, while sustaining me, it can weary others, although I hope I am not too presumptuous in attesting to your personal interest in this matter.

The sunsets and the quality of the light here are quite spectacular; of great interest to any artist, I would imagine. I think you would be favourably impressed.

Please write to me from Rome, if you are so inclined.

Yours truly,

Dr G A Cooper

Dr G A Cooper   Palazzo —————, Rome
————— Switzerland

July, 1863

Dear Dr Cooper,

Your letter was gratefully received; your work does not sound tedious in the least. I think you are too modest and in truth are blessed with the energy and zeal of a pioneer in your field. I admire that.

Rome swelters in the heat. I am as peaceful as I can be, awaiting the joyous arrival of a dear friend from whom I have been separated these two years.

I have abandoned my work in this extreme weather and become quite idle.

I read and eat fruit and dream far too much.

By all means call on your return to Rome.

Yours truly,

Emily Hudson

*   *   *

In her dream Emily was beside Captain Lindsay in a trench filled with water and blood. He did not know she was there. Mud splattered his face and his hands were bare and raw on his gun. She wanted to ask him what had become of his horse but she could not speak. She could not even convince him of her presence as she laid her hand upon his arm to stay him as he raised his gun.

She woke in cold sweat and shivered until she remembered where she was—the warm climate of Rome enveloping her, the smells and sounds of safety. Lighting her candle she crossed swiftly to her night table and wrote:

Miss Mary Cornford   Rome
Bluff House
Newport, R I

July, 1863

My dear Mary,

Your last kind letter was most welcome, thank you, and the details of your existence not in the least mundane. I am delighted that Matthew's leg wound continues to heal well, and that his spirits are good.

I expect that Newport feels a little dull after your season in Boston, but I am only glad that you have been in sufficient health and spirits to enjoy your time there, despite the anxiety and pain caused by this cruel war.

While mourning the calamitous loss of life in this recent push to the South, I am relieved to hear that under General ——— the Union appears at last set to prevail. I can only hope that the Confederacy will surrender at the earliest opportunity and therefore end the bloodshed that insults the sacrifice of our young men on both sides. It seems all words I can write upon the subject must appear both useless and empty, but let me assure you they are sincerely meant.

There is one question that has been burning in my mind despite the distance in miles and years since our last meeting, and which I feel a little awkward about enquiring over: the fate of our dear Captain Lindsay. While no soul is safe until the end of this war I feel I must know now something of how it has treated him. If he is alive—God willing—I should like to write to him, and any intelligence about his whereabouts would be greatly appreciated.

Here in Rome the heat increases daily, and we prepare to close the school for the summer. I had not anticipated idleness and must redirect my energies into beginning a new work, something painted outdoors. But I long for the sea. I think I will always long for it—or

indeed, always long for something!
    Affectionately,

    Emily

She had never couched an urgent request in such
evasive and formal terms.

Miss Emily Hudson   ——— Squadron
Palazzo ———————, Rome

August, 1863

My dear Miss Hudson,

    It is no use—I must call you Emily. I hope
that does not disconcert you—any more than
receiving a letter from me after so long might. I
have been visiting your cousins while on brief
leave at Newport not a week ago, and Miss
Cornford took the opportunity to confide in
me that you had been good enough to enquire
after me in your last letter. I am delighted to
hear that you are in good health, well settled at
Rome and pursuing the subject closest to your
heart.
    I must admit that I credit you with greater
bravery in asking after me than I have shown
where you are concerned. I have thought of
you many times without saying a word to a
single soul, and now that I am at last writing to
you it feels not at all as if it were real.
    The shore at Newport appeared especially
deserted without you. Indeed I half expected to
see you coming towards me from the sea in the

dazzling light—the strain of this war has made me rather fanciful, I am afraid.

I write to you (from an undisclosed place) on the eve of yet more bloodshed. Yet I am fortunate enough still to be in excellent health, if weary. Some charm seems to be protecting me: bar minor wounds I have survived the war remarkably intact. But thoughts of mortality are ever closer and after a long struggle with myself I have come to the conclusion that there are several things I must say to you.

First, and most importantly, you must know that it was your cousin, William, who revealed your illness to me, warned me of it and advised me in the very strongest terms not to promise myself to you. I believe that as you have always been to one degree or other in his power you should know this. I would not like to be killed without you having had the opportunity to understand what took place at so crucial a juncture of your destiny, just as I could not continue to fight without assuring you of my regard once again, and making it clear to you that while your cousin may have altered events, he has not altered my feeling for you.

Time may have altered many things, but not the high esteem and tenderness in which I have always held you. I should never have told you a word of William's letter, but I was younger and not the sturdy fellow I have become. You would hardly know me.

It is only because our human life is so short and so precarious that I have decided to write these—I hope not unwelcome—words. If they are unwelcome, forgive me for them, and for the wrong I did you all that time ago.

Should the war end and I survive it, I shall write to you once again. Please rest assured that I understand how much circumstances can change, and that you are under no obligation to me, ever were, or ever shall be.

I write this above all because you are entitled to see clearly your situation as it was then, as it is now. This may well be my last and only gift to you.

Yours truly,

Major J C H Lindsay

The letter induced in Emily a torrent of tears. She read it in the warmth of the balcony but had to put it away from herself in her pocket for fear of soaking it entirely. There are some griefs for another—equal to one's own—that cannot be quelled, and when she thought of him and how they had longed for one another and how very young they had been that Boston winter, she wept all the more. He had been noble and honourable to offer himself to her in spite of her cousin's words; she had felt proud and stained and ill and ashamed and it was so very sad. But William, it had been William who had engineered it all.

He had deliberately stepped between them and contrived to divide them from one another and he had concealed it from her, assuming the role of protector, deliverer, moral compass; this last was the grossest and most repugnant hypocrisy. He had tried to drown her in his soul just as the consumption had in its blood. She had always believed him to be so entirely trustworthy, so utterly beyond reproach, while he had sought to determine her very heart and soul and all her actions from then on to this day. So much of what had passed between them became clear to her. She felt sick that she had felt the guilty pang of having wronged him and used him ill. It was inescapable that while she and Captain Lindsay had been blinded, he had brought the darkness to their eyes.

She sat on the bench and cried; she paced in fury and cried; she thought and cried; she felt and cried; and with her hand closed over Captain Lindsay's letter, wished with all her heart and soul that she could stand beside him and tell him that she understood it all. That he should be so unhappy was unbearable to her. The tears continued to stream, the storm of grief and fury unabated.

She felt entirely alone. Miss Drake was taking a group to St Peter's and Anna had gone to the market. The dancing beauty of the summer day became visible to her anguished eyes before retreating again, to be replaced by her vision of Newport's shore and the generosity of spirit of her friend, who would fight for his country even though he was afraid, and encourage an angry orphaned girl to have the courage of her highest dreams.

Then she saw the snow at Boston and remembered his cheek against hers as he begged her to marry him, and she thought of the comfort they could have brought each other and the true affection. She mourned for the children they had been and the innocence they had shared.

Mrs R W Harper   Rome
Hotel Splendide, Vienna

August, 1863

My dearest Augusta,

I have had occasion to hear from Captain—
now Major—Lindsay. I wish you too had had
the opportunity to meet him—he is very dear
to me and the fact that he lives seems an
extraordinary miracle.

His letter has revealed an underhand cruelty
of my cousin in keeping us apart that has left
me reeling as if from a blow to the soul.

I long to go to him—stupidly—
passionately—but do not even trust myself to
write until I am calmer.

Forgive me this selfish letter.

With love,

Emily

[Letter unsent]

Major J C H Lindsay   Rome
——— Squadron

August, 1863

Dear Major Lindsay,

From my heart I thank you for your letter. It
seems we have both suffered terribly at the

hands of my cousin, you and I.

That he should be so sure an angel of destruction is almost beyond my comprehension, and yet I do believe it and see it clearly now.

I wish—fervently—that I had the power to pluck you from the war, its horrible dangers and corruptions, and keep you near me so that I could tell you that I too have never ceased to think of you as one of the purest memories of my heart. My strongest wish is that you should know how passionately I wish that you were safe.

Please write to me at the earliest opportunity to assure me that this is so.

In the meantime I shall attempt to find the key to patience.

Yours truly,

Emily Hudson

In London, William stood in Emily's empty rooms. He had insisted that Mrs Denham allow him to do so alone. From his previous searches he knew that she had left nothing he could find or keep, nothing of herself except the dresses he had bought her. It seemed ironic to him that her proud independent existence in this city had been—from the first— entirely funded by him, how in fact her life had differed in very few respects from that of the gaudy kept women he passed every day on the streets and whose glances he endeavoured to avoid.

With his hands he examined in detail the dresses in the wardrobe. Like their wearer they seemed to mock him still. He could not allow them to remain.

They must be destroyed and quite dissolved or he would have no peace.

CHAPTER NINETEEN

Telegram to Miss E Hudson, Palazzo ———, Roma:

ARRIVING ROMA 18th AUGUST 10PM STOP MEET US STOP CANNOT WAIT AUGUSTA

Augusta alighted from the train the same bright thing Emily remembered. True, her hair was now elaborately arranged beneath a fashionable hat, her delicate feet shod in the finest kid, but her merry smile and wave of recognition was the same.

Emily ran into her arms. 'You are such a lady,' she murmured into her hair. 'You are all in velvet!'

'I wish that I were not. Mr Harper made me wear this because he feared I would catch cold when the train journeyed through the mountains.'

Behind her, supervising two porters with a substantial array of elegant luggage stood Mr Harper. Turning to greet him, Emily saw that he was somewhat portly and quite of middle age. Augusta had never mentioned this in her letters and Emily felt touched by it for a reason she could not name.

'I am so glad to make your acquaintance,' she said.

'And I yours.' He nodded, as if to say, We shall be friends and we shall understand one another and all shall be as it should: decent and convivial.

The following days were taken up with such a riot and a flurry of gaiety, conversation, and visiting back and forth that Emily found she had little time to brood, but Major Lindsay remained constantly in her mind, his unhappiness like a thorn in the palm of her hand. She must endeavour to make her peace with his memory, but he frequently felt so close to her that she could not describe his presence only as that.

*   *   *

Emily and Augusta were cosily settled in the small sitting room attached to Augusta's bedroom in her apartments in the city. They could barely move because of the heat. Mr Harper was abroad hunting for a more commodious dwelling place for his young wife.

'We have not yet begun our confidences,' said Augusta comfortably.

'There are so many I do not know where to start.'

'But I do know one thing, Emily. You have been unwell and you have been concealing it from me. All this talk of resting and chills, it has gained no ground with me. Quite unlike you.' Augusta's voice was affectionate and teasing, but her eyes were full of tears. 'Forgive me,' she said, simply. 'I cry very easily at present.'

'It is only that I could not bear to intrude upon your happiness.' She did not want to add: And we are so different, you and I, the intimacy we shared has altered quite. There are so many things Augusta did not know the truth of and that she felt now she would never tell her.

'And you can never bear to compromise yourself, Emily, even with the truth. Was it . . . what we have long feared?'

'Yes. But it has left me. For the present.'

Augusta leant towards her. 'My dear girl, I was selfish in my happiness, and should have made you tell me.'

'No. I strive to believe that all has been for best. It is a difficult lesson.'

Augusta frowned. 'But why should it be so much harder—always—for you than for me? I have always been so coddled and spoiled.'

Emily smiled. 'To answer that question would take longer than an afternoon.'

The two women clasped hands.

'And what of your cousin?'

'He has gone.'

Augusta looked at Emily sharply. 'You are still keeping things from me. I do not like it.'

'It is the right thing, dear heart, for the present.'

Augusta hesitated but did not insist. It was not like her to want to look too deeply into another's soul. 'I am feeling not a little shocked to think that perhaps you are becoming wise.'

At that minute Mr Harper came into the room carrying a pretty box tied with coloured raffia, bowing his head as if entering a burrow.

'Aah. Here he comes now. Here is dear Mr Harper. It is a miracle that the gentleman has found Turkish Delight in this city with such speed. I must have some at once. Let us hope you have the same luck with finding rooms where we can breathe.'

Augusta's husband reached down and briefly touched his wife's neck as he passed her the box, and she looked up at him and smiled. Emily felt she was no longer needed.

She stood up. 'I must be going,' she said.

*   *   *

Miss Emily Hudson   Newport, R I
Rome

July 30th, 1863

Dear Cousin,

That I should be the one to bring you this news is only part of the pain of it.

Major Lindsay has been declared Missing in Action at Gettysburg.

I know nothing further of the circumstances, but from the way he spoke of you when last I saw him I know he would feel it my duty to let you know.

Yours affectionately,

Mary

Miss Mary Cornford   Rome
Cornford House
Boston, Mass

August, 1863

Dear Mary,

You are indeed both brave and correct to

advise me of this shattering news.
I cannot write more.
With love,

Emily

Miss Emily Hudson
Palazzo ————, Rome   Newport, R I

August, 1863

Dear Emily,

I feel I cannot attempt to distract you from the hurt the news of Major Lindsay's fate has clearly given you with trivialities but, nonetheless, I write in the hope that reading this letter will provide you with a few moments' diversion.

There is a strange atmosphere in the city, as if Boston were holding itself in readiness for a crisis. We have had so much of bloodshed and so many dead that here it is like a contagion, and yet we can see no end to it, despite our prayers. You are not alone in feeling a loss, my dear.

We expect at any minute to hear of something terrible concerning my dear brothers, because now that Matthew has returned to duty, there is no respite for either of them.

I suppose we are not the first country to believe naïvely that our war would be short and glorious, but even the most pessimistic of people could not have imagined this waste of years and youth.

A strange result of it is that I think of my own fate far less than I used to. I use what skill I have with the pen to record what happens around me, what this war seems to do to each individual creature. We all share the optimism followed by the dread, followed by the gritted teeth of endurance, and the slow blow of waiting.

My father continues wilfully blind to the sacrifice of the young, still buried in his study amid his books, but he cuts a more curious figure to me, somehow; he has ceased to influence me in quite the same way. My mother suffers in silence from whatever the particular ailments of her soul are, but worry for my brothers is never part of her conversation. Forgive me for I cannot understand this.

In Rome you are fortunate to be away from the disease of this fighting, although I know it remains on your mind.

I simply seek to assure you of my good wishes as ever.

Yours truly,

Mary

Miss Caroline Trelawney   Rome
Trelawney House,
Richmond, Surrey

August, 1863

Dear Caroline,

Thank you for your kind invitation, but I am not inclined to travel at present. I have heard that a dear friend of mine from Newport days, Major Lindsay, has been declared Missing in our calamitous war, and it has quite put paid to any thought other than his fate. Memories assail me, glimpses I had forgotten, things that he has said. He had recently written to me after a long silence and I had replied, so he has been brought very close. I cannot write of this further.

I long to see you, however, and hope that you might consider a visit, perhaps in the spring. I do not know if you are aware of this, but my cousin has had occasion to visit me, and it has somehow brought you closer but made you feel farther away at the same time.

I am directing this to your house at Richmond, but imagine you may well be taking part in a very English shooting party in some far-flung moorland house as I write. It is odd, not knowing quite where you are.

The summer is reaching its zenith and stillness has settled on the city with the dust. I imagine everyone who has occasion to has left it until September, including my dear Miss Drake, who is indulging her love of mountain air at the lakes. I expect her return within a few days.

Do not forget me. Time and seas may divide us, but that is all.

With much love,

Emily

Miss Emily Hudson   Trelawney House,
Palazzo —————, Rome   Richmond

September 2nd, 1863

Dear Emily,

It appears you have known many trials in your short life, and I am only sorry for your sake that you have had to bear another.

When I think of you it is with a kind of wonder that you have endured what you have endured and found so much for yourself at the end of a very treacherous path. I continue to have faith, though, dear friend: not only in you, but also in an outcome for you that should give you something of what you deserve.

Believe you are in my thoughts.

Hold fast.

With love,

Caroline

Miss Emily Hudson ———, Switzerland
Palazzo ———, Rome

September 4th, 1863

Dear Miss Hudson,

My work in Switzerland is now concluded,
and I am eager to return to London and take
up my practice once more. I feel as if I have
been absent for far too long.

I am to pass through Rome where I shall
change trains on the 10th of September with
very little time to spare. If you would oblige me
by taking the trouble to cross the city so that
we could meet close to the station, I would be
most obliged, as it would be a great pleasure to
see you again.

Yours truly,

Dr G A Cooper

*   *   *

'I will not offer to chaperone you,' said Miss
Drake wryly. 'You are quite your own mistress.'
They stood in the September breeze on the loggia
looking at their eternal city and sensing autumn in
the wind.

Emily shivered. 'I do not want to go.'

'If you have encouraged him, even slightly, you
owe it to him to be there.'

'I am aware of it.' Emily's face was serious and
she fidgeted with her purse.

'You must not believe it of yourself, my dear.'

365

Miss Drake's expression was kind.

'What must I not believe, Catherine?'

'That you are inconstant. I know that is what your cousin always delighted in implying. But in truth, it is merely that you are very young. I remember it all clearly, you know.'

*   *   *

By happenstance Emily had arranged to meet Dr Cooper at the same café where she had breakfasted with Miss Drake on her first morning in Rome. He stood waiting outside the establishment so that she would not have the indignity of entering alone and looking about for him. The punctuality and consideration were typical of him.

'Miss Hudson.' He smiled warmly, if somewhat guardedly, gauging something from her face, and shook her hand. 'It is kind of you to come so far to meet me.' They looked at one another briefly.

'It would be unthinkable in London. Quite disgraceful.'

Emily was trying to sound light-hearted, but succeeded, she felt, in appearing both stupid and flirtatious. She was deeply embarrassed and sensed that the doctor was similarly uncomfortable. After they had sat down she began to bite her nails, hoping that the waitress would come soon for their order and interrupt them. She had barely taken him in.

There was a silence. Then he leaned towards her confidingly and said, 'There is nothing untoward in our meeting, Miss Hudson. You are simply saying farewell to your doctor.'

She looked up at him and smiled. She did not see the feared disapproval in his eyes, merely the kindness and affection. 'I am afraid I have behaved more than a little impulsively where you are concerned.'

'Perhaps. But it is no matter. Your health and happiness, for a number of reasons, are important to me, and I have been keen to satisfy myself on that score. I would not have you fail me now with self-accusation.'

She smiled at him again and it was understood, just as he had always seemed to understand and sense how it was with her from the first days of their acquaintance. 'You are unnecessarily kind.'

He drew in a breath, seeming to become more reserved. 'I do not believe so.' He stated it as if it were a scientific fact. There was a further silence while the coffee was brought. He added sugar and stirred his methodically. 'What shall you do now that the year is waning? Remain in Rome?'

'I shall stay here. And I shall wait for news . . . that the war is over back home.'

'It is said that the end is not far off.'

'I hope and pray for it.'

'Would you consider returning to America at any time?'

'I have learned in my short life that plans are useless—but if I were to have the opportunity, I do not think I should like to return there to live. It is only that I have dear friends in that country whose future is connected to my own.'

'I see.' He did not press her to tell him more, and she felt the tension between them begin to dissolve and quite float away. They talked of the doctor's clinic, of the mountains, the lakes, the tumult of

London and the bustle of Rome, and Emily could
see his mind begin to close from her and turn for
home. When he began to gather his belongings,
putting money in the saucer and reaching for his
cloak, she said, 'Dr Cooper, I have never had the
opportunity of thanking you adequately for all you
have done for me.'

'It was an honour,' he said. 'I hope you never
have need of me again, but if you do, you know
precisely where I am to be found.'

Miss Caroline Trelawney   Rome
Trelawney House,
Richmond, Surrey

September, 1863

Dear Caroline,

I am so grateful to have heard from you.
Sorrow sharpens everything I find. Thank you
for your kind words. I endeavour to continue
with the pattern of life.

I am rising early and going to work on a
particular view of the city through trees that is
very dear to my heart. I paint out of doors in
the morning light and am often finished before
eleven.

After that much of my time is taken up in the
company of my dear friend, Augusta, who as I
told you has returned to Rome for her
confinement—although at present she is very
much abroad, immersed in preparations for the
arrival of her infant. I had no idea there could
be so many things to buy. She has recently

changed her rooms from the initial apartment I found for her—I feel not a little responsible for the inconvenience, but she will not hear of it, declaring that she and Mr Harper are far happier to choose their own nest than to have it provided for them—and furnishing it also keeps her happily occupied.

It is exciting but somewhat peculiar to watch her embark on this new part of her life without a backward glance, and I wonder whether she will remain in Europe for much longer after the confinement. She talks a great deal of her father and of Boston life and I do not think it will be long before she departs. For the time being I am more than happy that she is here after so long a separation.

Please write and let me know how you do. I should hate to feel you were out in the world acting and thinking and I am ignorant of it!

The closeness of death has made me value all the more the people who remain dear to me.

Affectionately,

Emily

*   *   *

In this light it was all memory that threatened to overwhelm her. Real bright life receded quite, and her peculiar, taunting, gold-suffused visions were in command. She could sit for hours quite idle on the loggia, looking at the vista of Rome without seeing it or taking it in. There would be a book upon her knee but she did not trouble herself with it. All there were were visions from the past or fears for the present and future: her dear friend wounded, her dear friend captive, her dear friend dead. It did not do to pine and dream and become submerged in dreaming, but she could not rouse herself.

One evening, laying her chin upon her hand and leaning on the balustrade, she remembered Major Lindsay's words, written clearly on the paper folded in her bureau drawer. *Paint me a portrait.* Those had been his written words a long long time ago, words written in a confident, bold, hurried script, the ink now fading. She considered this. It was true that she had embarked on a study of a Madonna and child. But that was different. She thought about his words for several days, they kept reverberating in her head. She should like to be able to paint a portrait of Major Lindsay himself from memory, but while on occasion she could recall his face quite clearly, on others he remained in shadow, just out of reach, somehow blurred.

He had wanted her to make use of the colours he had given her. He had wanted her to paint a portrait. In London she had kept his present as a reminder of him, but used only the materials William had bought. In Rome she had availed herself of the resources Miss Drake had at her disposal in the studio, preferring to keep Major Lindsay's box out of sight, precious and buried at the bottom of her clothes chest. It was imperative, she felt now, to find the paints and use them, and after much musing she resolved to paint herself.

*   *   *

A self-portrait was one of the most time-honoured

and reliable ways an artist could explore his technique, use his skill—but also, she knew, attempt to convey an innermost quality, the light in his own eyes. It would be a hard task, but she wanted to attempt it; not only for her long-ago Captain Lindsay, but for herself.

The decision made, she felt she could stand up straighter, that there was less shadow around her, the light had sharpened again. At first she must decide where to place herself. She wanted it to be in the open, where she felt most at home, on the loggia with the city and its heavens behind her. The background need not be detailed, but it must be inferred—she had the temerity to portray herself as an artist in the city of artists, an ambition that frequently made her want to laugh, but did not deter her. One cannot merely talk of one's grand plan, she thought to herself. One must execute it.

With the aid of her looking glass she took careful sketches of herself, trying to be as dispassionate as possible about the cast of her own features and the expression in her own eyes. You look like a person who has known a great deal, she said to herself once, and smiled at this hard-won knowledge. You are no longer a girl. Nor did she look like a lady, with her sunburned skin and her loosely arranged hair. But amid all the changes in herself, she saw much of that first eagerness in her expression, all the old curiosity, a courage that—truly—she had never known she had.

She wanted the light to be soft on the features, not only illuminating but extrapolating, almost as if she stood like a young tree in the breeze. Working on the portrait absorbed her totally. She

371

would spend all morning at her easel, concentrating utterly on her purpose: to convey what she saw of herself into the finished portrait, to use all the discipline and technique she had learned, and by examining herself so closely, lose herself in it and shake herself free. In the afternoons she frequently walked down the hill and into the city, feeling a curious lightness and adventure in her step, delighting in the taste of it on her tongue: the sight of the sinewy feral cats and the scavenging dogs, the markets and the stinking debris that was left of them, the sound of water running in the gutters and out of the fountains, the sight of washing strung along balconies and children playing in the streets. If she wanted to escape the light and noise she had only to go into a church or chapel to feel and see a different, far danker glory, look up at the arches and domes that reached out to God.

She adored tasting the city—not only its air, either sweet-smelling or rank, but its ice creams and granitas and cakes and all the manner of delights the cafés offered. She had no fear of sitting alone with her book and her coffee; she was a foreigner, she could be as peculiar as she pleased, and beyond greetings and appreciative words, she was left to herself. She did not mind that at all. She did not feel alone. She was working.

It was all the freedom of flight she had once imagined—more. Her solitude was not painful. Her absorption in her work was company enough.

Emily completed the portrait as the autumn descended. It was a satisfying piece of work. She was proud of it. It was complete. The balance of light and shade were as she had intended; the colour, both lustrous and muted, blended as she had planned, and the expression, of openness and lack of pretence that the look in her dark eyes gave the onlooker, was peculiarly arresting. She would not have been able to manage such a work even six months previously. But now she had the means to accomplish what she aimed for, the technique born of discipline and study. Looking at herself she felt she had created a creature with both fearlessness and tenderness in her eyes, and a kind of pride. It was finished. She felt almost at peace.

That autumn and the following spring, Emily began to paint portraits of the young ladies and gentlemen who came to the studio. There was a little money in it and this was a source of another kind of pride.

She painted Augusta and her baby and gave her the portrait when she left for Boston. She painted Miss Drake, who hung the picture in her studio; and Anna and Paulo—they wrapped theirs carefully and took it home.

Miss B Norton   Palazzo ————
South Kensington Art School,
London, SW

April 25th, 1864

Dear Miss Norton,
   It is a long time, I know, since I wrote to you to tell you that I was well-settled at Rome. But as I am still here, and far more contented than even I could have imagined possible, I thought it a fine idea to write to you to acquaint you of my progress.

In my early days here I struggled hard with being healthy enough to help our mutual friend Miss Drake with her business in her studio, but little by little I became stronger, and worked hard on my technique until I have acquired some skill at taking portraits. I cannot say that I have frequent commissions, but sufficient to occupy me. In my spare time I continue my attempts at painting landscape outside amid the movement of light and colour. The work is a tremendous joy to me. And I have found not a little society here—amongst Romans and visitors—to also keep me amused.

In short, your kind action in writing to Miss Drake when I appeared dripping and distressed upon your doorstep has resulted in a not unsuccessful life for me in this blessed city. For that I am eternally grateful, and feel quite appalled that it has taken me so long to write to you and inform you of the fact.

I hope the school continues satisfactorily. Miss Drake begs to be remembered to you. She asks me to convey that should you have occasion to make a visit to Rome, we should both be delighted to receive you.

With all very best wishes and salutations,
Yours truly,

Emily Hudson

*　　　*　　　*

In May of that year, Emily and Miss Drake travelled to the Amalfi coast, and investigated the ruins at Pompeii and Paestum. Emily was overjoyed at the blue of the Mediterranean.

'It is so sparkling and happy!' she cried. 'It makes the ocean at home seem so very humourless and earnest.'

'Oh, really, Emily,' said Miss Drake, 'only you could describe an ocean as humourless. In any event, all seas have their own qualities. You will come to know that by and by.' But she laughed. They laughed together.

Through the insistence of time Emily became accustomed to her visions of Major Lindsay as of her other familiar dead, mingled with the life that surrounded her, welcoming them to her heart as her friends.

EPILOGUE

Rome
April, 1865

Telegram to Miss E Hudson, Palazzo —————,
Roma:

RELEASED UNHARMED STOP PEACE AT LAST STOP
MAY I COME TO YOU LINDSAY

Telegram to Major J C H Lindsay, Boston, Mass:

WITH ALL MY HEART STOP EMILY

Miss Caroline and Mr Thomas Trelawney, Miss Mary Cornford, Mr and Mrs Richard Harper and Miss Drake all gathered at the little chapel at Rome for the wedding of Major James Charles Lindsay and Miss Emily Anne Hudson. They all remarked that they had never seen a bride laugh so much nor a bridegroom look more overjoyed.

ACKNOWLEDGEMENTS

First I would like to thank the great team at Little, Brown; especially my editor, Caroline Hogg, for her enthusiasm, energy and determination, and Emma Stonex for her excellent copy-editing; all at Conville & Walsh, particularly my agent Clare Conville; at Penguin US, my editor Pam Dorman, for her commitment to the book; and at HarperCollins Canada, Iris Tupholme. Thank you also to my sister, my parents, friends and beloved family.

I am indebted to *The Penguin History of the USA* by Hugh Brogan (Penguin, 2001) and the brilliant *London in the Nineteenth Century* by Jerry White (Vintage Books, 2008) although any factual errors are, of course, entirely my own.